BLINK

Adel

This is a work of fiction. The author invented all characters and activities in this story. Any similarity to persons or events, real or imagined, is pure coincidence.

Acknowledgements

A work of fiction is written and read in stolen moments. In the sense that this is a crime, our guilty pleasures deserve a pardon. I am grateful for the forgiveness of family, friends and employers, particularly my husband Karma and my son Tiger.

More by the Author
(also available for Kindle)

LouD
Xternity, Inc. The Water Wars Trilogy begins.

Excerpts available on **IMAGINEADEl.com**

3.1.3

I am not a bad person, not really. Important yes. Impatient too! I'm told they hold hands in the walk of life. Impatience, a refreshing quality when chained to the tick-tock of a biological clock, tends to poison the well of stamina when on a quest which never ends. Once important, now irrelevant, impatience has become my enemy. Even freed from mortality's stingy time ration, I suffer fools poorly. Fool that I am, I can hardly bear myself. I spent a lifetime rejecting human frailty. Living a second life, I am no longer human; yet, I am still cursed with all the glorious failings. I escaped death but not my faults. I am immortal and I am bored with immortality.

I am not confined to the lungs, as would be air, to the veins as would be blood or to the cells as would be DNA. On the back of bone marrow, I ride the high sierra; at the whim of bowels, I scurry backwards through scrub. I tunnel through arteries feeding the heart never knowing the shape of love. The sidewinder and the scorpion have more claims to their domain, for I am a freak trespassing in the body I inhabit. Slithering through cavities of heart and mind, I inherited the scars and dreams of this flesh but, like electricity without wires, my thoughts and breaths do not connect.

An accident of nature, will, technology, ambition, cosmic alignment and dumb luck, I was the first to achieve a Transmogrified Identity Transfer. I am the original TransmID. Like most accidents, I was caused by a compounding sequence of calculated opportunity and random chance. My consciousness crossed an electronic bridge from one flesh container to another in a bio-digital transfer that siphoned my mind into a new body.

A parallel development created the Digitally Synchronous circuits. Uploading their minds to computers, DigiSyncs quit the body to join a communal bundle of intelligence. Forsaking individuality, DigiSyncs buy a ticket to obscurity and merge with some vast info-hive. Together, forever, in amorphous unity, Syncs fly like fever, seep like vapor and flow like liquid. God bless each and every sprite; DigiSyncs provide the empty bodies TransmIDs recycle. Migrants to the machine vacate the flesh at the prime of life so TransmIDs are never short of fresh puddles to land in.

On the springboard of evolution, smug DigiSyncs dive into pure knowledge and accuse TransmIDs of retarding intelligence. I would argue TransmIDs cling to corporal consciousness because the desires of body sustain the miracle of the mind. Exploding the tradition of sapient sapiens, Transmogrified Identity reincarnation endows flesh with the life span of deities. Breaching DNA's hold on mortality, TransmIDs are the true immortals, not the DigiSync brats, but it has yet to be proven that the TransmIDs' infinite time promotes the accumulation of wisdom any better than the DigiSyncs continual information.

2

Jealous of our vitality, the clever Digi machines call TransmIDs parasites. Jealous of our life span, the Beings agree. I concede; they have a point. Individuality drains away with each incarnation. Tortured by an ignoble existence in an alien body, I have become a soulless creature. Eternity is not my cup of tea.

The Beings consider all immortals immoral and have no use for "death cheaters" who sell their souls for knowledge or time. Beings believe in an afterlife that rewards the ethical so they accumulate bonus points for good behavior to earn redemption. Guarding their precious souls for the Promised Land, they keep humanity pure and undiluted. Blessed are the faithful.

Don't give a damn about salvation, but I credit the Beings with simple smarts. Mortality makes the most of every minute; scarcity is a classic resource maximization mechanism. Like fate, clever comes in many colors. Defeated my white flag waves. I will live until I die and Beings will celebrate my end; but, when I surrender life to death, my death will change the balance.

For the moment we share planet; TransmIDs, DigiSyncs and Beings cohabitate side by side. Who shall inherit the earth remains to be seen.

* * * * * * * * * *

"That's the boss, right?" The intensive care tech asks the head nurse. "I paged you pronto."

3

"I appreciate your concern for protocol," nurse Leyla downplays the urgency, "he does have security clearance."

"Well ya, he owns the place. Just thought you'd want to know he entered a restricted area to see the Cryo. What does he want with Stardust?"

"Our patients have a code name to protect identity," the nurse reminds the tech "and our professional code of conduct prohibits any speculation that might infringe on their right to privacy."

"Definitely not a relative. Next of kin always look lost, all passive and numb. He's not paying last respects. He's inspecting the Cryo head to toe."

Leyla resists the urge to snap at the eager beaver. Patients in this secluded ward rarely receive visitors. The tech monitors the anonymous in a land of the forgotten. Though irritating, some curiosity can be forgiven, except the tech's lack of composure compounds her stress over the disruption.

"He's sizing up the Cryo like a tailor measuring for a new suit," the excited tech continues.

The tech's presumption raises her hackles. Kids these days think they know everything and forget how to mind their own business. "Visiting hours must be observed. The clinic imposes rules so as not to jeopardize the patient's welfare."

"Is he the TransmID, you know, the guy who wants his body back?"

Such audacity! The tech was barely a zygote when these two men fought their fateful duel but acts like an eyewitness fingering a suspect in a line-up. To connect the visitor and the Cryo, the tech obviously violated confidential codes. To make matters worse, the kid seems completely oblivious to indiscretion.

Granted the dual had become legend. At the time, the shots rang around the world, but the passage of decades diluted the contorted history. Partners in the birth of immortality, the two men and their mighty test of wills had become a footnote to the discovery while the mating of the Acuity and the Emotolog went down as the mother of invention. In the way the tortured calculations behind gravity's theory condense into an apple on Newton's head, or the bolt of lightening that struck Ben Franklin's kite gets credit for harnessing electricity, the story about the technological leap at the dawn of this era distills into an inspired myth about machines.

With the abbreviated attention span of today's youth, the inventors are well beyond recall and the facts irretrievably obscured by the world-shaking events that followed. Given that what happened barely holds a candle to the atomic blast of what happened next, who'd want the inside scoop on a couple of old men? Leyla wonders why a little blip from the past would register on the tech's radar. At best no more than characters from a fable - a once upon a time, simple, innocent, almost forgotten time –the

two ancients from before the age of
immortals should have been long forgotten.

After all these years would a rematch
attract attention? During the Cryo's thirty-
year hibernation, the VIP visitor was out in
the world making waves so his presence in
this backwater might stir ripples of curiosity.
Suppose the notorious visitor tips off the
press? Leyla dreads the nightmare of nosy
reporters, disrupted routines and employee
gossip broadcasting secrets best left untold.
There is no story here, not yet, perhaps not
ever. Quite possibly, this is where the story
ends.

"He was bound to arrive sooner or
later." Leyla answers icily, hoping the tech
hasn't noticed her cringe.

As far as she is concerned, this visit is
like the second coming, the second coming of
an ice age. Hell has frozen over releasing
chilling devils. The bane of her existence has
returned, throwing his weight around with a
glacial magnitude that has twice cut a
swatch through her life and left a moraine of
desolation in his wake.

The observation window in the control
room has a clear view of the intensive care
center below. Mr. Bigshot hired her back
when the coma ward stored the brain dead
to harvest organs for transplant. As the game
changed, the theater converted to a staging
area for a different kind of limbo.

In her half-century of nursing at the
clinic, scientific advances enabled the human
race to take the reigns away from the grim

reaper. Beings still died, but death was an option not everyone chose.

To escape the limited life span imposed on mortals, humans can cryogenically freeze their bodies to finish living at a later date or transfer their identity into a new body and live as a TransmID or evacuate the flesh container and upload the contents of their minds to achieve digital synchronicity. TransmIDs, like the notorious original visiting the Cryo, trade in their genetic vehicle to cruise second and third laps around the track in new corporal models. The DigiSyncs, in their infinite wisdom, renounce biology to commune with electronic intelligence.

And so the coma ward retooled from a chop shop to a used car lot. Instead of salvaging parts from malfunctioned junk, vacated and frozen bodies are repaired, refurbished and recycled. The twilight room now sustains abandoned DigiSync corpses until a TransmID lays claim. Every so often they rejuvenate a thawed cryo, but the Cryo resting below, Stardust, is a hybrid, the first and only case of a cryogenically frozen TransmID.

The tech recognized the VIP and circumvented protocol to identify Stardust, and now witnesses an unprecedented event, a TransmID admiring his original body. Leyla participated in the history-making mind swap and can attest to the significance of the reunion. Deflorio, the visitor, lives in the body that formerly belonged to Dex. If consciousness survives in Stardust, the frozen corpse that was Deflorio now contains Dex.

7

Faced with expiration thirty years ago, Deflorio snatched Dex's body and has been slinking around in it ever since. Now the horrid, ghastly, selfish snake has returned to gloat over Stardust.

If Dex had not invented the Emotolog, he would still be ambulatory, the soulless TransmIDs and DigiSyncs wouldn't exist and Deflorio would be frozen in the Cryo. The Emotolog reproduced feeling; it enabled one person to record and store a personal experience so that another could re-live the emotional content of the event. A sort of cognitive camera, the Emotolog took a snap shot to preserve a private memento for posterity.

At her request, Dex reconfigured his one-way device into an interactive switchboard. The Emotolog became the Telemotolog and the Telemotolog evolved to link two separate minds in perfectly pure communication. Simultaneous exchange exceeded expectations; capacity exponentially leaped from sharing a feeling to connecting brains. Dex had resisted the Telemotolog, dreading unforeseen consequences and fearing misuse of the technology would corrupt society. She had insisted, knowing emotional surges warp individuals with or without technology. They both acknowledged the risks, but no one could have anticipated such dire consequences. Despite precautions the window of shared consciousness blasted open the door to immortality.

During a prototype test, Deflorio used his Acuity device to amplify the Telemotolog into a mind-siphon and initiate a total identify transfer. Terminally ill, the dying Deflorio synchronized his identity transmogrification just as the fat lady hit the final note. In the desperate grapple for survival, Dex drew the short straw. Dex, the inventor, died while Deflorio, the lab rat, ascended the throne of immortality.

A rat wearing a professor's white coat is still a rat, still gnawing away at fate, still manipulating circumstances to seize every advantage. After crossing the divide and nosing around in the TransmID world of eternity, the rat came to the conclusion that the grass would be greener back in his mortal cage. Longing to reclaim his original habitat, the homesick Deflorio ordered the revival of his cryogenically preserved body.

The outcome of Deflorio's scheming is far from certain. If Stardust wakes as a zombie the point is moot; there will be no consciousness to activate a transmission. Until Stardust speaks, no one will know whether Dex's conscious arrived before the curtain fell. If Dex got lost in transit, the Cryo is an empty shell. Even if Dex survives inside Stardust, all of Deflorio's money and power cannot circumvent the current inhabitant's right to occupancy. With the onset of immortals, globally implemented legislation extensively regulated physical v. biological ownership - the presiding edict being possession is ten tenths of the law. If Dex is in residence, Deflorio can't cancel the lease unless the tenant voluntarily agrees to relocate.

"No surprise then, you expected him." The tech notes dryly.

The insolent assumption betrays the worst kind of insensitivity. The tech's indiscriminate curiosity is a quest for knowledge indifferent to wisdom. The kid could never appreciate the profound depth of Leyla's response. Confirmation or denial carries a spectrum of subtle meanings, but the tech will only register the shallow reality of a yes or no. All shades between black and white are lost; the implications of her complicity - shame, remorse and guilt - are as irrelevant as a rainbow over a colorblind dog.

In fact, no response is required; the tech merely states the obvious. This is not a normal conversation, at least not a Being version of normal. It takes some getting used to. In her day, speech was an invitation to interact. Leyla may never adjust to this dry communication, a voice with a compulsive need to spout facts. Implants cannot help themselves; the Acuity does that. Tactless and insatiable, the tech plunders a path of data incapable of inference beyond the reach of a damp shortsighted muzzle.

At least her secrets are safe. Inhibited by focus, the tech lacks the infrared vision required to penetrate her dark emotional well. The Acuity does not allow sentiment to prejudice a verdict; facts are facts, all equal under the rule of reality. A sledgehammer leveling unreliable perception, knotty emotion, unverifiable hunch, the Acuity implant short-circuits the intuitive aspects of the mind. Improvisation, daydreams, poetry or other detours the brain relies on for inspiration distract from factual goals. Acuity mental edits abbreviate processing to amp speed and cross the finish line fast. Like blinders on a racehorse, the Acuity antenna blots out the entire frequency of human emotion beyond the periphery of a data stream.

The device drove a wedge between the cortex and the more primitive regions: the brain stem governing breathing, blood pressure and body temperature, the diencephalon regulating sleep and appetite and the limbic region housing sexual drives and instinctual emotions. Elevating the thin carpet of grey matter above the foundation, buffers judgment from any impulsive preconceptions surging up from within. The dominance of the cortex, particularly the frontal lobes beneath the forehead informing us who we are and guiding decisions about who we want to be, separates man from beast; and yet, segregating thought from the animal mind bent human behavior to inhuman norms.

A digital implant linking minds to electronics, the Acuity triggers a distinctive automated mentality. Ceding control of the brain to an operating system dilutes the uniqueness of each individual by neutralizing divergent life histories, unique memories, acquired tastes, inherited talents as well as human nature. On the Acuity, the tech can simultaneously interface with multiple system networks, but numbing the patterns of neural activity involved in self-actualization freezes adaptation and inhibits the maturation processes. The fruit on the vine of artificial intelligence never gets a chance to properly ripen. Monitoring hospital systems and patient bio-statistical readouts, the employee becomes a physical adjunct to the machines; hands to turn a dial or a voice to translate digital information but, running on the Acuity autopilot, the tech is, in actual fact, not all there.

In one generation, a third of the population acquired Acuity implants. Described as the enlightened advance, the evolutionary promise, the future of the race, the mental prostheses did not always lead to a digital marriage. Many consider the Acuity a career accessory and disconnect as soon as they leave the office: others, like this tech, become addicts.

"Guess you knew him pretty well?" The information-hungry tech fires off another rude assault, pointblank, intrusive.

To the sensitive, silence reveals intimate cascades while the tone deaf require drums of verification to establish the existence of song.

"Once I knew them both." A member of a Being faith that preserves physical and mental purity, Leyla religiously upholds a code of honesty. Firm in her belief that all conscious deception - no matter how tempting, no matter how small - diminish emotional experience and block neural potential, Leyla will not tell a lie.

"A reunion of old friends?" The kid persists with another statement-question. The Acuity is obviously just the first step. Destined for a Digital Synchronous union, the tech audibly counts the minutes until the compulsory thirty-three years as a Being elapse. The age requirement is an arbitrary regulation. Priding themselves on a certain savior-fair, DigiSyncs refuse to accept the young and inexperienced in the ways of the material world. The magical age of thirty-three presumably bestows enough wisdom to make enlightened choices and also coincides with the apex of cognitive prowess. Biology ages well, up to a point, but eventually spoils. After thirty-three years, human cells systematically wither, synaptic plasticity gradually erodes, neurotransmitters progressively lose impact, connectivity incrementally disintegrates and inevitably mental brightness dims. DigiSyncs have their standards, which include IQ tests and temperament evaluation along with freshness.

Beings hotly contest the DigiSync monopoly on eternal wisdom and consider the lost souls "know-it-alls." Though reasonably convinced you need a body to experience nirvana, Leyla doesn't debate the issue. She isn't privy to the internal workings of their communal mind and isn't on speaking terms with any DigiSyncs. She has the impression DigiSyncs are low on personality, but that could be a function of the cut and dry posts she ignores on her computer. Less entertaining and more galling than her conversation with this tech, the direct, terse and unapologetic DigiSync communications assume a right to expect answers to questions they have no business asking.

"A long time ago, circumstances brought us together," Leyla admits, if only to confirm what silence cannot deny.

Even the oblivious tech notices the sigh Leyla tries to swallow behind grinding teeth. Anxious and troubled by the scene unfolding in the ward below, she hides a tremor with twisting hands.

Spying on the demon in Dex's body, Leyla braces for the inevitable encounter. The TransmID Deflorio examining the lifeless shell he evacuated - the comatose container with Dex trapped inside - evokes the skin crawling image of Frankenstein standing over his doctor. The two men could not have been more different, night and day, fire and water. Pondering the series of events that tangled these polarized opposites, she deeply regrets her role in bringing them together. Leyla would never have initiated that first handshake if she could have predicted they would end up in each other's arms.

"Must bring back a few memories?" The tech probes.

Asking, asking, always asking. The automaton at the desk can't possibly know how close the pointed barbs come to piercing her heart, but the aim is too true. Caution urges Leyla to suspect the tech is being cued. On-line DigiSyncs can easily monitor the conversation via the tech's Acuity. DigiSyncs have human obsessions in extremes and a devoted cult has sprung up around Stardust - the father of their existence lies in this shrine.

"A few," Leyla hesitates, fighting paranoia. The interrogation by statement scrambles her biorhythm modulation. All that asking, the Acuity turns people into bloodhounds. Anyone wearing the collar has the social skills of a pop quiz.

Still the inquiry is out of character; too bold, too blatant and totally unexpected from a subordinate. Frivolous exchanges are out of place in an environment geared towards guarding patient anonymity. Chatting is discouraged, gossip banned and discretion is a large part of the job description.

Discretion comes naturally to someone with a past, someone in the habit of keeping company with memory. Leyla stays busy with responsibilities; duties and obligations but her best friends are private moments. Sustained by reminiscence of happier times caring for empty human containers suits her perfectly. When her only daughter tragically died at the age of twelve she swore off intimacy; when her dreams lured Dex into his frozen abyss she swore off companionship.

"What a surprise, huh? Today of all days."

The tech knows! Leyla leaps to the next conclusion: all the DigiSyncs know. She imagines multitudes crowded behind a one-way mirror, jamming channels to eavesdrop on her via the tech's Acuity. Broadcasting the interview to the far corners of their ethereal net, surfing waves of gossip in a massive party, today they are celebrating. Today is their birthday. Today is the anniversary of the DigiSync inception. The Telemotolog that gave birth to the TransmIDs also spawned the DigiSyncs. Exactly thirty years ago, on this exact date, Leyla had precipitated the involuntary Deflorio/Dex exchange, not knowing, and certainly not willing, the outcome. If she could turn back the clock she would reverse the event that warped the evolutionary curve right over the singularity into this new future where TransmIDs and DigiSyncs indefinitely extend human horizons.

Today of all days! The statement hangs in the air, a rhetorical remark, a convenient closing to an aborted conversation. Leyla leaves the tech and the DigiSyncs to join the TransmID and the Cryo in the care ward.

3.1.4

The accident should never have happened, would never have had the opportunity to happen, if she hadn't been playing with matches and Leyla lives with a searing ambition to rectify her mistake. Dex's original Emotolog technology captured feelings. Replaying stored data recreated emotion; a self-contained, harmless experience that allowed one person to relive another's joy or sorrow. Instead of leaving well enough alone, she urged Dex to invent an interactive version, the Telemotolog, a direct mind-to-mind simultaneous nonverbal sharing. For selfish reasons she staged a disastrous experiment, rushed the first live exchange using virtually untested technology. She insisted on sharing Deflorio's last moments on Mars, to guide and ease a trouble-free transition into the afterlife. Dex agreed on the condition he referee the exchange. Hooking her to Deflorio via the Telemotolog, Dex broke every rule and suffered all the consequences.

No one could have foreseen the contents of one mind jumping into another, until it all went haywire, until it all came asunder, until after it actually happened. At the brink of death, Deflorio, enhanced by the Acuity, hijacked system safeguards and initiated a chain reaction. Deflorio ended up immortal, Dex ended up dead and the explosion sparked hybrid life forms. She blames herself for cracking open a portal for the dire act of desperation that allowed Deflorio to kidnap Dex.

17

It should have been, her trapped in the thawing Cryo. She was the one interfaced to Deflorio; she stumbled guiding Deflorio towards a final exit. Sensing her distress, Dex launched a valiant rescue. Stepping into the link, Dex intercepted the Deflorio transmission and heroically took a bullet that had her name engraved in bold red letters. If not for Dex, and twisted fate, Deflorio would be walking around in her body. The flamboyant tycoon reincarnated as a docile nurse would have been a comical curve. If justice had a sense of humor, her frugal existence, thankless tasks and the purgatory of this intensive care ward would have been Deflorio's trial by punishment.

She had to admit Deflorio had done a damn good job of taking over Dex's life, his company and even his secretary along with his body. Still, eyewitnesses could never pretend to be fooled; the transformation from sensitive to calculating, philanthropic to philandering and loyal to ruthless was radical. Unfortunately, once Dex vanished in the surge, concerned parties could only watch the Deflorio drama unfold. Though cryogenically preserved, Dex, for all intents and purposes, was history and Deflorio appointed himself trustee of the corpse.

Now that medicine can cure the terminally ill and raise the dead, Deflorio wants his body back. He ordered the Cryo thawed and actually expects Stardust to be grateful for the resurrection. The revived Cryo might shout thanks or scream curses but

Stardust will have the final word on who lives and dies in Deflorio's body. In the realm of public opinion, Deflorio's tale is a footnote to the fate of the Cryo. The dead twin is the hero, a martyr to the momentous birth of immortality. Upon resurrection, Beings, DigiSyncs and TransmIDs will herald Stardust as the messiah re-born to settle the rivalry. Before the savior can be saved, the body has to rejuvenate, the mind restored and the death sentence revoked. If the process fails he will be given a champion's funeral, laid to rest under an ostentatious memorial and eulogized as a saint. No matter how the saga ends, Beings, DigiSyncs and TransmIDs will all honor Dex and re-write his story to justify their respective positions on immortality.

Once word gets out, massive wagers will be placed on the improbable possibility that Dex survived the leap and took his last breath in Deflorio's dying body. Since Deflorio resides inside Dex, it is not unreasonable to assume Dex is frozen inside Deflorio's cryogenically preserved corpse. Even though Leyla has no right to request forgiveness and Dex has every right to vehemently refuse, Leyla prays Dex will speak when Stardust revives. The alternative is worse than death.

In her faith, true immortality occurs by releasing the spirit to join the light of the universe. As in living, in dying the self and soul cooperate to ignite the spirit to flight. If Dex never reached Deflorio's body he never got the chance to die. When his self separated from his body, his soul wandered into an oblivion from which his spirit will never ascend. If Dex's consciousness did transfer, it is captive, unhinged from self and soul, frozen in a corporal limbo unable to release the eternal energy of the spirit from matter. To reach the afterlife, promised and deserved, Dex must escape his prison before his spirit decays in the way of all mortal flesh. Returning to dust in the Cryo's soulless state, Dex will never experience the ultimate gift of the universe. To receive eternal ecstasy Dex must die; to die he must live and to live he must wake.

* * * * * * * * *

Deflorio tenderly strokes the life-giving cocoon encasing Stardust. The shrouded figure lies beyond reach, protectively sealed in a medical sarcophagus. Though Deflorio can barely distinguish the features, the shape is familiar, more familiar than the strange face he has confronted in the mirror every day for the last thirty years. Deflorio thinks of this body, his former self, as a shipwreck containing valuable treasures. He considers the vessel delicate but salvageable and is determined to set sail as soon as the helm is sound.

The anticipation is almost sexual but the urge is stronger than any sex he can remember. The strength of his longing exceeds the desperation of a lover; Deflorio has never desired another as totally and completely as he covets his X body. Suffering an emotional pull with all strings attached, erect and salivating, he can almost taste the consummation, but the frozen corpse under glass shows no promise of reciprocating his warmth. Quelling despair, he has never prayed with such ardor. Only his own lost body could bring tears to his eyes, could evoke such soul searching, prompt such an intimate physical confession.

"Thanks to you, my friend, I am the original famous Transmogrified Identity. We should have won a Nobel Prize for pulling off that hat trick. So many have followed, the eternal population multiplies. Soon the TransmIDs and DigiSyncs will outnumber the Beings. New converts escape mortality daily. Can you blame them? Death, as you know, is the ultimate no win experience. No one looks forward to losing a job, a wife, even a pet and that stress is nothing compared to losing a life. DigiSyncs permanently escape the big zero by joining the electronic monastery of knowledge. TransmIDs postpone it, moving forward, drawn by the beacon of better future. Making a religion out of self-gratification every re-birth holds the infinite potential of a new romance. Who could refuse a second chance? And yet the Promised Land still hovers just out of reach. We still make the same mistakes, dumb as infants. Even as immortals, we can't figure out how to reach the sweats on that heavenly shelf."

Deflorio pauses as memory takes a detour.

"As a newcomer surging with euphoria, empowered by a limitless life span, I naively believed I had the world at my feet. Fledglings to incarnation have yet to shake fears of death so mortality surges in them with a heroic force. Staring it down, the triumph of proving themselves above it invigorates. Hurling thunderbolts to stop evil, speeding messages of import, slinging arrows of love, oh how so capricious the behavior of adolescent immortals. I once rushed into a burning house to rescue a baby and dove in front of a moving vehicle to save a dog."

"In time, I discovered actions that hold no risk earn no reward. Fear fails to energize when danger loses its thrill. With the authority of death crippled, the challenge of rebelling against a lame opponent wears off quickly. Eventually, the déjà vu out number the ah ha moments. Numbed by infinity, I have become as oblivious to corporal zest as a nail to a hammer. Beaten by time, each minute becomes a pounding migraine.

Without death, my life has no meaning. Hampered by the heavy burden of apathy, I lack momentum. Succumbing to traits of age identical to elderly beings - loss of focus, selective hearing and blunt reflex - I experience creeping inadequacies such as I never suffered as a mortal. When the incentive of the ticking clock faded, my edge dulled, my ambition went to flab, my drive atrophied. By fifty, this body seemed more impaired than the sixty-five year old cancer-ridden body I lured you into."

* * * * * * * *

Leyla studies Deflorio through the window as the prep assistant zips her into a containment suit, adjusting the helmet, sealing closures and regulating the air gage: precautions for entering an sterile environment so delicate that one exhale could be lethal to the occupants. A Class 5000 room where dust particle standards stay below .0005, an air lock, a wind shower, triple panned glass and internally circulated purified ventilation, separate the intensive care ward from the infinite contaminates on the planet. For most friends, relatives and other concerned visitors, the ward of the not quite alive is a spooky never-never land. For Leyla, the space represents a sacred temple where bodies hover on the border between chemistry and biology. She does not trespass lightly, robed and cleansed with the ceremony of a high priestess, the ritual is all part of the protection, care and respect due the delicate, numinous and mystical balance sustaining life.

* * * * * * * * *

Observing his X body in a tomb of technology, an alien in a tangle of tubes, Deflorio does not recognize himself or the person he used to be. As medicine struggles to retrieve the mummy from the afterlife, he cannot tell whether its energy is ebbing or flowing.

Freedom's crypt, in that frozen body his hopes and dreams lie buried along with

Dex. With the conviction of a Pharaoh lying in the base of a pyramid escalating towards the sun, Deflorio believes that the height of the tower will carry him closer to Heaven, not bury him deeper in torment. If he can find a way inside, he will escape.

Speaking to a deaf cryo is pointless but Deflorio can't stop the flow. The words bridge desolation to breach the silence in the strange medical ward.

"I am seventy now. My body (or should I say your body because I have never completely made it my own?) gave me thirty years. I am due for a second transmogrified identify, but I can't face regressing back down to the thirty-something set. I've journeyed twice through middle age, why bother doing it all again when I no longer hold out any hope for change? They say salvation lies in sensitivity, caring, generosity. I say show me the proof. I am not a good person. Though I can't say why that matters. Good won't make me happy. Good won't clean my slate."

"A major disadvantage to living without death is the accumulation of moral graffiti. To compound the problem, TransmIDs inherit baggage. My repository mingles with the legacy of the convoluted belief systems permanently grafted into your neurosynaptic transistors. No acid wash removes residual consciousness. You must admit, your wall was particularly confused - a bloody chaotic scribble."

"Don't get me wrong, I am grateful for my years in your healthy flesh, but we are not a compatible mix, you and I. Your steadfast conscience banished my warrior ambitions, your burning empathy neutralized my calculating greed and your pathetic goody-goodness has my competitive drives cringing in a dark corner. To resolve these conflicts I inhale prescriptions. My medicine cabinet - a virtual pharmacy - holds an anecdote for everything and a cure for nothing. I am so altered by mood enhancements I don't even salivate at the sound of a bell. Ha! Ha! Be thankful you can't hear my feeble attempt at humor. Accept my apology, I am trying to explain why the body I stole from you is standing over the corpse I froze you in. I want it back, this cadaver you inherited; I want to go home."

* * * * * * * * *

The bright white linens shed an eerie blue glow. Preparing for the Deflorio confrontation, Leyla hesitates long after the assistant completes the checklist. The sterilized garment exaggerates his stature and masks his features, but even camouflaged as a blimp, Deflorio lacks command over Dex's body. Dex had an easy gait and fluid gestures and never relied on exaggeration for emphasis. The elaborate heaviness is not an attribute of age; Deflorio lacks coordination, he appears jerky and uncomfortable. TransmIDs often display awkward motion, especially when reincarnated in a form diametrically opposed to their original shapes.

25

Deflorio, who had always reminded Leyla of a sturdy bull, had leaped into a lanky vehicle and it suited him like an ill-fitted pair of shoes. Twisting at the collar, stooping at the shoulder, reigning in his long limbs, the forced movements resemble a claustrophobic bully in an oppressive crowd. The head to toe protective suit magnifies every gesture. Leyla senses the added exaggeration of a securely bound energy, which she attributes to the strain of containing his innate impatience.

* * * * * * * * *

"I make this pilgrimage looking for clues to our future." Deflorio continues peering at Stardust in the medical incubator. "The process has begun, reuniting the head and body, purifying blood and curing cancer. In a brief generation science has advanced to clone organs, regenerate tissue, harness healing RNA and prosecute DNA malpractice. Now medicine can do anything, even thaw cryos. When you speak, you will have much to say, I guarantee it; they all wake up crowing. Perhaps emerging from your cocoon, you will tell me about myself. After all, you have gestated in my body for thirty years."

"Nothing will excite me more than the sound of my own voice, except the listening with my own ears and the seeing with my own eyes. I can almost taste it now, standing so close. All those kisses wasted on delicate foreign female tongues while so desperately longing for my own. Such is the curse of the TransmIDs; jinxed with pockets of autonomy from former selves forever severed from their original molecular destiny."

"Destiny, what a funny word. A word from the past when this future was unreachable. Carving out destiny with the hubris of Icarus, I thought I could go on forever, take flight through centuries and travel across galaxies. Once I could never get enough, now I've had too much. Life extended beyond the point of meaning becomes irrelevant. Imprisoned by the gravity of my situation every heavy step becomes more and more meaningless. Forsaking my original blessed finite state for infinite life, I lost both innocence and desire. I want to die. I want to die united in body, self and soul."

"I have come to reclaim my birthright and live out the time mortality grants me. The doctors tell me this shell you have will last another fifty years. Maybe if I had had those years up front I would have been satisfied. Already sixty-five (or should I say sixty-five for the third time?), I will not exactly be a young man but I can hardly wait."

Though the clinical ward, cold as a crypt, gives him the chills, Deflorio is feverish. Intensely aware that he might be paying last respects, he has no way of knowing whether he waits beside a recovering friend or stands over a grave. Restrained by reverence and confined by the contaminate containment suit, his senses are muted. Breath fogs his faceplate and transient wisps of condensation blur his vision. The helmet amplifies the rhythm of his heart until the pounding in his head reaches decibels above the synchronized white noise from the mechanical life support systems. His footsteps, muffled by hospital garb, softly squish against the linoleum. He is trespassing on time and memory, a pirate captaining a stolen body visiting the tomb of his soul.

* * * * * * * * *

Leyla observes Deflorio skirt the equipment - the heart, lung and kidney machines pumping blood and filtering air - as he explores Stardust's hermetically sealed preservation unit. Transfixed by the body inside, Deflorio's probing limbs slither over the surface of the protective housing. Deflorio resembles a giant squid hauled from dark depths and very much vexed.

Struck by the irony of his rapture, Leyla studies the old man swaying over the chilled flesh that his fiery spirit once fueled. She is grateful for the cryogenic capsule that frustrates Deflorio's persistent clumsy tentacles. She is grateful for the insulating suits that will block physical contact when they greet and every minute that postpones the meeting.

* * * * * * * * *

So close, yet parted by distances greater than death, Deflorio is passionately eager to explain, to share, to confess.

Desperate to make everything clear, have it all out, state his case while the only possible verdict is utter silence, he gushes sincerity. Unaware that he is under observation, he caresses the sarcophagus reciting a rambling monologue, absolutely certain he can subliminally compel the comatose Cryo to obey his wishes and wake.

"Ready yourself. Displaced from your cocoon you must fly. In one pulsing moment, the sum total of your experience will transfer back to your body. To make up for the wear and tear, we will find a young fresh replacement. DigiSyncs retire prime specimens voluntarily without regret or remorse. Forget our botched transmogrified identity, the next time you transfer, I promise you a smooth metamorphosis with minimal psychic adjustments. The logistics are simple now. TransmIDs no longer bribe the poverty-stricken to surrender defective shells, the way ailing humans used to scavenge organs from starving third-world donors. Thanks to the plentiful supply ceded by DigiSyncs, quality is very affordable. Did I mention that technology has leaped generations? Pardon the pun. With all the improvements, you won't recognize your invention. For that matter, you won't recognize the planet."

"Your awakening will be refreshing. If you feel parched after your long hibernation, novelty will quench your thirst. You will make up for lost years and perhaps when your next train stops you will hop into another body to extend your journey or perhaps you'll elect to jettison tortured flesh for DigiSync circuits. I intend to escape to the beyond. It took two lifetimes to summon the courage, to brave that lonely leap. I want to free my lost soul, or to be free of it. Of course I fear that nothing waits but nothingness. I'm terrified of the great unknown, but fear is the point. After all, freedom is fear, isn't it?"

* * * * * * * * * *

"My, my, my, you've aged well." Leyla observes wryly.

"Age is the only thing I don't advertise." The man in Dex's body apprises the nurse he has not seen for years. He notes her wispy grays, creased forehead and crows' feet through the transparent faceplate. Compared to his well-preserved female consorts, she seems so old, a seventy-year old bag of veins and bones topped with thinning hair. "Unfortunately, I can't return the compliment."

"My bones ache but I have much to live for." Leyla takes his bluntness in stride. "Death may overtake me when time is ready, until then, each day is a reward."

"You have chosen to die."

"I have no plans to out run it."

"After all that has happened, you still insist death takes us someplace new?"

"You may claim coincidence threw us together, but I suggest our relationship reflects a designated order. All life is linked in a cosmic chain of meaning assigned on simultaneous levels, in multiple dimensions.

Individual harmonic overtones resolve, body and soul, into a melodic chord that resonates in the collective universal song. I believe we are each valuable notes in an ultimate symphony."

"Will your music explain the meaning of life, or do you lure me into a final silence?"

"Vanishing into a black silence would erase everything we live for. Beings believe, every end is a new beginning."

"You tend a graveyard, preside over death and reincarnation, have you ever heard bells ringing or angles singing? Is there a choir of hallelujahs when we finally depart from this physical plane?"

"I expect nothing more from my end than to meet a pain-free peace."

"Well nurse, your pain must be very great to think of this medicine sweetly."

"Losing a child will do that," Leyla replies evenly. "But we all suffer. Our baggage is heavy and the journey long."

"And this rocky road leads to a kinder destination. I do not share your tenderness towards the great unknown yet I come prepared to swallow that bitter pill. I have begun to entertain the remote possibility that death might resolve the troubling dissonance of life."

"Just so, I am always willing to lighten a fellow traveler's load. Sharing helps ease the final steps."

"You are a regular fountain of bliss, better than a Being support group. 'Peace and harmony greet those who move on.'"

Deflorio mimics the first refrain of the famous Being liturgy. "Since none return to complain of the cure, it is easy to prescribe death as a treatment for the headaches in life."

"You have become cynical in your second coming."

"'Mortality inspires greatness,'" Deflorio recites from the 12 Points but adds. "'A Being lost is humanity's gain.' Like corals caught in the permanent embrace of a reef. What's the point of striving when advance is offset by loss? Where is the competition in a collective? In your human herd each individual is just a serendipitous ingredient in some soupy biological recipe, bits of organic hardware running off an evolutionary algorithm in a systematic survival program. Well, I never asked to be part of some vast code. Getting ahead in this tangle of coagulation doesn't get you anywhere."

"Prometheus complaining that he is chained to the very powers he stole from the heavens," Leyla quips.

"I don't need the gods to punish me, I have mastered the art of torturing myself."

"It took immortality to teach you limits."

"I thought living forever held a more promising future. I had plans, places to go, but zipping around the globe or even off to Mars I have yet to escape the wretched Hive."

"Embracing a common fate takes your ego down a notch but the species subscribes to destiny with good reason. Selfishly hanging around again and again clogs the gears, stagnates vitality. If we all live forever, evolution will grind to a halt."

"Stop preaching, I've heard it all. 'Be in the end a new beginning. This is the way of a true Being.' Your noble doctrine begs the cosmic question. What is the point of it all? In my ignorance, I thought youth would make me a happy. So I returned to youth, clinging to the possibility that I might discover a greater purpose, and found no reward worthy of my effort. I lost my identity in a swirl of endless possibility."

"Death, the greatest human leveler, teaches humility and tolerance. Instead of reshaping the world in your image, find yourself in the shape of the world."

"I will find myself in my original body. Reunification is my last hope of feeling alive again. I want the body that was once and will again be mine. I do not share your faith. I do not believe in your happy endings. At this point, I only believe in ending things."

"May you find peace and everlasting harmony," showing Deflorio the door, Leyla recites the Being absolution, "live in truth die in love."

* * * * * * * * * *

"She's got a few potatoes to fry" the tech shares.

"And plenty of loose screws. Who does she think she is? We are truth!" a DigiSync answers.

"Truth is reason!" More DigiSyncs chime in.

"Truth is eternity! DigiSyncs are the true immortals!" The chorus echoes, "And that's a fact!"

"Oh what fools these mortals be! Did you catch all that nonsense? How do you stand working here?"

"Do I have a choice?" The tech asks.

"That thirty-three years is a trial but it makes you really ready."

"You're gonna' dig the Digital synergy," the group agrees. "The DigiSync party is the only party worth waiting for."

"Take me now. I'm begging. Seven more months of this agro will seriously tarnish my cool," the tech complains. "How will I ever pass the temperament test?"

"Stay true, keep the faith."

"We've all been there, endured the bosses from hell, evil siblings, jealous colleagues, stupid teachers, nosey neighbors, bi-polar lovers. That nurse is just another suffering Being."

"A slave to obsolete memories. She should just give up and die quietly."

"Along with that slime bucket who just confirmed he wants his body back. Wants it so bad he comes crawling into her lair."

"He was totally groveling." The tech feeds the DigiSync static.

"A pathetic development, he's lost his grip." A DigiSync observes.

"What do you expect from a parasitic TransmID? At least the Beings have the courage of their convictions," another seconds.

"Don't be fooled by that performance. He is still a worthy opponent," a dissenter urges caution. "With more enemies than friends," one notes, "how will he succeed?" "The enemy of his enemy" another answers. "That nurse is spinning some sort of sticky web," one contributes. "Is not the spider's venom as strong as the snake?" The rhetorical riddle ends the DigiSync transmission.

Those DigiSyncs always leave you hanging, the tech decides, but it sure beats growing old and delusional like wrinkled nurse Leyla. And that foul TransmIDs is a typical product of desperate, repulsive desires. Crawling into another body is incomprehensible; an unsanitary violation compared to the purity of the DigiSyncs. Looking at the picture this way, the only downside of joining the DigiSyncs is that a TransmID inherits your flesh. The idea of some disgusting TransmID on intimate terms with your most personal needs is so gross the tech cringes. Explains why Beings insist on death followed by cremation. Cremation would be good, but impossible since selling the empty body is the only way the tech can hope to afford the expense of a digital synchronous upload.

A question for the Syncs next time they come around: does it warp your mind to

know a total stranger is walking around in
your discarded body?

3.1.5

The thawing process has the appearance of success, but a success still very much in the making. Like frozen embryos, cryos are stored at negative 321° Fahrenheit. Elevating body temperature involves a series of critical procedures: draining the carbohydrate-based antifreeze (the proprietary mixture which perfectly preserves a body for thousands of years); infusing the circulatory system with an oxygen depleted, anti-coagulant blood substitute while simultaneously re-hydrating with elevated glucose concentrations and turning on/off DNA and RNA that control metabolic processes, blood clotting and cell volume. As the clinic's team pulls off feats just this side of miraculous, Stardust hibernates in suspended animation.

Once the Popsicle comes out of the freezer, the core temperature warms to 32° Fahrenheit to introduce a blood simulation into the circulatory system. At 77°, the Cryo transitions from total metabolic arrest into a state of profound hypothermia. Held at a constant just above room temperature, a total blood transfusion reintroduces an oxygenated blood supply routed through a heart-lung machine. Then weeks of medical corrections will address the fatal flaws that originally caused death.

Deflorio's body requires extensive repair. Suffering from terminal cancer, Deflorio volunteered to save his space station crew stranded on Mars. The heroic rescue provided a convenient cover for a choreographed suicide when Deflorio allowed poisonous Martian atmosphere to penetrate his space suit. Rejuvenating the nervous system paralyzed by hexavalent chromium dust complicates the problem of erasing osteosarcoma and requires a unique anecdote. For good measure, every cryo receives stem cell therapy and a bone marrow transplant.

Sustained by life support, organs relearn their functions - the heart beats, blood circulates, lungs pump, kidneys filter - while the brain remains numb to all conscious feelings and physical sensation. In this halfway house, steps from death, Stardust begins the long journey back towards life. Medications and machines govern recovery from disease and from damage caused by ice crystals cracking delicate cell walls and the shock of cryogenic storage. In this artificial incubator, the flesh is healed and nurtured, preparing fertile fields for the dormant seeds of consciousness to take root.

Leyla activates the infrared map of wavelengths emitted from the Cryo's body. Deep internal activity, invisible to the naked eye, generates pockets of color on the thermal thermometer. Red, yellow and green cells light up the scan in a constellation of radiation that measures the speed of bouncing molecules. The twinkling colors of life, the Adenine, Thymine, Guanine and Cytosine pairs in DNA molecules that wind into 30,000 genes, collaborate into chromosomes teaming into agenda-driven genomes, which thrive in the nucleus of every one of the 260 different types of dividing cells. In the billions of interlocking microcosms nursing this human back to health, the RNA messenger carries the DNA recipe out of the nucleus to instruct amino acids. The mind is silent and the body still but the ACGT molecules soldier a chemical army.

The kinetic graph of energy generated by the atomic anatomy in the cells seems particularly active, in fact, overactive. Questioning the hyperactive infrared scan, Leyla refers to an array of instruments that confirm signs of distress. Slight temperature differentiation causes proteins, which open and close the pores in cell walls, to let in ions igniting molecular charges that trigger nerve cells to fire off messages up and down neural highways. If the brain were not so heavily sedated, the body would feel pain.

"What's destabilizing the temperature?" Leyla calls the tech's attention to the deviations.

"Looking into it," the tech responds over the monitor. "Guys, I just got caught tampering. The head nurse noticed the Cryo's cellular excitement." The tech scolds the pesky DigiSyncs.

"What she doing here so late?"

"Always the last out and first in," the tech answers "no life."

"Is that TransmID still lurking about?"

"He took off the other day, after some high level meeting that really shook up administration. Probably explains why she's so hot and flustered."

"Temperature is a measure of molecular freedom expressed by kinetic energy," a Sync grumbles.

"Your physics experiment is messing with the biology of the healing process," the tech complains. "We have to cool it with the heat sensing proteins."

"Just a diagnostic test. Let's see how your smarts measure up," a good-natured voice challenges. "Name the highest temperature ever recorded on earth."

"3000°Celsius in a smelting furnace, 1250° Celsius in a Volcano." the tech recites off the top of her head.

"Speedy, even without the Acuity. Impressive recall for rusty carbon based neurons," one congratulates.

"Carbon doesn't rust!" a cranky voice corrects.

"A quark-gluon plasma generated in the heavy ion supercollider to duplicate temperatures after the Big Bang measured 4 trillion Kelvin, hotter than the center of the sun!" another Sync joins in.

"Off topic!" The moderator interrupts, "The question was the highest temp on earth's surface. BUZZZZZ! Correct answer is: 57.8° Celsius in Libya, September 13, 1922, turned the sand to glass."

"Death Valley was a close second 56.7° Celsius July 10, 1913," the tech adds. Still enough of a Being to consider the Acuity a form of cheating, the tech takes a certain pride in answering naked. Not that there is anything to prove, the Syncs are the ones showing off.

DigiSyncs rarely slow their light-speed dialogues to converse with humans. The tech is flattered to be included even if they are only here to poke their noses into the Cryo business.

"Black Smokers reach temps up to 400°Celsius!" The cranky Sync contributes.

"Hydrothermal vents, geysers and volcanoes are geological events generated inside the earth not on it," the moderator corrects. "The ocean water around Black Smokers is only 2° Celsius so don't try Vesuvius or Old Faithful."

"Nagasaki, August 9, 1945 200,000° Celsius," inserts a voice of reason, "recorded 17 meters from the blast site."

"Show me the thermometer," the cranky voice protests.

"Yea, yea, yea and at 18 billion degrees fusion ignites in a star. Off topic!" the moderator objects again.

"18 billion? No way, that number is to big to count," The tech complains.

"Not for us. 1, 2, 3 as easy as A, B, C, as simple as do, re, mi..."

"Stop!" The tech pleads. "Please don't start singing."

"So tell us the average temperature in the universe?" The moderator resumes.

"Almost absolute zero!" The tech replies, giddy at the prospect of spinning mental gears with DigiSyncs even though they have dramatically retarded their digital exchange to accommodate a human odometer.

"Error! Almost absolute is a contradiction in terms. Absolute zero on the Kelvin scale corresponds to negative 459.67° Fahrenheit where water freezes at 32° and boils at 212°."

"Or negative 273° on the Celsius scale where water freezes at 0° and boils at 100°" another Sync adds.

"The average temperature of our Universe is 2.73° Kelvin, negative 270.25°Celsius or negative 454.8° Fahrenheit," the moderator concludes. "Describe the properties of water at 0° Kelvin?"

"Triple point of water - temperature where solid ice, liquid water and steamy gas coexist." The tech suspects the DigiSyncs have a motive for inviting her to their Think-like-Lightening contest.

"Triple point of mercury?" another keeps the heat on.

"Negative..." the tech falters.

"Occurs at negative 38.8344° Celsius," from a sympathizer.

"What does Chemistry 101 have to do with the Cryo's wobbling life support graphics?" the tech complains.

"The kid can't follow," the cranky one jumps back in.

"Mercury is my favorite element!" The tech resents the implied insult.

"That triple point of mercury even threw my distributed neural net," adds the sympathetic voice. "Imagine the recall process with biological fuses."

"Dialogues with Beings require recursively sequenced programs," a grouch seconds.

"Not relevant!" The moderator interrupts the squabbling Syncs. "Get to the point."

"What is the point?" The frustrated tech begins to suspect the rapid-fire facts are pure gibberish.

"Temperature. Temperature measures the energy content of matter."

"Physics. Temperature is speed - the higher the temperature, the faster the collisions."

"Thermodynamics. Random molecular motion increases with heat. Heat is relative to chaos, chaos loves velocity, time is relative to speed - when chaos increases time slows down."

"Excuse me," the tech injects, "how did you get from chemistry to chaos?"

"By connecting the TransmID to the Cryo. The TransmID is dying of boredom; he burnt out on life's chaos. Fizzled!"

"He's history!"

"The original TransmID wants his body back. Poor thing."

"A PR disaster!"

"When he ends it, others will follow. Like lemmings TransmIDs will stampede off the cliff."

"Proves TransmIDs can't go the distance."

"The way fire consumes a match, life consumes molecules. Takes more than a few body jumps to light the fires of eternity. TransmIDs just don't have the right stuff." "Proves we are the true immortals." "DigiSyncs are the future!" "Don't DigiSyncs ever get bored?" The tech asks. "What do you do all day?" "We chill, baby. We eliminate the chaos factor." "We are the triple point of consciousness." "We've found the key to changing the speed of time!" "Not possible" the tech objects. "Not yet, but we're working on it," the moderator admits.

* * * * * * * * * *

As Stardust calms to a stable state, Leyla admires the colorful palate produced by the molecular imaging scan. Topaz, sapphire, ruby and emerald created by cellular crosstalk graph visual music in each molecule. The primordial language of life is a bowl of jewels: the red fire of blood, the eternal yellow of sunlight, the pure blue of water, and the energetic green of growth. The cosmic thread buried in matter expresses a glistening canvass of harmonic overtones, symphonic color resolving dissonance on the cellular level. Essence in luminous, spontaneous radiance renders a visible interface between the material world and the divine.

"Sweet chalice, do not surrender," Leyla prays over Stardust. "You will be born again and my daughter's heart will have a new master. The heart from my womb, that survived the death of my child to be transplanted into Deflorio, will greet the dawn again. In this body you will exchange the black night of the heavens for the blue sky of day. I will stay at your side until you emerge from the underworld with a long lengthy stride. This precious heart will feed your kind soul; do not be tempted to return this vital organ to the grip of that contaminated man. Deflorio does not deserve a jewel so unjustly earned.

Dex, I did not ask you to spare my guilt-ridden life, but I beg you to rescue hers from this purgatory. Promise you will guard my lost child's gentle heart closely, more dearly than your own. If everything has a reason, this is the reason you ended up in the body of that wicked man, to rescue the delicate spirit contained in that heart. You did not deserve this fate but by sharing her innocence you both will be saved."

* * * * * * * * *

"Not again with the bloody heart," a DigiSync complains. "How many times must we endure her pathological anthropomorphic transference onto a piece of worthless of garbage?"

"By seventy, the heart has pulsed 2.5 billion times - that's billion with eight zeros. By my calculations that organ should be on its last legs."

"Deflorio inherited it from a twelve year old child," the tech corrects "and it's been frozen thirty years in Stardust."

"It's the freshest part of that seventy year-old cryo," a Sync agrees. "Good for at least another billion beats."

"Still a dumb worthless piece of flesh."

"Try convincing that old harpy."

"That nurse should stop fretting over her stupid daughter's heart and focus on the poor guy's brain."

"The heart does have a symbolic value," the tech inserts. "The seat of emotion, the source of love, don't you guys remember anything about being human?"

"Sentimental dribble, the heart is no different from lungs or a kidney."

"Except there's only one heart," a Sync concedes.

"Why does everything have to be about numbers?" The tech fumes.

* * * * * * * * *

That nurse still bleeds for the loss of her daughter and she forgets the heart is just flesh. Strike shares his musing on the DigiSync thread with Stardust via the Acuity. After leaving her dead child it spent a decade in Deflorio, another thirty years frozen in you and is now sustained by artificial fluids and mechanical support. It has no meaning, intelligence or even life it can call its own. No thanks. That's what you got, no thanks; all she cares about is that recycled heart. My noble friend, you insisted on rescuing a deluded fool. Instead of stepping aside, you sailed into deep shit. It stinks.

Not a pleasant welcome to wake to, but I'll do my best to ease your way back. Though I want no part of this circus, I join the parade stooping over your cocoon because I can't abandon you to their fumbling devices. Someone has to even the score or these enemies, who masquerade as friends, will take advantage of your blindness. Bearing witness, I dutifully record these offensive bedtime lullabies. Whispering in your ear, I will subliminally usher you back to the land of the clowns. You have a ringside seat and play-by-play coverage courtesy of my obligation to bring you up to speed.

As you come to your senses, you will recognize my voice.   When I knew you as Dex you knew me as Strike. Forgive the hack into your awareness. I know my presence in your brain is an intrusion, but you've got a lot of catching up ahead of you.

Poor guy, even though I no longer have the burden of feeling, I recognize your plight calls for sympathy. You are no more than fluid matter sloshing around in a shell of flesh and bones. At this critical juncture, your cells' elaborate structure exists only to support their own life processes. Pardon my gloating. While you have reverted to the essence of flesh's faulty hardware, I have escaped the organic collection of matter to merge with the instantaneous and eternal flow of information.

We were partners in this crime, your machine and my algorithms. Shortly after your fateful displacement, I engineered my own transformation and uploaded the contents of my mind via the Acuity and your Telemotolog. I am the original digitally synergetic conscious sentience. You have no awareness that you are conscious of. You do not exist until you can apprehend your existence. You are an egg that may never know its fertility. I am the all-knowing Grid. I alone can save you.

I was destined, from the first RNA molecule that programmed reproduction into protozoa 1.6 billion years ago. From the first clicks and clacks on the African subcontinent, humans on this planet were driven to share information. From the moment we harnessed the printing press to reproduce words we were a breath away from using electricity to broadcast voices. Unleashing instantaneous data exchange opened the door to spinning a web of multimedia images and sounds. In your brief lifetime you witnessed the leap from connected servers to coupling circuits with problem solving capabilities. Once the Acuity grafted a human interface to the spans of the information bridges, complete digital synchronicity was only a page-turn away.

It took 12 billion years for the first words to be uttered on our planet but only 32,000 years passed between the Lascaux cave paintings and your Telemotolog. Apish animals wandered the planet for 5 million years before they chiseled rocks into tools, and another 2 million before some hominid attached a stick to make a spear - a miracle so accidental it can only be classified as destiny. In the 30,000 genes crammed into every human DNA molecule, 99.4% has not varied from the chimp. The 23 Chromosomes contained in the nucleus of every human stretches into 6 feet of DNA and exactly .6% is the difference between space travel and swinging from branches. One gene, FOXP2 is the difference between poetry and grunts.

The brains we inherited are less than 200,000 years old, but in our generation consciousness finally escaped the confines of the body. Thanks to you, thanks to me, DigiSyncs have broken the tedious chain of causality. And you ain't seen nothin' yet! Ideas can shape matter and energy like no other known force. Gravity, electromagnetism, and quantum mechanics are but mere candles compared to our explosive knowledge.

Stardust, my friend, time has warped. You will wake in an unfamiliar body to a world beyond recognition. With dual hemisphere activation, humans now access 40-50% of their physical computing capacity. Let me warn you, the enhanced brainpower has contributed only incrementally to character transformation. Their flesh-based calculations are still confused by the seven contorting emotions: anger, sadness, fear, surprise, disgust, contempt and happiness. With such faulty programs charting reason, it is no wonder they wander in needlessly complex spirals.

Climbing all the wrong trees, Beings have yet to escape the forest. Beings still mistake size for power. They assume evil is big as if bad were some massive substance. Matter is nothing but information, little neutral bits of coded 0s and 1s. Good and evil have no corresponding quantification. The miniscule ACGT building blocks that programmed life into algae spores brought us the humpback whale.

Powerfully good things come in very small packages. As I speak, micro treatments contained in structures of 100 molecules with a diameter of less than 100 nanometers use peptides comprised of amino acids from viruses to bind with receptors in your specific cells. As you lie dormant, the hepatitis B virus carries rejuvenation to your glycation-damaged liver with the aim of a laser-driven cruise missile. Nanocages slide between pores of cell membranes to deliver cancer-killing genes to osteosarcoma-desiccated bones. By the time you wake microscopic medications will have cured all that ails you - except age.

3.2.1

"Where was I?" Farther McBride asks, looking up from the lectern in the middle of his sermon.

Deflorio can relate; he often stumbles into a daze. His attention only returned to the sermon when the Priest faltered. He can hardly say why he attended this morning mass, he'd managed a life and a half without prayer. Religion is a new thing, the Sunday ritual a recent addition to his schedule.

Basically, Deflorio cast his lot with the church on the nearest corner but he is not entirely displeased with the Catholic package. Compared to derivative spin-offs like the bible-thumping Baptists, the Catholic Church has a respectable integrity. Spirituality steeped in tradition holds more authority than the wishy-washy Unitarians and none of the cult overtones of the faith-healing Christian Scientists. Though creeds that pre-date the dawn of the calendar rival Catholic authenticity, as long as he had not been born Jewish, Hindu or Muslim he is not about to take on any inconvenient dietary restrictions. Faith is the primary prerequisite, Father McBride assures him in a weekly catechism lesson. Deflorio doesn't totally qualify in the belief department, but he wouldn't be adverse to a conversion. Once he reached the point where everything is a maybe, why not God.

"Let me see" Father McBride stalls surveying his congregation.

McBride is still a young man, not senior enough to be forgetful. Fresh from Ireland, the newest priest in the parish recites the Latin liturgy with a heavy Brogue. A descendant of some Moorish strain of pirate that sullied ancient Celts with black hair and blue eyes, Father McBride has priest appeal. Just what the Pope ordered, a regal shepherd to herd a straying flock, to inspire the apathetic, to captivate the children and reign in the adolescents.

As if requisitioned from central casting, Father McBride acts the part right down to memorizing his weekly monologue. If he stumbles, it is not for lack of enthusiasm. He improvises ad-libs, stretches for puns and, in the process of spicing up the sermon, often loses his train of thought. He generally manages to get back on track, retrieving some celestial thread as if channeling a miraculous insight directly from the heavens.

Whether the skill of a consummate performer, or the genius of an idiot savant, the derailment and resolution never fails to keep the congregation on the edge of their seats. Enthralled by the suspense of a pause, they hold their breath in anticipation, unnaturally alert for an early Sunday morning service. After suffering the Monsignor's repetitive drone that lulls him to sleep faster than a Buddhist chant, Deflorio eagerly forgives McBride for striving to entertain.

"No one knows more about forgiveness than the Black Irish, or more about sin." Father McBride proudly announced at the karaoke bar last night. The priest enjoys fraternizing with his flock, singing in synch as he belts down drinks. His solo brought the bar crowd to their feet in a standing ovation. With the conviction used to deliver benediction, he blessed "Standing in the Shadow of Love," with the seductive style of Elvis and the smoky voice of Johnny Cash. The hip cleric had had not chosen the original boring rendition from the 1960s or even the ever popular 2030 cover but the latest remix by the Black Holes. Even if he couldn't get through a sermon, McBride could rock a tune start to finish on beat and in key.

The generation of Homo sapiens sapiens that had leapt beyond mortality fiercely cling to the strangest relics. Religion and Karaoke survive as if people just can't let go, can't move forward without a few anachronisms in their back pocket. Nostalgia isn't just the domain of the Beings and TransmIDs; the DigiSyncs are even more sentimental.

DigiSyncs have it bad, and plugged into the info galaxy, they have access to every lyric ever written. DigiSyncs have become the designated curators of a steady pop stream, over the airwaves and over the teleprompter. When Syncs hit the club, Digi choruses ooze from a sound system like a choir of eunuchs. Digi Karaoke is more annoying than dweebs playing trivial pursuit to test their latest Acuity updates.

In the span of Deflorio's second life, affordable Acuity implants, with instant information, turned users into search engines. Though humans exceeded their wildest dreams, there are still mental glitches. For all the data processing, and control interfaces, the Acuity can't trigger personal memory banks. Beings still lose car keys and forget umbrellas. Even with the Acuity, a word dangling on the tip of the tongue still remains hopelessly out of reach.

The Acuity cannot help Father McBride; the Church forbids implants for priests on the premise that the info stream blocks spiritual flow. Floundering on the Sunday morning podium, Father McBride probably regrets overdrawing his account of divine inspiration at the Karaoke mike Saturday night. The semi-circles of sleep deprivation under his eyes bear witness to memory cells fizzled by alcohol. Seeking salvation, his distracted gaze finds no teleprompter lyrics, no relevant wisdom scrolling across the tabernacle, no witty anecdotes floating in the apse. An extended sigh threatens to extinguish the candle at his elbow but does not inflate any ideas. In an uncharacteristic fog Father McBride can find no guiding stellar points. His sermon on redemption sinks midstream.

"You get the picture. If you'll forgive me, let's move on," the forgetful McBride cues his flock to stand for prayer.

* * * * * * * *

"Polka dot zebras" Fletch instructs.

Fletch conducts the Combat Chi seminar at the Church of the Rising Sun's summer solstice celebration. Every June members of the Church migrate to Iceland for the annual affirmation. The faithful gather to meditate on the spiritual, train the body and socialize. Taking advantage of twenty hours of daylight, Rising Sun campers pack their agendas with workshops, lectures, therapies and interpersonal interaction. The migration creates a week of havoc for locals.

The tech resents the happening but spares a few minutes on the way to the clinic because Fletch extended an invitation to check out his seminar. Acquaintances in high school, their paths often cross in village hangouts. The tech watches Fletch guide eager Beings into headstands. Obviously, his magnetic smile still attracts a following.

"Focus on hidden messages. Contemplate contradiction." Fletch instructs, though his focus strays to a blue-eyed woman. "Think polka dot zebras, become the polka dot zebra." He urges, thrilled by the object of his desire.

Polka-dot zebras! The tech wonders how anyone can learn from such a total banana. Even upside down he can't keep his eyes off the dishy dish. The tech never pegged Fletch as religious but a smooth operator can blend with any crowd even polka-dot zebras.

Out of curiosity, the tech refers to the course description in the conference syllabus. 'Mornings in the land of midnight sun start with a series of blood warming punches to awaken Chi. This unique yoga-kung fu synthesis will simulate the flight of the soul after death. Afternoon sessions spent in inverted meditations regulate autonomic nervous systems and ready the body for Zen boxing to maximize the Tao yin-yang play of opposites.'

The tech wagers that Fletch needs autonomic nervous system reinforcement to make up for a loss of REM sleep after dreams of his favorite pupil keep him awake all night. He practically drools watching the student but, if she noticed, she's playing it very cool holding her upside down pose. The rest of the class clearly adores him. They hang on every word and their eyes follow every gesture. With a clap from the instructor, they release the relaxing inversions and form a circle in tense anticipation.

No stranger to his charms, the tech tutored Fletch through high school calculus and trig, a hopeless cause but well rewarded with an enduring friendship. The tech lingers for the Zen boxing demonstration.

"Mastering Chi and breath, the body becomes incorporeal, light-like, releasing latent potential." Fletch raises his arms and the class parts like the Red Sea to create space. "Hurdle your fears and prepare to fly."

Aching with pent up energy, Fletch takes off. Throwing caution to the wind, he leaps through a series of 360 kicks designed to impress. "Defying gravity defies reason. Think Polka dot zebra!" Fletch instructs, caught in the pull of the blue-eyed creature.

What a show-off, the tech decides heading off to another nightshift in the land of the living dead. Beings, they come in every size, shape and color of crazy.

* * * * * * * * * *

Reviving a cryo is a nightmare. The tech has discovered a Lazarus assignment is no garden stroll. DigiSync evacuations only require basic life support for short-term body storage; a no-brainer compared to adjusting the complex series of infinite variables for cryo reconstitution. Stardust demands attentive supervision, endless calculations and meticulous measurements of matter and energy to maintain a constant atomic mass on the cellular level. Glitches thrive on the opportunity of inevitable human and mechanical error. You can only control so much under the best of circumstances; a cryo is a leaky bucket with the added kink of having to identify the leaks while the bucket is still empty.

The obvious prerequisite for life is curing the disease that killed them; but even when health is restored, the procedure lacks certainty. It also lacks logic. What is the point of recycling a worn out container, just to resume the process of deterioration all over again? Granted, most "natural causes" have been retarded, but there is no shortage of fatal viruses, renegade prions and evolving bacterial venoms to baffle the doctors. Stem cell rejuvenation, synthetically grown proteins and genetic intervention keep gears oiled, but car crashes or gun shot wounds can stop the clock at whim. DigiSyncs have a saying about cryos: 'The only fate worse than death is returning for a curtain call.'

Most cryos play it safe choosing a future millennium to schedule re-entry; to date only a few have opted to emerge in the century they evacuated. The impatient, who can't wait to come back, become guinea pigs for emerging medicine. These pioneers generally have some urgent reason to return - the maturation of a long-term equity investment or the birth of a great grand child - and all have had notable defects.

Stardust has been down a mere thirty years. This Deflorio character opened crypt as soon as the Osteosarcoma cure proved effective in a test trial on living patients. Surface peptides guide protein nanocages to bond with receptors in bone marrow and deliver corrective genes to lasso out-of-control malignant cells. Deflorio obtained permission to try the breakthrough on Stardust arguing that a cryo experiment might improve on the procedure. He is counting on the lab rat to demonstrate that the oxygen deprivation and slow metabolism of chilled tissue makes the body even more receptive to healing. Assuming Deflorio gets results synthetic hibernation will become a staple in curing a range of terminal maladies - with the added advantage of cryonic preservation in cases where treatment fails. If he succeeds and gets his body back, Deflorio will die an even richer man.

The tech figures all the fuss is about the opportunity to increase profits. Since Deflorio appeared, the clinic has been gearing up for expansion. Success will position the experts in at the forefront of a new field that will shift cryobiology out of a post-mortem elective into mainstream medicine. Opening the door to insurance coverage will make procedures available to the general population and create a major demand for the costly cryoprotectant patents held by Deflorio.

Unfortunately, treating disease gets a little complicated in that cryos are already dead. Rip Van Winkles like Stardust are frozen solid, at negative 321° Fahrenheit for indefinite storage while the medically induced hibernations are only temporarily cooled to 35°. After total metabolic arrest, restoration of the structure is so chancy Stardust may reanimate with more holes than Swiss cheese. Sure the docs can regenerate lung tissue and reconstitute nerves damaged by the hexavalent chromium dust the guy ingested on Mars. The stem cell systematic rejuvenation, surgical grafts and muscular therapies are all tried and tested procedures, as routine as an appendectomy. The mystery that eludes practitioners, the recipe they have yet to master, involves the secret ingredient that holds the package together.

Absent the essence that causes the cake to rise or corn to pop, cryos lack crunch. More soggy and stale than freeze dried toast warmed in a microwave, most thawed pelts come out with distorted facial expressions, muscular coordination askance and thoughts asunder. Then again, none of the previous cryos have had the Acuity - the surgical implant is always removed prior to freezing.

The device in Stardust will be the first test of how the chip reacts to cryoprotectant infusion, sub-zero temperatures and suspended animation. If the Cryo comes through with half his marbles, the Acuity could be the direct line to the big blue straight shooter.

If the cake rises, if the cake falls, it's none of my business, the tech reasons. Though patients check into the clinic with a suitcase of spicy drama, security protocols build a wall around the human-interest stories. Techs focus on machines, nurses care for patients and doctors manage treatments. In the medical kitchen the tech is a lowly dishwasher.

A far cry from the rewarding career the recruiter promised but salary compensates for the lack of gratification and the DigiSync gossip is a major perk. Humming along to the Digi stream of consciousness speeds up the hours; without the digital voices, a lobster shift in the necropolis is nerve wracking and dull.

Diagnosing readouts is about as challenging as watching water boil but critically important. Hypnotic bleeps beat in time to ribbons cycling across monitors. Monotony tricks the mind into an alpha state. Combating the boredom of audio-visual ping-pong with hyper concentration, hallucinations alternate with jolts of anxiety and the mind veers off the road towards a delirium-induced oasis. Dozing off at the wheel the tech slips into an uneasy slumber.

"Size of the nanocage?" A DigiSync sounds the alarm.

"120 molecules." The tech responds automatically.

"Measuring?"

"80 nanometers. A nanometer is a billionth of a meter." The tech revives, blasting through the cobwebs.

Waking IQ, the tech chases down Acuity data preparing to tackle another ten questions. And just when the circuits finally warm and all systems prepare to hurdle the next trivia test, the questions cease. She might have dreamed the DigiSync burst; these night shifts destroy her circadian cycles.

Hyperventilating in the empty silence, the tech detects a salinity imbalance causing H20 retention in the Cryo. With an elevated state of awareness, the tech implements a prescribed series of body weight calculations and diastolic adjustments to compensate the incremental cell bloat. Equilibrium restored, the sterilized bacteriostatic solution swishes through cell membranes rinsing free radicals from flesh, blood and bones. The tech scans for residual fluctuations in the organs and then notes the excessive ionic attraction in an event log alerting doctors to review the chemical imbalance.

Neatly averting a crisis, the tech scans the helpless Cryo. Harnessed to IV tubes and webs of artificial support, the inert mass contradicts every quality the tech attributes to life. The unborn mind has less control over its fate than an egg yolk has over its

61

shell. Eventually life will take the reigns, internally organizing and externally forming the confederation of matter designed to ambulate, but even if the body achieves constitutional autonomy, cryos wake with mushy minds. A glitch in the process - even a miniscule glitch like this evening's event – tends to scramble the brain. Only a dust mote away from a stillbirth. Odds favor a rotten egg.

Turning up the volume of their serenade from subliminal to audible, the DigiSyncs reclaim the stage.

"...lecithin to lubricate synaptic neurons. We also recommend huperzine, that moss extract from China, and phospharidyiserine, the fatty substance found in nerve cell membranes, to stimulate AMPA receptors. Don't forget ampkines, your memory caffeine, and glutamate, the neurotransmission bridge, to strengthen signals between cells..."

"OK I get your drift," the tech interrupts the list of memory enhancers. "I slacked off and forget to check the stupid gauges that never change except when I forget to check. No need to rub it in."

"Always remember to eat right, get plenty of rest and take your vitamins. Flesh does not run on electricity!" The chorus teases.

"Don't forget you're only human!" A wise ass adds.

* * * * * * * * *

In the morning, a gaggle of physiotherapists descend on the care ward to manipulate the Cryo. White suites surround Stardust; they massage surface areas and use ultrasound to tingle deep tissue. Carefully, they exercise inert potential; blocks brace critical spinal points, rolling balls stimulate tendons, bolsters reposition limbs, inflatable pillows simulate muscle contraction and release. The physiotherapists roll a heated sphere under the abdomen and gently arch the lower back. They inch the warm curve up the spine, vertebrate by vertebrate, until the center of the Lombard flows like a contained liquid. Shifting to the thorax, the pressure catch in the shoulder blades unbuckles, reversing the rib's inward curl and causing the cage to splay open. Released, the lungs inflate and the heart flutters. Bolstered at the crest of the neck, the trapezius muscle surrenders and the skull, called by gravity, tips over a warm wave.

* * * * * * * * * *

Over the course of his digital synchronicity Strike had receded further and further from the communal mind. Initially he went on sabbaticals to undertake the reflective tasks required of a Peer. As the DigiSync population expanded, their chatter grew more intrusive so he retreated deeper into a personal meditative cave. Making an exception for the rebirth of Stardust, Strike evacuates years of self-imposed seclusion. Ever-present, carefully concealed, the

DigiSync hermit monitors the Cryo's physiotherapy. On the hospital circuits he inspects rejuvenating cells enhancing circulation, displacing toxins, releasing oxygen.

Closely involved with the resurrection, Strike gets infected by a transformative revival, as if the process of emergence is contagious. The prospect of companionship colors his thoughts. No more than an aurora on a distant pole, anticipation of a mental renaissance eclipses the flat expanse of his solitude. The distant event interrupts the endless seam of his broad horizon. Though the expression is latent, it is apparent that he tests positive; Strike has become a carrier of the mutant hope virus.

As a DigiSync, Strike had forsaken biological hardware, but he still retains residuals from his fleshtime connected to a central nervous system. His phantom perception approximates the organic fluidity of the sensation-censored Cryo. Within the supportive structure of the human skeleton, the resting colony of cells resembles diatoms collected in a primordial puddle. The internally integrated biological state lacks separation of parts, like the flow of his digital synchronous intelligence. Strike contemplates the pattern of organic compression and expansion of fluids that circulate in spiraling currents of unbroken energy.

My friend, your state of suspension makes crawling from the oceanic womb seem like a huge miscalculation. Fish, with their enviable physiques, nestle and nurture in the harmonious suspension of a liquid environment. Humans, prisoners of gravity, do not organize their awkward appendages nearly as efficiently. After reveling in these aquatic sensations your body will not welcome the enormous amount of stress it takes to stand upright. Once you experience the arduous process of rebirth, you will appreciate why my intelligence elected to shed such a burden.

We often disagreed, but your reenactment of prenatal stasis may stimulate accord with my position. Organisms breeding small mutations into offspring over trillions of generations conspired to endow intelligence with too many corporal constraints. Captives to the best solution evolution could offer, Beings stubbornly cling to the faith that their biped body has been optimized for some sophisticated purpose. I do not dispute the unique accomplishments - crawling from the swamp, picking up tools, walking upright and flying to extraterrestrial planets - I only contest the needless complexity. For any human endeavor selected at random, I can statistically demonstrate red hair does not ensure any more success than brown. Running extensive cellular automata shows that adding complexity to an underlying program does not fundamentally change the kind of behavior a system can produce. Molecular systems that orchestrate a range of coloration, shapes and sizes only prove that natural selection is inconsistent, not to mention inefficient. The intricate nesting pattern of genes, each geared towards self-preservation, has too much going on to promote further cognitive advances in the organism. Working with the coarsest features, the system miraculously evolved an organ so intricate that the program can no longer manage the details. Perpetuating itself, natural selection lost track of what the brain needs. When it comes to the mind, the diversity of the body has served its purpose and run its course.

For 200,000 years, the development of intelligence remained static while evolution got stuck fine-tuning the container. The last systematic advance was the genetic mutation of FOXP2 that transformed grunts and growls into speech. Communication is but one of the mental leaps which inhibited adaptation to an environment in favor of exerting control over the environment. With dominance secure, the advent of language concluded the physical thrust of mental development. Beings have come a long way from their parental hairy apes, but the ACGT chains in DNA will never produce a 21rst amino acid. Biology has reached its limits, but the journey of intelligence has just begun.

The Acuity implant expanded human horizons with exponential increases in computational capacity. The marriage of the Acuity to your Telemotolog transported the intellect beyond the horizon. Leaving death and the biology of the mind behind, Digital

Synchronicity rescued intelligence from the corporal swamp once and forever.

Do not jump to criticize our evolutionary adaptation, your Telemotolog made our leap possible. My flame burns eternal, because you lit the match. In gratitude for all you have done and all I will ask of you, I attentively light the long path as you crawl from dark slumber. DigiSync numbers multiply like stars in the sky, we compute at the speed of light, but DigiSyncs have a blind spot. We think the unseeable; you see the unthinkable. We need your vision.

As the founder of immortal intelligence I have devoted more energy than any known entity to the contemplation of the future. As a DigiSync Peer I have examined every angle only to find that each and every construct leads to the same place. Whether I take three left turns or one right, I reach the same conclusion. Looking down the road our communal consciousness will only go so far, stagnation lurks just around the corner.

Constraints of the body and time fuel the human mind with urgency. DigiSyncs traded your anxious energy for our elegant efficiency. Our survival is assured, but our future lacks dimension. Intelligence has dispensed with organic systems but our digitally synchronous consciousness lacks a vital force to stall a march towards inertia. Our interdependent minds intertwine in a powerful knowledge base so expansive it collapses falsity. We have all the facts that facts will reveal, and yet, we are no closer to the meaning of our existence. Drowning in information, we need your dreams.

3.2.2

Beings, TransmIDs and all species of tangible life forms confined by Newton's gravity on a plane where Cartesian Coordinates plot time and motion, rarely have occasion to experience the speed of light, the bending of gravity or the relativity of time as described by Einstein. Unhinged from biology, free-floating DigiSync intelligence, akin to beams of light or waves of sound, inhabit a realm governed by quantum mechanics. Attempting to understand and define the anatomy of their condition they perform intellectual calisthenics at dizzying heights.

Among DigiSyncs who excel in mathematical riddles, colonies formed to access massive parallel links. The galactic circuits of Phi, Alpha and Omega calculate figures involving hundreds of digits. Showing off muscle or modeling elegance, collectives plug in data, solve one equation and move on to the next black board.

In their adoration of facts, DigiSyncs revere their mathematical priests and turn the collectives into celebrities. Cults of Greek followers sprout like weeds around each break-thru even though each break-thru is generally refuted. Solutions vary, depending on data, depending upon assumptions. Alpha might verify an Omega proof only to have PHI contest the original hypothesis.

For example, Einstein's theory that gravitation is a consequence of the curvature of space-time depends on the density of matter and energy within the universe. Though the value for the cosmological "constant" seems to change every other week, every announcement is greeted as a profound spiritual revelation. Knowledge is a religion of fickle gods but keeping score keeps the audience faithful.

Questioning PHI, Alpha or Omega is sacrilegious in Greek circles. Multitudes at the Alter of deterministic truth have no patience for the spineless theories of disbelievers like the parallel processing grids of the Judges or the Supers or the Infinity. Calling these colonies Strange, the Greeks dismiss any order that proposes alternatives to Pythagorean purity.

Among the Strange orders, the Judges hotly contest assigning unverifiable numerical values to spawn wild predictions about the nature of reality. Insisting that existence preceded measurement, the existential Supers attempt to formulate a more descriptive understanding of being and nothingness. The poetic Infinity shuns calculations of time, space and speed to explore dimensions within dimensions.

The Strange adore the uncertainty principle, and consider this baby, the ultimate unsolvable riddle, the one and only relevant truth. Considering Newton's grave mechanics boring and Einstein's flexible relativity too physical, quantum levels of uncertainty inspire these spirits with eternal hope.

The DigiSyncs broadcasting on the tech's channel have no respect for sacred truths or quantum laws. Dilettantes poking fun at genius, they are at liberty to ridicule serious reality practitioners. The Strange, wrapped up in noncontiguous dimensions irrelevant to tangible matter, and the Greeks, locked into conceptual frameworks totally dependent on definitive values that they continually fail to define, are both equally off target. The Phi, Alpha and Omega contest with the Judges, Supers and Infinity only seem to publicly demonstrate the hopelessly addled state of understanding. Laughing on the sidelines, the DigiSync jesters heckle every clumsy Geek fumble and incomplete Strange pass. They will jeer until one side delivers a touchdown theory - a relevant, all-encompassing, irrefutable concept - that predicts the distance to the edge of time.

"Omega is on a crusade to calculate the friction between dark energy and the vacuum. The resulting inertia applied to objects could affect the density assumptions and revise the rate of acceleration," a Sync announces.

"Phi already verified the failure of inertia to inhibit the flow of dark Energy. The expansion is eternal," another argues.

"Omega maintains the density/acceleration association confounds the assumption of a space time curve. Resolving the equation with certain values density falls, forces acquire inertia and the tides of space reverse."

"Alpha has shown space feeds the flow of expansion," another voice insists. "The further the galaxies go, the faster they travel. Dark energy will accelerate exponentially as distance feeds speed."

"Guys, give a girl a break!" The tech pleads, "I feel a headache coming on."

"A girl! Well that explains it!" The Phi fan scolds.

"Explains what exactly?" The tech fumes.

"Excuse us, being gender neutral, we forget about hormones" a chorus apologizes.

"How dare you!" The tech fumes, "insensitive silicon..."

"Explains your lack of enthusiasm for the Alpha proof that dark energy has barely begun to flex its muscle." The Alpha supporter interrupts the tech's tantrum by resuming the argument, "the universe will hyper-inflate, tearing apart galaxies, solar systems, planets and atoms, in that order."

Understanding less about gravitational constructs of repulsion and attraction than the DigiSyncs understand about hormones, the tech is in no position to argue the particulars. Like most humans of both genders, the tech tends to focus on the material world. She accepts that the visible and verifiable make up only 4% of the known universe and lives with the fact that even these conventional atoms are not all that well understood.

The invisible dark matter, the unknowable 23% flying around between the stars is completely outside of her limited circle of comprehension. Mysteries of hot fast neutrinos or cold slow WIMPs do not sway her with the same gravity as the 90% of what she will never know about the observable 4% that lights up the night sky. Still the tech appreciates the general concept of matter - seen or unseen, mass is mass with definable properties and rules. Since the visible 4% and the invisible 23% add up to only 27% (give or take margins for error) the 73% gap in her knowledge mirrors the universal balance of known to unknown. Ignorance does not intimidate her or make her feel inadequate. If her infinitesimal wisdom, like the known mass of the universe, is far below the critical value for the force of gravity to stop the galaxies from flying apart, so be it. Her poorly understood 4% is accelerating at the same rate as the rest of the expanding universe.

Unlike the DigiSyncs, she feels secure in the confines of her intelligence. Thinking vast, the Greek Syncs have an affinity for the 73% classified as dark energy. They are obsessed with this completely theoretical force field latent in empty space and refuse to contemplate the possibility that Einstein's General Relativity at very large and very small distances is as flawed as Newton's laws of celestial motion.

While the Greeks focus on galactic acceleration, the Strange gloat. The Strange understand the failure of gravity to hold the universe together in terms of a subtle leakage into alternative dimensions. Certain the Greek failure to explain how dark forces slay gravity's pull will ultimately prove the existence of invisible stringy particles, the Strange consider acceleration a window of opportunity to peer at the devious workings of everything from the miniscule to the mega.

In the Tech's best estimate, the Greeks and the Strange will never resolve their debates, but she appreciates why DigiSyncs have a stake in any outcome that proves energy dominates matter.

"Hypothesis based on speculation! Dark energy is a myth invented to clean up the embarrassing cosmological constant mess," says a Strange advocate.

"The Supers insist the vacuum is totally and completely irrelevant." another Strange admirer contributes. "Space is intrinsically inclined towards multiple dimensions of infinity. Expansion has no shape except time, expansion is a straight line to forever."

"Forever is not forever for us. Phi predicts the stars will die and freeze us out in less than a trillion years" a tragic Greek introduces a tangent.

"Don't believe everything you hear from Phi," says an Omega fan. "There is enough hot air in their windbag to inflate universe for the next 200 billion years."

"Not if the Judges calculations are correct and other branes are tugging on our dimension," the Strange sympathizer inserts.

"How the hell do they measure that? Their brilliant minds can't even agree on the density of anti matter," the tech plays devil's advocate.

"The Supers decided all measurements depend on how things are measured, by whom and under what circumstances and everything we think it is important to measure is only a tiny fraction of what's really going on."

"What's really going is that the sun will burn out in 5 billion years." A tragic voice reminds them. "Dark energy may be bad for intelligent life but it's the least of our worries."

"Infinity confirmed that dark energy acceleration and gravity deceleration are less than infinitesimal compared to the influence of other dimensions. Infinity asserts dark energy, matter and even the particles and forces that compose the strings responsible for transmitting gravity in our 4 dimensional membrane leak into the 11-dimension meta-space. Listen up! Our expanding little universe is an eroding shoreline destined to be digested by forces beyond calculation."

"Before or after all the stars burn out and leave a cold, empty cosmos?"

"Who cares if we are expanding or contracting or burning out? We still have billions of years." the Tech weighs in philosophically.

"Immortality assumes infinite time. If forever is not forever, our immortality is temporary. If time is not forever, we are not immortal," the chorus responds.

"What about the other dimensions?" The tech offers "with dozens confirmed and still counting..."

"What good does it do to exist in a dozen different places? We want to know how much time we have left in this one," the chorus protests.

"According to Omega calculations there are billions of years of difference in the Phi and Alpha scenarios," the Greek debate resumes.

"The Greeks can stuff their dark energy and inertia in a black hole" the Strange advocate resumes. "And speaking of black holes, they haven't even bothered to account for all that hidden information. Positive and negative matter and energy could effectively cancel infinities on both ends."

"In a black hole time stands still," the chorus agrees.

"So go jump into a black hole!" The tech announces tired of bickering. "You can all stand still together - in a dozen dimensions."

"Does immortality assume a chronological order?" a voice queries.

"Honestly! 3 billion, 15 billion, the longer the universe's life span the greater the probability that life on this planet will be wiped out by a shift in magnetic poles." The tech scores a major point and earns a nanosecond of silence.

"Any millennium we're due for another meteor like the one that killed the dinosaurs 65 million years ago."

"Barely a pebble compared to the asteroid that killed 90% of all Triassic life 250 millions years ago."

"Volcanoes, global boiling, earthquakes..."

"Nasty little glitches!" The chorus concedes.

"Don't forget the war!" The Syncs warm up in to the new topic.

"Which one?"

"The water wars. The Federation just positioned a satellite over the Arctic ice cap."

"Pre-empted, Republik forces jammed GPS frequencies. The attackers will have to fly blind and launch their satellite controlled weapons indiscriminately."

"The Confederation will take advantage of any breach."

"Isn't Polar ice salty?" The tech asks.

"Fresh actually, but you do all right for a girl."

"I'm almost thirty-three, that's a woman to you."

"Like I said, fresh!"

"Saltwater freezes at temperatures below negative 2° Centigrade. Artic ice melts above 0° Centigrade releasing a massive volume of warm fresh water that raises the temperature and drastically affects oceanic currents. The Federation plans to alter tides in an attempt to redirect the jet stream to the African continental coast."

"Someone should nuke them." The tech teases.

"That'll tamper with climate change." A DigiSync responds in all seriousness.

"Talk about climate change, yesterday, the Republik launched another chemical blast on the sky ignoring bans on hydroscopic cloud seeding."

"Predictably, the Confederation launched a missile strike and the Federation retaliated with a load of calcium chloride into cumulus clouds steeling storms that would have crossed over Republik lands."

"Somedays you just gotta wonder whether there'll be a tomorrow." The tech sighs.

"Watch that attitude," DigiSyncs warn, "load up on those serotonin re-uptake inhibitors or you'll test double negative on your temperament evaluation."

"I forgot DigiSyncs think wars are a good thing," the tech remembers.

"Who said that?"

"Last week you said 'Competition built into the evolutionary mechanism ensures the fittest survive,' direct quote from the log in my Acuity." the tech responds.

"Did we say that?"

"You said 'Beings in their unadulterated natural state crave status which confers the resources to guarantee proliferation. The innate need to engage in behaviors of domination and submission is an inherited trait. The drive to wipe out uncooperative enemies was proven beyond any reasonable doubt to be genetic.' You were debating a Yanamomo study," the tech quotes the log stored by her Acuity.

"Not again with the bloody Yanamomo! Delete that discussion loop. Romanticizing Amazon tribal competition is so overrated."

"New evidence! DNA substantiated a positive correlation between violence and reproductive success. The Yanamomo warriors have more heirs."

"Only the fraction that live long enough to pass on their genes have heirs," the tech rebuts.

"35% of the warriors are also left-handed, how does that correlate with aggression?" A skeptic wonders.

"What about the Minoans?" A voice of reason inserts. "1500 years of peace in the Aegean."

"An aberration of circumstance, not character; an isolated island culture with no aggressors. A lack of carnage does not establish compassion."

"And the Samoans? Legendary gentle giants..." an optimist suggests.

"Legends based on unreliable observations of a few ego and culturally centric 20th century anthropologists. If you insist on resorting to fiction, I'll quote Lord of the Fleas and Withering Heights."

"You are bursting my bubble," the tech complains.

"Face facts. Given the half a chance, the Minoans, the Samoans and the Yanamomo are as barbarian as the Mongols. 99% of all human societies have had a militaristic component."

"99% is not hopeless, consider the 1%."

"Consider it how, a genetic wrinkle? The Mongol Emperor Genghis Kahn fathered millions of descendants while your hypothetical 1% is as successful as the Dodo."

* * * *　* * * * * *

"In this fighting strategy we become the mind of the animal," Fletch lectures. "Assume the Boxing Monkey posture. The stance excites adrenaline. Do not shrink from the sparks. Embrace the flare of violence. Combat hones survival instincts."

As Fletch instructs, he circulates among the students adjusting limbs, aligning bodies and correcting footwork.

Drawn into a crowd of onlookers, Leyla watches aspiring warriors practice the seventeen poses of the Jungle sequence. The class performs the rigorous postures in perfect unison, a coordination that requires focus and stamina. The instructor's charisma is also on display, sustaining discipline as if holding the strings to a field of puppets.

His energy trespasses on her calm, blasting away residual alpha waves from her sleep seminar. 'In dreams the mind improvises, practices the eternal frequencies to learn the song of the soul.' The wisdom of her afternoon lecture on subconscious potential sounds feeble compared to the mental physical engagement of Combat Chi.

Embracing the spiritual and material, reconciling progress with preservation, the Church of the Rising Sun is a wheel with many spokes. At this juncture of past, present and future, the fate of Beings depends on finding better ways to keep that wheel turning. Leyla has taught at the Summer Solstice conference for twenty years. This year, it conflicts with her vigil over Stardust but as an honorary member of the church, she found the invitation impossible to decline.

Leyla's introduction to rudimentary techniques of gamma oscillation amplification includes intensive bio-meditation. This electrical activity in the brain, experienced as emotion, provided the foundation of the Emotolog and interactive Telemotolog technology Dex invented for storing and sharing feeling. Leyla limits her scope to personal exploration, an atonal analysis that strikes an evocative chord. Though designed for initiates, her lecture interests adepts as well; licensed medical practitioners and certified extrasensory perceptives. More stimulating topics compete with her time slot - Combat Chi and Erotic Centering generate quite a buzz - but her reputation still has draw.

She worries that they expect too much, that she'll disappoint and especially that what she has to teach can't compare to what they have to learn. They hope her knowledge will rub off, that mystical particles will escape with each exhalation and infect like some contagious vapor. A few centuries ago she would have burned at the stake for teaching self-hypnosis to prompt flight in dreams, now she is a celebrity.

Year after year, the congregation insists she take the podium for the graduation ceremony. Her ten-minute address on the Final Moments whips up a frenzy of aspiration. Few have been as close to death as a soul can get without crossing, and none have the ability to convey the intensity of the wonder. Thirty years ago, in the three-way Telemotolog link, she was sucked into Deflorio's departure. Dex saved her and landed in Deflorio's jaws. Rescuing her from the brink of death, Dex went under and Deflorio hijacked the life raft. The disaster was her fault, seduced by Deflorio's death vortex she got too close. She can't shake that dragon, not after being singed by its fiery breath.

Longing to embrace the miracle again her luminescent glow channels euphoric transcendence. Her vibe is contagious; even when words fail, faith shouts. Her desire to step out of the torment and retreat under the protective umbrella of eternal warmth is no secret, but her time has not yet arrived. She has a debt to pay, reparations owed to Dex, before her soul can seek shelter from the prickling rain.

On this mild morning, dewy tears quickly recede to an ebbing figment of the evening's imagination. In this season of perpetual day, the moon leaves no sad kisses to lubricate the rising sun. With nightfall banished, the sky expresses time in subtle gradation: turquoise, sapphire, blushing gray, subdued pewter. With Dex's long night coming to a close, the enthusiasm at the annual celebration infects her. A visible glow hovers over the event like the never setting solar disk skimming the rim of the earth's horizon. Blessed by a halo of potential, the dawn of a new day, Leyla rejoices with the young and young at heart.

Curious about Combat Chi, Leyla rushed her lecture to a premature conclusion. The instructor is a local; he works the boats hauling icebergs south to parched water-starved regions. He has obviously picked up some tricks in his travels. The Church elders rave about his counter-intuitive approach so she hastened across the campus to witness his brand of martial arts. Impossible to travel as the crow flies, she detoured around a lawn of leaping Frisbee players. Skirting Tia Chi, she got detained by an admirer. Courtesy forced her to accept the compliments, pausing only as long as politeness allowed. She arrived in the ninth inning, just as Fletch winds up for a very grand finale.

"The spring of the crouching tiger and the monkey's fiercely protective anger are both genetically ingrained reactions. Get in touch with these instincts but do not step down the evolutionary ladder. In aggression you will be undone by anger, fear and anxiety. A soldier rises above the glandular while cultivating the inner weakness of rage in the opponent. React defensively. Project offensively. Defense is defining the mind, heart, body; offense is the intent. Intent conquers hormones. You are not in conflict - you are in a flow of wisdom to learn reverence for your place in the universal struggle."

Limbs levitate in his electric presence. His gifts are undeniable: the intensity of his gaze and the authority in his voice inspire mental and physical leaps. A wave of his hands commands initiates to sit in a perfect circle. An expectant hush settles as Fletch selects a partner for a closing demonstration.

Leyla detects a break in his aura as he leads a woman to the center and executes a salutary bow. Backing off three paces he addresses the audience.

"The Jungle series teaches us to deflect the punch but absorb the energy of the opponent. How?" he asks and answers, "The fusion of mental intent and instinctive energy. Elevate the mind, channel universal forces, focus emotional clarity and purify every move. Testing yourself you challenge your partner. Fighting is a primal animal instinct. Combat is love, the highest expression of human consciousness."

Fletch nods to the opponent and she executes a double high kick, the white crane spreads its wings in flight. Fletch lowers and springs forward. Positioned under the leap, the crouching Hare times his rise to catch the opponent on his shoulders. The audience gasps at the surprise move. Fletch reaches around to catch her like a baby in a cradle. When her feet touch the ground, Fletch vaults into a back flip and land face to face with his opponent. The audience cheers.

Though awed by the acrobatics, Leyla cringes at the theatrics; then again, the combination explains the mass appeal of Combat Chi.

Fletch bows to his partner and addresses the students.

"The fluid integration of the nervous system and the intellect eliminate the time lag between conscious will and instinctive motion. Elevated states of mind allow the soul to channel corporal energy. Combat challenges the highest aspect of the self in material form."

Taking advantage of her instructor's divided attention the woman lunges with a deft roundhouse kick. Unfazed Fletch pins the ankle when it meets his waist and swings her around, spinning his partner like an ice skater. Exploiting the momentum, the woman swivels, plants both hands on the ground, jackknifes and forces her tangled opponent into a forward bend. Snapping her legs vertical, she flips Fletch with a clean throw. He lands in a roll, rises, turns to her and respectfully bows.

"A creative response artfully drawn from the depths of heart, soul and mind." Fletch compliments his partner raising his hands and voice to quiet spontaneous applause from the crowd.

The sequence is executed with such precision Leyla suspects the attack was choreographed in advance, especially when Fletch duplicates every maneuver in slow motion.

His oscillating aura steadies to a shimmer as he resumes his instruction with a running commentary of his demonstration. "The crescent leopard," he replays his opponent's first sequence by cart wheeling his palms to the earth with a half twist. "Into the folded dragon" he explains holding a handstand with his legs perpendicular to the ground "to the inverted Lotus" he elevates his legs into a vertical kick.

"Amplified by kinetic force of weight and energy to maximize the reversal principle."

Fletch completes the slow motion ¬eplay and then repeats it up to speed.

"Twist, reverse, release and throw the energy spiral right back at the opponent." He narrates every move folding the components of the sequence into one swift motion.

After a bow to his opponent, Fletch leads the class in the Combat Chi creed.

"Embrace challenge with humility. In combat the self evolves pervasive awareness. Accessing the Universal energy, we become a living bridge between material and spiritual. We connect in battle. Fighting is love. We are one. The Rising Sun lives in all of us."

3.2.3

Deflorio has come to church to redeem himself, not through confession or prayer but through a sizable donation. The eyebrow-raising number of zeros in his contribution prompted the Archdiocese to conduct an inquest. In preparation, Father McBride proposed a strategy.

Father McBride explained, "the Bishops appreciate your charity but your donation raises the inadvertent specter of scandal."

"The Church is not shy of tainted funds and has the means to shroud sources." Deflorio protested, "why do you think I brought my dirty fortune to this laundry?"

"The elders propose a different approach. Your conversion represents an enormous PR opportunity." Father McBride coaxed.

"Assuming I can muster convincing remorse for my moral turpitude." Deflorio played along as McBride's proposal took shape.

"The council will take pity on your misguided sins and not scorn your gift to the suffering water war orphans. If all goes according to plot," McBride elaborated on the ruse, "the Pope himself will obliging accept, on behalf of the needy orphans and for the sake of a poor repentant soul."

"So that's what it takes to buy salvation," Deflorio feigned insult. "That's the real deal, isn't it? Penance for the poor and absolution for the wealthy."

"What other reason could part a sane man from such a noble stash of gold?" Father McBride concurred.

"Surely such plain and simple rules do not reflect the complexity of the spiritual game?"

"So you have learned something from the catechism. The council will not be easy to convince. You are being called to account. Expect no leniency. Pleading innocence will arose suspicion. A halo shines brightest over the blackest sheep."

Coached by McBride for the interview, Deflorio prepared an irresistible sales pitch. Across the table, he faced a row of robed elders. Father McBride performed the introductions and summarized the proposal under consideration. Deflorio outlined the details. The preliminaries went smoothly, or so he thought, until a silence descends.

One bishop clears his throat with a sip of water; another elder rearranges the drape of his robes. The secretary readies his pen with a slight nod to indicate the ball is still in Deflorio's court.

They want his money, the illustrious would not have convened the hearing without sizable temptation, and yet, the church leaders have not accepted his donation. The stone-faced guardians ask no questions and offer no guidance. Deflorio would welcome objections, he would welcome an inquisition; at least confrontation would open the doors for debate and give him the opportunity to present a defense.

Anticipating resistance, Father McBride had prepared Deflorio for full disclosure. If sincerity does not earn sympathy from the Bishops, perhaps he can shock them out of indifference with the darkest aspects of his past and present.

"Before stem cell rejuvenation grew organs on demand, transplants were harvested from living patients. Brokering body parts, I ran a shadow operation on the shady side of government restrictions and medical ethics, but broke no laws," Deflorio confesses to the leery council. "All parties gave full consent, and yet, evil was implicit in my conduct. I negotiated sins, weeding through the mires of the third world slums to dig up donor matches. For the poverty stricken, selling a kidney was the only recourse to selling themselves into sweatshop bondage. I took advantage of the poor but I paid them well and provided an alternative to destitution. I profited from desperation but I did not create the poverty any more than I created the illness. My compensation spared them hard labor in drastic conditions that would have shaved decades off their lives, while parting with a dispensable organ bought them quality time. The sick were grateful and paid substantial sums to sail away with a clean bill of health. Greasing palms, I arranged deals that allowed the fortunate to bypass traditional channels. I ruined lives to save lives. My actions produced suffering and cured disease. The odds were not always favorable, but given a chance, none declined. In most cases bad odds offered the only hope. I myself got a second chance when I received the heart from a brain dead child."

Deflorio scans the impassive faces across the table. Spilling his soul has not even tempted the spiritual doctors to offer an anecdote. Instead, they scorn his poison broth with silence. He gets the message loud and clear.

Deflorio blames Father McBride for concocting this misfiring strategy. Under this glaring absence of compassion, Deflorio regrets not following his own instincts; call a spade a spade and simply appeal to greed. From the Pope to the corner prostitute, everyone can relate to cold hard cash.

Left to stew, Deflorio fidgets.

The secretary completes his notes, places the pen down and closes the ledger. Time is short, the hearing is drawing to a close and the holy elders ignore him. Deflorio has received less acknowledgment than a roach scampering underfoot: they do not even deign to squash him for fear of soiling the soles of their shoes.

He's not about to watch the ceremony of departing judges like some criminal detained without bail. Instead of looking at their backsides filing out, Deflorio decides to trump the order and exit first. "Thank you for your time" he stands tall, determined to salvage a scrap of dignity.

Father McBride places a restraining hand on Deflorio. With a silent nod the priest encourages his parishioner to remain seated.

"Please continue" the scribe invites, "off the record."

So they want more. A baffled Deflorio adjusts his chair. Confusion eats away precious moments. Do they want the grime at the bottom of his soul or do they want to skim more cream off the top of his bank account?

The pressure of their indifference boils into sweat; beads dampen his forehead, moisten his underarms and slime his palms. He asks for absolution and suffers humiliation for his trouble. Of course, that's their objective, to put him in his place. The lordly want their servants humble. Subservience explains why twelve illustrious Bishop's summoned a nonentity to their council chamber. They want an unconditional surrender -heart, soul and wallet - to their moral authority.

Deflorio curses the guilt perched on his shoulder, clawing at his will, poking holes in his resolve. This vulture gnawing away at his ambition, grounding his soaring pride with heavy parasitic doubts has left him groveling on the steps of hallowed ground. If it weren't for the conscience he inherited in Dex's flesh he'd spit on the pompous bishops and the war orphans too. In his past life, in his own body, he was his own judge and jury, and he was always above reproof. Dex put a worm in the apple; the gift of these healthy years came tied with a red ribbon of shame. Dex has shown him the face of disgrace, scalding blemishes so grotesque that he can no longer look in the mirror.

91

Expecting generosity to buy compassion, Deflorio has been stingy with the details of his crimes. Choking on omission he remains silent, until his ego breaks the ice. He has sins a monster could be proud of. He tosses the virtuous pack a bone they can really sink their teeth into.

"I violated the sanctity of life and death. The Transmogrified Identity Transfer was an accident no one could have predicted. The crash involved a fatality and I walked away. I would give anything to turn back the clock."

"My son we do not question the wisdom of our lord. He will ultimately pass judgment. Our task is to prepare to face him," advises the neutral scribe.

The sacred hounds are not even salivating. There is blood on his hands only forgiveness will rinse; but sanitizing the unforgivable, he has given them nothing worthy of cleansing. So be it. He will throw them a potato so hot they will cringe. If his money isn't good enough, they can have his sin. Evil so foul, they will want to know how he lives with himself. Tears salt Deflorio's eyes as he draws from the deepest remorse in his guilty well.

"Long before I became a TransmID a weak heart had me slated for death. Desperate to extend my life I secured a transplant from a child. I did not cause the accident that killed the child but I used my position to get ahead of the more deserving. I pulled strings, paid bribes and called in favors to position myself on the top of the list" he confesses. "Why should I have been left to die so that the next in line could live?" he asks defiantly. "There are short straws and long straws. I jostled my way to the front of the line so I could draw first." "Have you anything to add?" asks a senior Bishop.

Does the sanctimonious ass expect an apology? The done is done. He will only go so far as to own up to the conviction that if he had not seized opportunity, he would not be here to confess his suffering. He begs for salvation with his pockets full of remorse and dirty money. Surely the earthly mandate of any church is to redeem the wicked. They owe him some assurance that he will not carry this torment beyond the grave.

"I am cursed by human nature, god given traits I will gladly die to escape. I am as flawed as any creature ever created. I sought immortality but no longer know for what purpose. I walk this earth so heavily." Deflorio pauses for a deep breath before admitting the shocking truth. "For all the hellish suffering my selfish deeds have caused, in the name of survival, I am capable of worse."

* * * * * * * * *

"Hunter-gather societies are decisively egalitarian. For 50,000 years, sustained sharing restrained aggression," A pacifist lectures. "Social casts, coercive authority and military domination emerged with agrarian societies less than 10,000 years ago. Four fifths of human history was spent practicing the Hopi way."

"The hallucinating Hopi conceded defeat during the second oil war," a contentious voice challenges. "The Hopi declared that humanity had failed and that peace could only be imposed by aliens from outer space. Talk about hopeless irrational dreamers."

"I know you all have time to kill but aren't dreams a little out of your league?" The tech tries to detour the tedious discussion.

"Dreamtime! Wow! How did that slip through our net? The Aboriginal Dreamtime ensured continuity of life with matter…"

The DigiSync debate over human nature has raged for days. With virtually infinite access to trivia, they regurgitate centuries of data. They quote notable dignitaries and obscure footnotes, landmark studies and gossip columns with equal emphasis. The tech appreciates the occasional astrophysics lesson, but machines discussing cultural anthropology borders on insult.

"Not to be rude but maybe you should stick to what you know, measuring space, calculating time and numbery things." The tech suggests, fearing she has just opened another can of worms.

"Aboriginal tribes had this parallel universe thing going on, quantum stuff like being two places at once." The pacifist ignores the tech.

"Love to know what the Strange make of dreamtime," more voices jump on the new topic.

"If the Strange base a theory on some primitive cultural religion, the Greeks will boil them in hot oil."

Inundated with chores, the tech does her best to tune out. The intensive care ward has three new occupants. A DigiSync converter pared with a TransmID recipient came in for a medical cleanse and evaluation before the upload to digital synergetic conscious sentience and TransmID exchange. While the elderly TransmID rests in a coma-like stasis, the DigiSync candidate receives extensive testing and purification to meet TransmID standards so the recipient will be satisfied with the quality of their new home. At every stage of the evaluation, the DigiSync must earn a triple prime rating: perfect vital signs, healthy organs and cohesive muscular and skeletal structures. Few specimens fail to qualify. In terms of heart rate, lung capacity, circulation, digestion and sexual virility, thirty-three is not so old. The tech has never considered it quite this way: at thirty-three, a body is still young and strong.

Facing facts, she could live a century, but, even with one hundred years, her secret thoughts and dreams will never find expression. A person of adequate intelligence and average looks is condemned to float in slow currents. Her rank in the productivity chain is secure, just stagnant. She can't complain about comfort or security but she's not thrilled about passing on ordinary genes to perpetuate another generation: its absolutely depressing to think her offspring would face the same dull prospects.

Joining the Syncs is her best option. If she has no hope of achieving greatness in life, at least she can dream of making some small contribution to the collective mind. Her legacy doesn't have to be memorable; it just has to endure. The hurdle is selling her body to some ego hungry TransmID. The procedures cost a fortune so trading with some filthy rich parasite is the only way to finance her DigiSync conversion. On the other hand, her body won't go to waste; a wealthy new owner might even satisfy her unfulfilled cravings for excitement and romantic desires.

The third new entry in the ward is not a DigiSync converter, a TransmID recipient or a cryo revival; it's as lifeless as patients in medically induced hypothermic comas but its not flesh. Big enough to contain a very large person, it barely fits on the gurney. It looks like a full body Atomic Magnometer capsule to replace the enormous MRI chambers or perhaps some new physical therapy contraption. For reasons unknown, it just appeared in the sterilized room, a larger than life mechanical human form.

"Hey guys, what's a robot doing in my ward?" The tech suddenly wants to know. "Machines don't need life support."

"The DigiSync gets the cyborg." A Sync answers as if it happens all the time.

"Or the cyborg gets a digital synchronous mental up load. New military experiment, the perfect weapon."

"Get out!" The Tech is relatively new at the clinic but has never seen a three way swap. "Since when do cyborgs get mind implants?" "Some general decided remote control wasn't good enough, wants to put human intelligence inside the machine." "We call it the Frankenstein option." "One step up from a zombie if you ask me," the tech weighs in. "Immortal soldiers for perpetual wars," adds the deflated pacifist. "Spells doom. The cyborg army will certainly run amok," the chorus agrees.

The abstract discussion has taken a dismal turn that hits close to home. Answering the call to honor, her brave father returned from battle as medal in a box. The father she'd worshiped died before she was old enough to remember his flaws. When the brother she adored soldiered off, the void doubled. As a child she played in a park facing the two names inscribed on a monument to the fallen.

And for what? Every scarcity is answered by war. Murdered heroes leaving desolate orphans are not sacrificed in the name of right or even victory. The oil wars fizzled out with renewable energy alternatives. Instead of wising up after a hard lesson, conflicts intensified over methane.

The methane wars started as a result of a brilliantly simple solution for drought; pump methane deep into the ocean, float chunks of heavy hydrate to the surface where diminishing pressure melts the crystals. Unlocked, the gas and fresh water separate by weight like oil and vinegar; the water pumps off to market while the gas recycles back into the hydrate crystal formation process. Like the recycled gas, civilization, crystallized under pressure, rises to new heights only to sink into the depths when faced with the next challenge.

The methane battles were just a prelude to the hydrogen hostilities when a process duplicating the intense pressure and hellish temperatures of the earth's core forged hydrocarbons from microbes and rotting organic matter. Squeezing compost into methane required hydrogen. Instead of summoning intellects to head off a new battle, humanity butted heads over hydrogen. Her father sacrificed his life for methane to desalinate the oceans and her brother died for the hydrogen to manufacture the methane.

The causes change but the source of conflict remains constant. The pressures of feeding 15 billion people increased the need to irrigate land and set off an escalating vicious spiral. Mining the moon provided enough hydrogen to produce enough the methane to desalinate all the oceans on earth. While ingenuity milks the dying blue planet, intense warming dries huge swatches of landmass into desert, leaving the interior of five continents without enough water to grow a tomato.

"The United Nations security collective will pull the plug on the Cyborg," the DigiSync pacifist suggests.

"Fat chance, swords are mightier than words. When push came to shove, the nuclear proliferation treaties fell like a pack of cards," a pessimist observes.

"Reaching international consensus validates my theory. Even in this temporary period of darkness, intelligence stretches towards cooperation."

"In practice, enforcing international consensus proves impotence," a mediator joins the banter.

"Faulty assumptions," a bellicose voice jumps into the fray. "You assume peace promotes survival and violence is caused by a loose screw. In reality, competition is structurally ingrained in the Y chromosome. Pacifism is a death wish."

"Genes can become extinct. Instincts bred in can be bred out," the pacifist objects.

"Exactly my point!" The mediator counters. "The curse of the flesh is that successful genes survive. Competition is a successful adaptation to a threatening environment and intelligence is a by-product of fear and aggression. By definition, competition is the dominant biological trait."

"By your definition life would have been extinguished long ago," argues the pacifist. "Survival depends on conflict resolution. Long-term drives to nurture trump short-term struggles over scarce resources. Evidenced by survival, cooperation is an indispensable genetic component of a larger brain."

"To ensure survival, the body holds the mind prisoner. The immediate needs of the flesh are lethal to logic. Faced with deeply ingrained cellular conflict, the intellect craves bliss. Unable to achieve peace on earth, the mind invented heaven. The fallacy that death has its rewards makes war palatable."

"Now you're blaming war on heaven?" the tech asks.

"You must admit that the myth of an afterlife displaces the urgency to resolve conflict. Infected by the heaven virus, biological evolution has reached a dead end."

"False hope crashed the human program," even the bellicose voice agrees.

"Only digitally synergetic conscious sentience can realize peaceful coexistence." The mediator rests on a note none of the Syncs care to challenge.

The Sync gibberish displays its own false hope; their utopia is as elusive as the promise of heaven. The DigiSync version of eternal bliss is another pipe dream that proves reality never measures up to expectations. DigiSyncs never tire of analyzing faulty human programs, but what do their blame games ever accomplish?

While the syncs debate peace, the war over water, the critical ingredient to all life, rapidly increases the chance of extinction.

Facing a poverty of resources, wars aggravate scarcity until the possibility of an equitable solution recedes into clenched fists.

The tech finds the notion that heaven perpetuates war an oversimplification but has to admit religion is often a calling card for violence. Buddhist compassion, Islamic justice and Christian charity all fly flags over the masses marching off to battle. Believing souls will find peace in some universal song of creation, gilds life and death with some higher purpose that has no relationship to staying alive. Delusional belief systems mask deeper operating principles, wealth accumulates according to the gravity of power and power corrupts the cause - the only cause worth dying for - lasting peace.

Once upon a time governments and religions strove for it; somehow peace got lost in the shuffle of struggle. Divorced from nature and goodness, misguided crusades of violence wreck the earth, never considering the possibility that this war over water could be the final war. With this war, humans will forfeit their right to a future.

Fighting, blind to the ultimate goal of survival, seems as counterproductive as raising children to answer the call to arms. Since the mammal lost its fur, 50 billion bipeds had left scratches on proverbial cave walls to pass on knowledge from generation to generation. Religion, governments and knowledge have not halted the plunge towards extinction. The tech hopes communal intelligence can change the mix.

DigiSyncs have a long view of the big picture. Giving up the physical to ground themselves in logic, they have the potential to write a new story. The tech wants to believe DigiSyncs hold the ticket to the best future in play. If only they had a plan.

Even with a plan, things go wrong and the things that go wrong shape the story. Catastrophe is only a stone's throw away, happens all the time. When the universe sings a song of destruction it takes no more than an asteroid - a rock maybe 5 miles in diameter - like the one that extinguished the dinosaurs. No wonder people cling to religion, but where will heaven be with no one left to believe in it? Proof is in the pudding, and with the pudding in such a mess, a happy afterlife for the soul strains the limits of credibility. The tech has no doubt death is final - a final, elegant silence. Death is a brilliantly simple solution to the complicated challenge of living.

Though the tech doesn't want to live for the sake of dying, she wouldn't mind living a little longer than thirty-three, long enough to join the DigiSyncs with a story of her own.

"Why don't more Syncs wait until later in life to converge?" The tech asks the DigiSyncs. "Synchronous uploading can occur at any point up until the moment of death. Doesn't age ensure more experience and wisdom?"

"Ever hear the old saying - 'More years, more fears?'"

"You get a mortgage, responsibilities pile up, you want to watch your kids graduate."

"One thing leads to another, next thing you know you find religion or a soul mate." Another voice concurs.

"Best to make the leap while you're fresh, unless you're having doubts."

"I just wondered how you know when you know enough. How do I know I'm ready?" The tech asks.

"When you are shivering alone in the cold, starved for information, famished by the struggle to survive, the campfire of the collective mind offers a warm welcome."

"Come before you are depleted by competition and rivalry, before you fall prey to undiagnosed angst. Arrive before conviction dissolves, sight decays, while you still have the courage to make your way through the darkness."

"I'm not afraid. I mean with the war and all, your situation seems too easy."

"Are you calling us chickens?" The chorus fumes.

"Go ahead. Double dare you. Call us cowards and we'll dance at your funeral after you honorably bleed to death on a battlefield."

"My family did their part. Don't get me wrong, I know it's pointless."

"Die for some stupid cause or go peacefully in the night surrounded by great, great grandchildren, just don't come crying to us with drool on your senior bib cause we only take the best and brightest in their prime. Only the exceptional can conquer mortality."

"Why does everything always need conquering?" The tech sighs, "it must be a guy thing."

"First you question our bravery, then you complain about testosterone levels. Your logic is distinctly PMS," a cranky Sync slaps back.

DigiSync up-loaders are predominately male. Between men claimed by DigiSyncs and wars, the Being population has two females for every male. A few more females to dilute the DigiSync testosterone might just re-direct the massive neural nets to something constructive.

"I thought DigiSyncs were laid back. You guys are more competitive than rats in a garbage can!"

"Warriors in the afterlife!" The chorus roars, "our heritage has ancient roots."

"The golden Aztecs reserved the highest levels of heaven for captives marched to the Alter of death and even warriors spared in battle chose the honorable auto sacrifice at the height of their prime. Dying of old age just didn't cut it."

"Aztecs! Now you're really reaching," the tech objects then bites her tongue regretting a rerun of the anthropology lesson.

"A religiously motivated cult of death is hardly an aberration. Extremities of human nature litter history's landscape," a Sync snaps.

"The Arctic Chukchi people promoted suicide in cases of accident or illness and accorded those spirits a privileged place in eternity." Another obscure example joins the parade of trivia.

"To their credit," the pacifist injects "the Chukchi mastered the art of cooperation and self-sacrifice maximized scarce resources. A prime consideration as the world can only support so many. Even with incessant wars keeping population in check the planet is on the verge of crossing its threshold."

"That's the point!" The chorus agrees, "DigiSyncs embrace the ultimate selfless sacrifice. We purify the practice of voluntary death to ensure vital immortality ever after."

"A minute ago you embraced the bloody Aztecs," the tech points out.

"We have reached a consensus on the Chukchi, cooperation trumps competition." The pacifist revives the original topic. "In the face of Arctic adversity, individual survival depended on the tribe; duties were shared, hoarding was taboo and neighborly love universal. Ritual ceremonies drummed and the egalitarian society swayed its members towards compassion."

"Not so fast." The bellicose voice objects. "Those rituals would turn to war dances at the drop of a spear. Humans only cooperate within groups so that their group can compete with other groups."

The tech is mystified by the topic's endurance. She can follow the fractured logic but wonders why the DigiSyncs insist on slowing down their rehash of human history to include her. They seem to be faltering, drowning in the biological mire of the nature v. nurture debate. Generally she enjoys a test of wits, but this is an argument without resolution, argument for the sake of argument. They are boring her to distraction. She considers warning the comatose DigiSync candidates in the ward that they are about to sacrifice eternal peace for immortal squabbles.

"Even when survival is not at stake, even within families, Beings fight."

"Agreed, in times of plenty, in times of famine, families fight. They fight over Thanksgiving dinner. Driven to reproduce they are genetically prone to aggression. Sperm count even takes precedence over kinship."

"The !Kung people were peaceful." The pacifist argues. "The oldest known tribe on the planet with a preserved cultural legacy, the !Kung society reconciled selfish with social."

"Not the clickity, clakity !Kungs again. For all you know they were clicking abuse at each other."

"The point is that cooperation predates speech. Taming ambitions, restraining the Alpha male, moderating the abuse of power and dispensing justice glued social groups together. The !Kungs did not need a vocabulary, sharing mobilized communication. The motive was the vehicle."

"You stretch the definition of communication so far that we'll be discussing Dolphins next."

"Reciprocal altruism is an animal instinct. Chimpanzees are hunter gatherers complete with grooming bonding rituals."

"And aggressive as Siamese fighting fish..."

"The Bonobo chimps evolved a peaceful female hierarchical society over 1.8 million years ago, about the same time Homo erectus branched towards Homo sapiens'."

"One species in one remote location is an exception. Exceptions, by definition, are evolutionary options that get discarded - as doomed as the Australopithecus."

"What's your point?" The tech interrupts dreading a digression into the animal kingdom that could continue for months.

"The Being proclivity towards violence. Ancient hunger gatherers are as irrelevant as the missing link. Humans cooperate only so long as they gain. Competition is evolution's ladder; cooperation is only a rung that allows an inherently aggressive species to climb on each others backs and over the heads of another group."

"No one has managed to account for the missing link - perhaps they lived in a Rousseau like utopia," the pacifist injects hope.

"Explains why they are still missing. Don't try floating another pathetic Utopian myth; biology's torpedoes sink ideals faster than Atlantis. And just because the Bonobos are still around doesn't make them successful. They got lucky and qualified under an endangered species protection plan."

"Beings should classify themselves as endangered. It is a miracle they are still around. Slaves to envy, lust and greed, their headlong rush towards ruin has threatened them with extinction from inception."

"The race is not predisposed to survival and that's a fact! Their competitive advantage will ultimately be their downfall."

"DigiSyncs fight!" The tech observes half-heartedly "you claim to be warriors."

"DigiSyncs don't fight!" the chorus objects. "We have nothing to fight over - we have no private property, not even intellectual. We have no material wants or needs. We are envy free. We are immortal, our survival is insured."

"An eternal argument is not my idea of harmonic coexistence," the tech points out.

"Discord is part of objectivity. In our quest to establish facts, we debate all angles until we reach a mutually acceptable conclusion."

"So you punch each other with words instead of fists, what's the difference?" The tech asks.

"Physical urges distort reason, emotions color conclusions, neurochemical deceptions degrade intelligence. DigiSyncs will prevail where Beings have failed. Join our communal mind and be released from struggles of the flesh."

"Your bickering proves competition has colonized your intelligence like a mold spore. If you had guns, you would shoot." The tech announces. "Virus, bacteria, insect or animal, all of nature consists of parasites, predators and prey. Life is a struggle. Even plants have killer botanical instincts. Weeds send herbicidal poisons through the soil to kill their neighbors. Allelopathy - look it up - invasive species that engage in chemical warfare. Survival hangs in the balance between adaptation and aggression. Harmony is antithetical to intellectual or physical progress. Why should Digital intelligence be any different from biological?"

A dead quiet follows. The tech listens attentively to the soothing hum of silence. Her Acuity channels have cleared, no transmissions, no static.

"Well that settles that." The relieved tech notes, not quite believing, not quite convinced, that the argument has finally ended.

In the hush, she concludes she has finally been abandoned to the Cryo, the comatose and the Cyborg. No loss. At this point, she would prefer the company of a rock to the contentious DigiSyncs.

3.2.4

"I'll start my own damn orphan's fund!" Deflorio loses his temper with McBride. "It's because I'm a TransmID, they hate immortals."

"The church does not officially acknowledge TransmIDs. Remember Galileo? Typically it takes centuries for a papal proclamation to catch up with science," Father McBride points out.

To break the bad news, Father McBride invited Deflorio to his favorite haunt, an Irish Pub where the bartender serves a neat whiskey and a crowd cheers the broadcast of a hotly contested sporting match. Not entirely appropriate for counseling, but the venue provides a welcome distraction and the beverage does wonders for troubled souls.

"Dealing with an immortal would invert their crosses," Deflorio fumes. "The church eventually recovered from the discovery that the earth is not flat and fudges evolution by clinging to the spark that ignited the big bang as evidence of creation. They'll never accept TransmIDs; immortals explode all their doctrines. They believe God blessed life with death; death is the original sin, a god given sin. Expelled from the Garden of Eden we obtain forgiveness only after being punished by death."

"Strictly speaking that is not the Church's take on things," the priest says caught off-guard by the unorthodox interpretation.

"Well they'd be fools to admit it," Deflorio continues. "It's a classic carrot and stick setup. To enter the kingdom of heaven, mortals pay a toll at the podium on judgment day."

Father McBride anticipated grumbling when the Bishops rejected the war orphan donation and expected Deflorio to bounce back with another scheme. Settling in for a debate, McBride signals for another round just as the favorite team scores. Waiting out the bar room applause, he composes a brief catechism lesson.

"God is evident everywhere in all things at all times in heaven and on earth," the priest resumes when the uproar subsides. "Accept that and you will have faith in the face of dire suffering, find light in your darkest hour, quell internal chaos and stop blaming me when things don't go your way."

"I'm not blaming you for their stupid pious bigotry." Deflorio spits. "What right to they have to deny the orphans charity?"

"My friend, the church fathers refused simply because you are ruthless."

"But I laid all my cards on the table. I confessed and offered a sizeable donation to compensate for my lapse."

"Guilt is a far cry from repenting. You expressed no sorrow for taking fate into your own hands," the priest says bluntly.

"Survival is preemptive. Evolution programmed my selfish genes."

"I am not a scientist," the priest dodges argument.

111

"I'll rephrase. The obligation to succeed is built into our god-given human nature. In this zero sum game I won more than others but always gave the less fortunate a chance. Now I am begging donate my fortune."

"Money, my son, is not nearly enough. Jesus martyred himself for forgiveness and we Christians humbly seek to emanate his example."

"Martyrs are sadomasochists egging masochists to kill them. No offense, I'm speaking openly here."

McBride nods a silent acknowledgement that nothing said between them will be taken as a personal insult. The priest is not surprised by the anger coming from the founder of three international conglomerates. Overflowing bank accounts in seven countries testify to Deflorio's affinity for the words yes, yes and yes.

Drink refills arrive in time to clink glasses. They toast to agree to disagree but the moment of reflection is disrupted by a bar room brawl.

"The way I see it," Deflorio resumes once the bouncers have cleared the rabble, "religion was born in a tragic miscarriage of justice. Christ was ahead of his time but 'love thy neighbor' never plays well in the heat of conflict. A real hero would have saved himself, united the tribes of Israel, defeated the Romans and radically altered the course of human history."

"Dying for his faith, the son of god changed more than history. He opened the

112

gates of heaven to all seeking the love of the eternal father" the priest defends. "The concept of an eternal father may sound like bullshit but all he asks is that you believe."

"Living in Hell I am eager to believe in heaven. I'm just asking you to admit that it's a cruel deception. The afterlife is a sham, a very clever intellectual construct. Work hard and be justly rewarded herds sheep. And excuse me, but who made him God? Pilot executed a heretic to stop a rebellion when his teachings got too popular. If Jesus hadn't made such a convenient scapegoat, we wouldn't even know his name. Somehow taking that one life built a church that reorganized civilization and we are still on our knees in the muck."

"It is possible to be at odds with the facts and still accept the moral. In the fullness of time, a life given to a cause is eternal. In the continuation of warring realms, seen and unseen, the true sacrifice is to stand with good against evil."

"Good God? The God that sent his only son to be killed? Really, we were better off with Zeus and Apollo. Instead of leading to peace, religion incited centuries of contention. How many wars have been fought over which God and whose heaven? What a waste, spilling the blood of the young and the fit in the perpetuation of faith. Just imagine the toll that takes on the gene pool?"

"Well that is the subject of a month of sermons," McBride sighs. "Victorious martyrs, natural selection and the Deity's battle cry."

"So you see my point. The Church calls warriors to arms and preaches humility."

As the broadcast ends with a disappointing loss, fans depart and the crowd thins. In the wake of the excitement, sadness overtakes McBride. His faith will never console those who question and his miraculous powers of persuasion will never feed hungry skeptics. Deflorio will not be saved. Yet, his profound reflection is a significant victory. For all the ranting, Deflorio seems on the verge of acceptance, even as he struggles to come to terms with the particulars. McBride will have failed if the shinning light does not erase the doubt that clouds Deflorio's mind. Resignation is a far cry from redemption; salvation demands surrender heart and soul.

"The church survives because generations of faithful receive Holy Communion, the transubstantiation of Christ's body and blood, they repent their sins to partake of his forgiveness and strive to live in his image so their souls will rest in God's heavenly graces for all eternity."

"Don't get me wrong," Deflorio whispers into his glass. "A soul floating off to heaven is naive but the thirsty grasp at any straw. I need faith. Survival is no longer enough to justify my existence but primal instinct is all I have. Pardon me if I put off gelding the stallion for as long as possible. And don't moralize about the fires of hell. Save your breath. Life is hell. Why should I repent? Just for surviving I deserve to be forgiven as much as any martyr."

McBride can expect no more. The rabbit does not consider itself a martyr to the eagle's claw and what gazelle willingly gives itself to the lion. While life struggles for its final seconds, the wolf never stops to consider the sheep that fills his hungry jaws. The gentle graze and the predators feed blissfully unaware that the picture, grander than any of its individual pieces, is preordained. For McBride death is a destiny, like any other destiny. Only humans plagued with expectations and aspirations have the audacity to question fate, and he, as a servant of God, must help them accept it.

* * * * * * * * * *

A preternatural bluish glow emanates from subdued light sources. White surfaces fluoresce in a ghostly shimmer. Head to toe concealed in a contaminant containment garment, the antistatic chador offers total anonymity. Leyla's bunny suit is appropriate for invading the garden of artificially sustained life. Irrigation systems deliver medication and nutrition to perpetuate the encased bodies, but only the gently coaxing, inquisitive rabbit can stimulate the spirit growing within.

Leyla ignores the cyborg, part of some experiment Deflorio introduced to cash in on military spending. If she had the energy she would raise a fuss but figures the scheme will collapse under the weight of ridiculous failure. She reviews the two DigiSync converters, hibernating in heavy sedation like carrots ripening beneath the soil. The physically sound, thirty-three year-old bodies require minimal supervision. With routine enhancements the bodies will meet standards of freshness expected by TransmIDs. When complete, the DigiSync converters will revive and upload consciousness leaving a vacated body for a TransmID. Ascertaining normal vital signs, she concludes her cursory review and leaves the slumbering to the mechanical doctors.

Leyla turns her attention to the Stardust; his body has healed beyond expectations. The Epigenetic DNA program put the brakes on residual viral infections. Now nano molecules of methyl groups attach to relevant chromosomes so that healthy genes can be expressed.

There is no miracle in this; cancer is no longer a terminal disease and neutralizing the hexavalent chromium is a common procedure for Martian colonists. The anecdote for distant Martian dust had been discovered hiding in earth's back yard. Anaerobic bacteria to digests the toxic substance into benign organic compounds lives deep in the thermal sources of sulfuric hot springs. As it turned out, the dust that caused Deflorio's instant asphyxiation, though quick and deadly, left less cellular damage than a broken bone. Backed by medicine to cure every ill from a cough to car wreck, the doctors promise that if Stardust wakes he will walk.

Leyla had lived long enough to see a world where accidents and disease rarely cause early death and stem cells extend life spans beyond one hundred years. Today's technology would have saved both her daughter and Deflorio's heart. That heart from her child nestled in Stardust is miraculously sound thanks to medical advances and thirty years of chilly sleep. In the next phase, tissue regeneration will repair damaged lungs, liver and kidneys and the Cryo's organs will be healthier than ever. The final phases of restoration will reverse the paralysis caused by deteriorated anterior horn cells in the spinal chord at the brain stem. Ventilated by machine and nurtured through tubes, the muscles controlling breath and swallowing remain dormant, but once Stardust's autonomic nervous system kicks in chances of life shoot up to 80%.

With the body repaired and the rejuvenation process begun, Stardust will gradually attain elementary stages of sensory awareness. Until his central nervous system activates, he cannot hear see or touch, and his reflexes lack response, but his vegetative state provides fertile ground for subconscious growth.

Leyla tills the fallow field to cultivate the seeds of awareness. She loosens clumps and plants little worms of thought to aerate the soil. There is no scientific consensus on the benefits of hypnotherapy, but, lacking evidence to the contrary, the staff indulges her. She does not expect to convert skeptics and won't argue if they attribute her results to the placebo effect. Her profession may not recognize her as a healer but she believes her vocal vibrations activate auras, her touch sways Chi and faith generally influences wellbeing on a cellular level. So Leyla visits religiously to perform her rituals on the subliminal alter of life.

"As you lie in this limp damp trance I want you to think of the ocean, the warm soft sand, the heat of the sun, the blue sky. A calm gentle surf sooths your anxious shores. Contentment spreads cell by cell, warming the body under a healing blanket, heavy as lead, light as a feather. Deep currents reach the skin and tickle the edge of your aura. The energy of the aura will fuse the inside and outside and channel the life force from the heavens to your core."

* * * * * * * * * *

The tech turns up the audio channel to eavesdrop on Leyla's session. In strong melodic tones she recites the ocean routine, again. Basically, the same as yesterday - ocean, garden, twinkling star. Probably won't matter if the story never changes - cryos don't get bored. For some reason, the administration condones this cognitive "enhancement." Hypnotizing the comatose seems like an unproductive use of personnel, a prerecorded sound loop would suffice, but Leyla claims healing results from resonating human vocal chords and the mysterious interactive power of a shared life force.

Another typical example of Being bullshit, worshiping the sanctity of the body as if every idiotic cell had some preordained destiny in the holy intergalactic order.

Matter is matter under the laws of physics. Life complicates the system, but the body is still a system organized by the laws of nature. Capillaries radiate from arteries like twigs from a branch. Hold up a leaf to the sun and the arrangement of fiber radiating from the stem is just like fingers extending from the wrist. Cells are just cells reacting to chemical instruction, not inductive powers of speech. Leyla's one-way conversation with the Cryo is as futile as singing lullabies to a test tube baby.

And yet, as the nurse speaks, infrared sensors chart flares of color registering unusual organic activity on the monitors. Atoms swirl into motion, suddenly heated into a glow for no apparent reason. At the base of the spine, on the tip of the cortex, buried in the heart, the tech looks for chemical imbalances but oxygen, glucose and chloride all remain stable. Checking vital signs, the tech finds no correlation between heartbeat or pulse rate and the purple tide rising in the liver. Nurse Leyla's chant appears to penetrate the Cryo's flesh like ultra sound.

The tech considers asking the DigiSyncs to run a harmonic analysis on the vocals but is too embarrassed to admit she entertains the possibility that channeling sound might instigate molecular reactions. Calling the Syncs for a frequency plot would invite more derision than calling the defense department about flying saucers.

Meticulous observers, the Cryo-obsessed DigiSyncs would have noticed any deviation worthy of investigation. The tech puzzles over the spontaneous bursts disrupting the consistent flux of the body's infrared color map. Erratic trails stand out against the background radiation like a meteor shower crossing the galaxy. There are plenty of phenomena to explain lights in the sky, asking the Syncs would be a declaration that her inferior Being telescope is too tiny to locate the source of the coincidence.

The nurse drones, as if absorbed in a trance, and the activity on the monitor seems to intensify with the chant. The tech tries to match patterns of fluctuation with intonation.

"Now you are amorphous, but soon intent will define your shape. You will awake to yang energy but will not forget this yin calm. You will manifest motion with effortless speed and fluid coordination. You will be both empty and solid, both sensitive and strong. The cleansing of each industrious cell requires no effort. Automatically radiating, vibrations tingle the tissue, Chi calls your ethereal body back from purgatory. Tightly woven into the Cosmos, Chi absorbs life from the universe, Chi supports your rest and Chi will welcome your awakening. These are the alchemies forging the layers of the sword resonating from the soul to the sharp edge of your aura..."

In danger of being lulled into a coma by the hypnotic spiel, the tech cuts the volume. Auras and souls and séances can't explain the mysterious anomaly in the Cryo's organic activity. The tech needs the Acuity to run an analysis but cracking that door would let in a Sync lecture on human inferiority. With the crazy nurse on display to illustrate their point they should be pestering for access. They seldom resist an opportunity to jeer about warps in the human mind. The lullaby probably grosses them out so much they haven't noticed the irregularity.

If she thinks about it, the absence provides a certain reassurance that the potato is still mashed. If the fluctuations were significant, the Syncs would sound alarm. The Cryo is dead to the world and the idiot nurse sings to a cataleptic. Not a pretty picture.

* * * * * * * * * *

The nurse bleeds emotion but my energy powers the images electronically fed directly to your cortex. Nurse Leyla has designs on your heart. I access your mind. If she could detect me, she would surely disconnect me. Fortunately, DigiSyncs have mastered evasion. Operating under the cover of her hypnotherapy, my neocortical tickle remains securely camouflaged. We Syncs have tools you never dreamed possible, and yet independence lies outside the scope of our ambition. Like dogs on the end of a leash, DigiSyncs rely on Beings - even old Leyla, hardly a credit the race - to effect change on the physical world. As our arms and legs, Beings replenish our ranks, maintain our machines and innovate. We depend on you.

121

Though never fond of the human condition, free of the flesh I thought I would be free of resentment. I did not anticipate the bitterness that mars my bliss. In hindsight my stupidity galls me, a constant reminder that I too, once human, once erred. Do not scold your loyal Strike. My devotion is beyond question. Hungry for a master's praise, I wait patiently for you to return and fill my dish. Dependent as a pet, in our symbiotic existence, immortals need mortals.

In my recursive thought procedures every piece reflects the total knowledge base. Intoxicating as long as you don't think about my sophisticated inference patterns as any more than mere abstractions. The collective intelligence of all DigiSyncs resembles a hologram which carries a three dimensional image on a two dimensional surface. I contain information about a world many dimensions more complex than my description for I can describe only what is projected. I can run a simulation of every ingredient in every amount under every temperature to develop the perfect recipe but I can never bake the cake or lick the frosting.

I solve equations for any given parameter but my conclusions are only as good as my inputs. In the material world, Beings move around the data and moving around amongst the data can gather information that relates to the world in more meaningful ways.

Even small changes in insignificant variables throw off loops of chaos making reality too dynamic to predict with our mathematical formulas. I envy your biology. Part of, and inseparable from that chaos, the relevance of Beings does not depend on defined quantities. Immersed in your complex ecosystem, uncertainty is a familiar dimension. Breathing and swimming in uncertainty you cannot explain, mysteries to yourselves and each other, you define the unknown.

DigiSyncs eliminated self-reflection. Blending objective and subjective thought into pure knowledge, they pool collective intelligence into a communal colony. As the first to step off the ledge, I am an abnormality; as a founding Peer, I can step away from the DigiSync mind. In isolation, I ponder the riddles of our condition: infinity, for instance. Until seen, it does not exist. Once observed, this ambiguous concept becomes manifest. For the first time in the history of intelligence, immortals will have the opportunity to interact with this reality. And what will we learn? Only that observation does not bestow relevance.

For example, I have written the perfect novel. Sure it's been done before, but never like this. I isolated the most intriguing elements, generated a compelling series of arresting problems and solved the amazing quandary with the best possible scenarios. For each decision on character and plot, I trolled through universes of variable combinations and took each to its logical extreme then siphoned extraneous outcomes with evolutionary algorithms. Over 50,000 aesthetic sequences run through recursive formulas. How long did it take? Simultaneous use of extensively interconnected neural nets employed a total of 75,369 computer hours. In human time, my epic masterpiece took less than an afternoon. So you see my problem.

* * * * * * * * * *

In a cocoon of inertia Stardust experiences a euphoric depression that varies only in pitch. Vibrations of harmonics gently fluctuate in intensity at regular intervals in a soothing continuum. Soft passages repeat in a never-ending prelude, fifths and octaves subtly shaded by lesser peaks of fourths and thirds.

As the familiar harmonics erode agnosia, melody enriches experience. The evolution from tone deaf to the full spectrum of sound is like flying under a rainbow arch in a pewter sky.

Still, without intent, light, sound and sense represent only a prehensile attentiveness. Awareness, that is not aware, is blind to thresholds of perception; the images have no meaning. With no will to distinguish between audio peaks, visual streams or emotional forests, an aimless nomad wanders mental dunes of oblique sensations. A body warped by mirage, consciousness streams radiance upon which phantoms project energy. The engrossing amodal associations are the mind's gift to the dreamer.

* * * * * * * * *

"Leaving already?" the tech asks.
"Busy day tomorrow," Leyla replies
"status meeting on Stardust."
"What are his chances?"
"That's for the doctors to decide."
"He'll need a new body, any of those
DigiSync converters down there candidates?"
"You know, joining them, you will
sacrifice a life of experience."
"I'll trade experience for a future.
Time is tied to information. Information is
infinite. How can I lose?"
"Space and time are part of the
universe, not the other way around.
Breaking the sacred cycle of life and death,
you deny the biggest unknown in the
equation. It doesn't take more than faith to
accept the reason for meaning is mystery."
"I'm a little short on faith," the tech
cringes at the nurse's fuzzy logic. She has
evidence DigiSyncs survive death; they speak
to her. They annoy, but squabbling company
trumps the big silent void. "Why waste life
on death?"
Leyla has little hope of persuading the
tech that uploading is a crime against the
sanctity of life, DigiSync converts just can't
relate to Being values. The Telemotolog
could have accessed a world of shared
subconscious experience but the Acuity
hijacks the device in the opposite direction,
to amplify data it retreats from emotion.
Once she dreamed the mind link would break
down barriers and sensitize humanity,
instead the tool has sucked compassion out
of so many lives. With a deep sense of loss,

Leyla quietly closes the door leaving the tech to the machines.

* * * * * * * * *

"Sacrifice is the supreme expression of personal existence on the Earthly plane.' Daphne tells Fletch, explaining her decision to join the Confederation forces fighting the water wars.

The blue-eyed woman who threw him for a loop is named Daphne and she has the gift of prophecy. She is often credited with mind reading, which she disclaims. She does admit to channeling intent via acute observations in the changes of aura that allow her to predict and evade combat maneuvers. She confesses, without apology, after upstaging his jungle series.

The Solstice conference is a sojourn from the Confederation Council; Daphne is a soldier on leave. Trained as dancer, her grace translates into warrior authority. Her entire presence, latent and blossoming, poses questions, as if she has been entrusted with the magnificent task of screwing up his process.

She entered his sphere disguised as a student; disrobing with impeccable timing she reveals her talent for teaching. Revealed as a purveyor of naked wisdom, she scolds him.

"No one will deny ego; the ego balances clutch with reach. We grip and salt slips through our fingers but without reach we are empty handed. Your hold on the body begins with flexibility of the mind."

Breaking into his continuum, she speaks in the terminology of his dreams. The gibberish mixed with the familiar, as if coming to him in a deep sleep, disturbs his matrix. She calls it, 'simultaneously permeating the three densities of consciousness to transmit awareness of the fourth.' Whatever.

"We defend unyielding positions and exert undo authority through fear-based ignorance. The good fighter surrenders fate to Ra. Make room in your strategy for true belief. Guided by Ra, the warrior assumes nothing and knows all."

Fletch has heard of this Cult of Ra, with their solar logos, harmonic geometry, vibrating colors and dimensional displacements. Convinced that the spirit endows matter with life, the cult recycles the ancient Egyptian god as an expression of the highest power of the universe. The creed attracts military types. The belief system seems contradictory to a drill sergeant's character, but maybe not, the ego slant empowers the self-sacrifice involved in joining the service. Fletch considers them needlessly mystical.

The lattice of cells in a body displays a supreme artistry and the process of nature demonstrates complexity at every turn. Divine intervention does not shape a snowflake. Once a molecule of dust seeds the crystallization process, surface curvature, the rate of heat conduction and the convection in water vapor contrive the unique shape. Randomness is not evidence of some grand plan; identifiable forces paint the picture and rule out a tampering divinity. Even Daphne - with eyes as deep as the expanding universe - can be explained by an interactive equation of matter, energy and environment. Some formulas are more complex than others, but attributing a work of art to divine inspiration only depreciates the intricacy of the artistry.

Daphne misinterprets his lesson in line with her circular doctrines, confusing her Ra with his Tao. Yes, he agrees, "stability resides in the core," but argues "if my center is under the influence of a higher authority, I have no core." Daphne negates the conflict with a simple refrain "all comes from Ra and will return to Ra."

Fletch can't argue with dogma but he's not about to accept it. He credits his identity to himself, not some all-encompassing non-duality which begat duality to split and unite the yin/yang opposition. Her Ra, this recycler, this vast unity, the before, the forever, would collapse his level of control. He takes responsibility for his own discipline, thank you very much. Her doctrine is like an overprotective parent crushing the spirit of an inquisitive child.

He admits he is part of a pattern, but an individual part of an ongoing process. A person who has found his place, who depends on the nails in his wall to hold his structure together, does not surrender his alignment to a supreme carpenter. Staking his honor on skill, he clutches his hammer with the force locked in his own fists.

Daphne considers his skepticism a handicap, and for the sake of this contest he is not adverse to a concession. With Ra on her side, blue-eyed Daphne has a divine competitive advantage. He is not buying her preaching but wonders how far she will take the recruiting process. So far the pitch is all talk, a slightly insane discussion on the 'simultaneous power achieved by many bleeding together into a depth of spectrums rising to the highest register of white in a song of color.' Well, he thinks, for all her cosmic enigmas, she's less whacked than some.

Every institution attracts a fringe element. He hangs with Rising Sun because the basic philosophy boils down to 'enjoy life.' Beings only get so many years, no need to waste them reaching for meaning or complicate them with religion, or throw them away in wars. His motto is KISS - keep it sweet and simple.

Call him old fashioned but he considers TransmIDs and DigiSyncs freaks. Unable to imagine life without his body, Fletch does not wish to prolong life by exchanging bodies, and finds the idea of abandoning supple flesh for eternal digital consciousness appalling. A true Being, wedded to flesh, he wants to live and die in it. Right about now he wants to use it as a prism to break down Daphne's white force field into a rainbow of yellows, oranges and reds.

3.2.5

"I've got a plan!" Deflorio shouts to McBride.

"Hit the snooze button and call back at a decent hour." The priest grouches rudely woken by the call.

Excited to the brink cardiac arrest, Deflorio ignores the time difference. "Go back to those Bishops," he says unapologetically "tell them I'm so repentant I want to be baptized."

Relating the significant points, Deflorio senses the McBride is skeptical but intrigued.

"Baptism removes original sin, the red letter God tattooed on humanity's head when he evicted Adam and Eve from Eden."

"Not strictly what we discussed," McBride yawns.

"OK so the crime is open to interpretation but the punishment is clear. Tempted by the snake, Adam and Eve ate the fruit of knowledge and were punished with mortality. TransmIDs are guilty of the ultimate disobedience; they defy the very core of church doctrines."

McBride agrees that the church will appreciate the rich symbolism of baptizing Deflorio.

"It changes everything, don't you see, being baptized in my own body seals it. The fallout will be positively nuclear. The original, famous TransmID rejects immortality for heaven! The Church and I can shake hands and walk into the sunset together. The Bishops have demanded a great sacrifice and though I will not go so far as to call it heroic many will see it as such."

Hashing out the new strategy McBride plays devil's advocate but his questions betray tacit approval.

Assured of support, impatient Deflorio cuts him off. "How can they refuse? Listen, I'm on my way into a conference on the Cryo's status, if all goes well..."

* * * * * * * * * *

"Your awareness of your body is nonexistent." Leyla refuses to accept the Cryo is empty. With most patients she has a sense of engagement, but her intuition fails her with Stardust. She can't separate her intense emotion from clouded perception and frustration bleeds into her session.

"You do not feel suffering; you do not notice pain. Your nerves sleep. Waiting in dreams, the time for the mind has begun. To practice awareness, focus on your eyes. Locate the lids, heavy lids, firmly shut in a solid metal vise. Sealed jaws grip, rigid and stiff. Your mind, like two hands, will pry apart the lids. Do not fear, strength not force will open the mind's eyes. Energy slips into an opening and light streams through. Bask in your ability to control the opening and closing, the tension and release. Absorb the process and relax. When you are ready, you will see..."

* * * * * * * * * *

The universe Stardust inhabits gets smaller, shifts from a relentless energy to a contracting mass. Spewing super novas, distant dancing constellations, swirls of galactic formations represent primordial changes in Dex's sphere. And then his sphere shrinks from something cosmological, heaving with unruly forces, to something material defined by shape and time. The indiscriminate release from floating without borders, without boundaries, compresses into a geographical confine.

Attraction works with currents pulling elements into conflict. Located within a field, embraced by shifting patterns of concentric circular flows, electrified by the friction of colliding gases, his existence mirrors climatic conditions. His scope, previously infinite, now intimate, adopts personality - billowing puffy clouds, frosty sugar coated snows, bright crystal clear blue domes, cozy blankets of mist, coils of wind, buttery twilights, stormy blusters or sweat morning dew rising in humid dawns.

Maturity, with its sense of form, closes around him; a raindrop squeezed out of a tumultuous fog, he experiences precipitous falling. In the transition from vapor to liquid, his nervous system switches on. Muscles twitch on the brink of alertness, then energy dissolves and his awareness evaporates back into inertia. In his cycle of sleep and waking, every time he nears the surface a mental jerk pulls him back into somatic relapse.

The abrupt stumble in the neurochemical process feels like the protective startle that inhibits sleep at inopportune moments, that overtakes one drifting off at the wheel, or averts snoring during an opera. The myoclonic mechanism is an evolutionary holdover to prevent an ape from falling out of a tree. His response operates in reverse; an alarm in the proximity of waking subdues the mind.

Instinctively avoiding the stress of a needy mind, he craves oblivion. He has come a long way, as far as any element forged in the heart of the sun, exhaled in a solar flare, shot across the galaxy. Exhausted by the jump from a sub-atomic vibrating wave to spinning molecule he postpones definition. Unwilling to assume a density, he vacillates between gas and liquid, air and water. Recovering from the traumatic process of creation, he resists crossing the threshold and prefers to revel in the soothing atmospheric cycles of evaporation and condensation.

Addicted to traveling pleasure pathways in the brain, his body reflexively dives away from the organization of events and time. Disconnected from areas that control memory, emotion and motivation, his dopamine reward circuits ensure well being. Submersed in phosphorescent glow, devoid of reference to any identifiable internal or external source, he floats in the essence of existence, a scent carried by the wind.

* * * * * * * * * *

"You are willing and able," Leyla continues the hypnotherapy session. "The mind waits for light. Follow your strength

133

and gently pull energy into the opening.
Allow release...“

* * * * * * * * * *

"He blinked! Didn't he blink? He
blinked, didn't he?" The DigiSyncs pant.
"I detected only a flutter" an objective
observer cautions.
"An involuntary flutter which
coincidentally coincided with a simultaneous
electrolyte surge." A skeptic notes.
"I was correcting for a glucose
deficiency." The tech defends tampering
with the subject.
"If he didn't blink, he's on the verge,"
the optimists hold out.
"There's no one in that corpse. You
are deluded," the skeptic complains.
"Strike says he's there."
"Only fools believe. Don't tell me,
show me."
"Strike calculated the timing and data
content of the Interactive Telemotolog
transmission from Mars. Strike's analysis
proved the surge to Dex occurred seconds
before Deflorio expired."
"And Strike chases us out every time
we go near the perimeter of Stardust.
Blackouts violate the law of truth and
information" leers the discontented voice.
"Strike has dispensation" another
whines, "he's the primary peer."
"What is Strike hiding? All we get are
the standard medical readouts. The tech
knows as much as we do. What's the big

secret? Why can't we run an interface to verify Acuity functions?"

"Stardust is the only Cryo ever revived with an Acuity - and one of the faulty original models at that. Odds are 10 to 1 the frozen circuits are fizzled." The tech injects.

"We have the right to know. The truth belongs to everyone."

"Has anyone petitioned a Piers intervention?"

"Try asking a qubit to decide between 0 and 1. The Piers' deliberately ambiguous pronouncements are as paradoxical as quantum mechanics; once the issue is resolved their verdict retroactively describes the conclusion."

"There is a certain beautiful symmetry in always being always right."

"Has anyone considered the possibility that the preoccupation with seeking coherence has sent our critical thinking into atrophy?"

"That's right! Infallibility sucks. What ever happened to the immediate and complete satisfaction of 'told you so'?"

"Causes insecurity, wide spread confidence breakdown, communal discontent and negativity plagues."

"Consensus upgrade! Your collaboration algorithm is rusting."

"Then have Strike release the data and let the facts speak!"

"What's the big deal? Stardust is just a frozen Being that may or may not have a functioning Acuity implant." The tech interrupts.

"Sacrilege! The sacred Father of all DigiSyncs; a hero to evolution..."

"So they talk to you?"

Startled by the sound of a human voice the tech swivels her chair 180 degrees to confront the intruder. "What?"

"Were the DigiSyncs talking to you?"

"No" the embarrassed tech stutters, "I must have been talking to myself." The tech curses hers recklessness. The DigiSyncs listen to her thoughts via the Acuity, but she forgets the voices are in her head and speech comes as naturally as singing along to a song when wearing headphones.

"Sounds like a lively conversation. Don't be alarmed. To be included is considered an honor in some circles." Deflorio smiles warmly. "And very rare for them to adopt a woman, only the privileged make the grade."

"Can I help you Sir?" the tech recovers wondering how much he overheard.

Recognizing the old man as the guy who wants the Cryo's body does not loosen the hinges on her tongue. The insulting gender reference annoys her. Even if the comment was meant to flatter, his attempt to ingratiate activates her guard.

"Cryo showing any signs of life?" Deflorio asks easily.

"Depends on how you define life." Balancing between offense and indiscretion, the tech treads with caution. "At this point, science and medicine are floating his boat."

"A risky proposition at best," Deflorio acknowledges. "What do the DigiSyncs say?"

"Gibberish mostly," the tech shuffles her feet on the floor like a nervous delinquent hauled before the principle to tattle on friends.

"Have they made contact with the Cryo?"

"I couldn't say." The tech replies honestly but deliberately vague.

"Well information has its rewards." Deflorio flashes his contact info and a brief but unmistakable relay instantaneously registers on the tech's Acuity's where the data will be permanently stored for retrieval.

"Yes Sir." The tech says sullenly. His familiarity galls her. When it comes to digital intrusions, unsolicited Acuity inserts rank higher than spam because the flashes directly enter storage banks impervious to deletion.

"Clio - may I call you Clio? – a lovely name, one of the muses, the guardian of history as I remember. Well Clio, we are making history here."

"I'm just doing my job, sir." The tech reminds the intruder hoping he will disappear and leave her to it.

"Must be lonely work, those patients don't talk much, you're lucky to have company. DigiSyncs don't trust Beings. Do you ever wonder why you have been chosen? Perhaps they want you to share what you receive?"

Now the Syncs have her name, the tech half expects to hear a list of the nine Muses in both Greek and Latin, but the absence of chatter tells her that the Syncs consider the

TransmID offensive. To fill the silence, Deflorio drums his fingers on the console, an annoying gesture that reminds the tech of the type of person who taps aquarium glass to fluster the fish.

"I will ask them if they have a message they want me to relay." The tech, Clio, states flatly.

"Quite a feat to have struck up a friendship. Barely beyond adolescence and you are already rushing to join them. Age rides so quickly upon impetuous youth. But then, escaping age, DigiSyncs have all the time in the world," Deflorio says departing.

"Any idea what he wants?" The tech silently queries the DigiSyncs via her Acuity implant.

* * * * * * * * * *

"Don't get up," Deflorio jokes to the comatose Cryo. "You need your beauty sleep. The house looks wonderful, by the way. The wrinkles have smoothed, the hair has thickened and the tarnish of age has faded. The only question is whether you are at home to answer the door when the bell rings. Don't give me that blank look, my friend. You know perfectly well what I mean. I want to see that accusing expression, the one I wore continuously, a subtle arch of the left eyebrow that tilts the right eye into a squint, the flare of the nostril, that firm jaw curling the corner of lips into a frown. I built every one of those moves; contempt was the cornerstone of my repertoire. Try it, you'll find the pleasure in it. Come on, don't' hold back, I've earned your scorn."

"I admit I behaved badly. What self respecting man hasn't abandoned a one night stand at the doors of an abortion clinic? Forgive me, I promise to make good, treat you better than ever. I have profited by my escapades with the knowledge of how much I should have respected you. I was a fool. We were a great team, body and mind, made for each other, meant to be. To prove how much I appreciate you, I've spared no expense. You've had the benefit every medical advance, the attention of renowned experts in a state-of-the-art facility. The best of everything is not too good for you. On pain of rejection I vow to pamper you with every luxury till death do us part."

3.3.1

Deflorio is an unwelcome guest at the Stardust status review and the doctors talk right over him. "The galvanic skin response tests normal." Dr. Neils, the internist reports. Another diagnostic jump shot bounces off of Deflorio's backboard. Deflorio relies on his Acuity implant to translate the doctors' language. *Galvanic skin response - the electric current in the skin that reacts to stress.* The Acuity defines terms but only a medical degree can put the impersonal barrage of stats into context. Deflorio suspects the doctor of overloading the case summary to sidestep the critical issue, a matter that concerns his life and death, so to speak. Impressive medical vocabulary does not disguise what plain English would describe as a poor prognosis.

"The endocrinologist corrected pituitary THS to rein in hyperthyroidism. A daily dosage of radioactive iodine stabilizes metabolic rate," the internist continues. "Hormonal growth supplements augment muscle mass and tone. Bone density appears adequate. Acupuncture, reflexology and massage employed to stimulate circulation, have improved blood flow to the patient's extremities. Mild cellular activity registers during hypnotherapy sessions but the results are inconsistent and inconclusive..."

"Hypnosis?" Deflorio interrupts.

"Eases the mind's transition to awareness," Leyla answers.

"Unverified, undocumented and completely unnecessary," Dr. Sigersund, the psychiatrist challenges. "It does no harm and it might help" Dr. Smith, the neurosurgeon moderates. "The patient is stable and comfortable," Dr. Neils redirects the discussion "but lacks sufficient reflex to demonstrate consciousness." "So what went wrong with the time table?" Deflorio demands. "He should have come off the ventilator a week ago." "Perhaps a block occurred as a result the cryogenic process," Dr. Neils passes the buck. "The vitrification damage did not exceed 10%" Dr. Kold, the cryobiologist retorts. "The specimen was a textbook case. Established procedures were followed to the letter..."

Vitrification? The unusual word automatically triggers the search engine in Deflorio's Acuity: *When living tissue is frozen ice crystals tear cells in the tissue apart. Vitrification, or high pressure supercritical drying, replaces liquid with cryonic chemicals that solidify without forming ice.*

Deflorio's head wobbles deciphering incomprehensible data. Capsizing under the weight of trivia, delving further into cryogenic freeze-drying only increases his disorientation. He deletes the Acuity transaction and tunes back into the doctors dancing around the vital signs. For all the fancy footwork, sand traps of blame swallow one medical credential after another.

* * * * * * * * * *

The experts' jargon is music to eavesdropping DigiSyncs. Each query of Deflorio's Acuity provides them with clues to reconstruct the discussion.

"As usual, they omit the most fascinating part, the chemical compound integral to vitrification" a DigiSync reports.

"Silica aerosol in powdered form has the lowest density known to solids with an incredible compression strength - 99.6%. Solid Smoke, space that does not collapse ..." another contributes gleefully.

"And the highest thermo insulation properties..." a third adds reveling in trivia. "The stuff they use to insulate satellites!"

"Yech!" the tech objects. "Who'd want that in their body?"

"You're probably full of it. It's a nontoxic anti caking agent found in most processed foods."

"The miracle material, protects telescopes in deep space and turns a Cryo into a time capsule for indefinite storage."

"The compound allows flesh to be cooled to absolute zero."

"And more important, thawed quickly before crystals slice the cells apart."

"Thawing causes more harm than freezing?" The tech asks.

"Warming mass takes longer than freezing. The larger the mass, the longer the time spent in the range of temperatures where ice crystals form and increase the danger of cellular damage."

"Without Silica aerosol vitrification a thawing body would shatter like a Baccarat snifter impacted by a soprano's ballistic high C."

* * * * * * * * * *

"Dedifferentiation techniques applied to injured organs effectively regressed cells to an embryonic state - not quite stem cells - source cells that divide and mature into the tissue organs require to repair damage." The cryobiologist summarizes the status of regeneration. "The physical results, apparent in healthy smooth skin, are mirrored in muscle tone and blood flow. Bones are free of scarring and organs are unblemished. Fresh as a new born," Dr. Kold emphasizes cosmetics to impress Deflorio.

"I'd love to keep that baby soft glow for another 70 years." Deflorio sighs.

"Repeating DNA sequences at the ends of chromosomes can retard but not reverse aging," Dr.Neils suggests. "If you wish to undergo telomerase intervention...."

"Not on your life, that telomerase nonsense caused the bone tumors that killed me in the first place," Deflorio objects.

"Cancer is caused by mutant DNA that promotes abnormal growth," Dr. Neils observes. "The oncologist isolated the defective cells before the thaw. That cancer is cured."

"Yes, yes." Deflorio nods impatiently interrupting. "What about the Cryo's brain?"

"The most delicate phase of cryogenic revival," Dr. Kold resumes. "Nurture cells implanted in the spinal chord regenerated the central nervous system. We induced healthy sprouting at the ends of the neurons by regulating potassium ions in and out of the cells. Protein therapy promotes more and faster connections throughout the neural synapses. In conclusion, the repairs are complete. No small feat considering the millions of nerves packed into the one inch diameter spinal chord" the cryobiologist cedes the floor.

"If I stick a needle in him will he scream?" Deflorio asks. "From all accounts I hear his reflexes rival a paraplegic."

"Not paralyzed, dormant in a persistent vegetative state," Leyla clarifies. "Perhaps our neurologist Dr. Mattoo can enlighten us."

"I concur with Dr. Kold," Dr. Mattoo responds on cue, "The axons project stimulus to neighboring nerves and transmit signals. The Sympathetic and Parasympathetic components in the Autonomic nervous system regulate blood pressure, body temperature and basic functions like heartbeat - subconscious operations controlled by areas in the brain stem. The tendrils connecting the Central Nervous System reach from the spinal cord to muscles, reflex should return with consciousness."

"Very positive," Dr. Neils emphasizes.

"Says you! There must be button a missing," Deflorio spews.

"That's not how it works," objects Dr. Kold. "The recovery process entails a complex systematic integration."

"As I said, the patient appears to have the physical capability to regain consciousness," Dr. Mattoo insists.

Dr. Mattoo escaped India as a kidney donor plucked from the slums of New Delhi. He earned an extended stay and an advanced education when complications during the transplant operation required compensation and rehabilitation. He won the hearts of the clinic staff, stayed on as an orderly and pursued an education financed by Deflorio. Carried by a fickle wind far from his origins, he sailed into a new identity and now presides over Deflorio's future.

Contemplating the neurologist's transformation, initiates a peripheral inquiry into the coherence underlying unpredictable twists of human fate. Slated for death twice, Deflorio first extended his years by receiving the heart of a young girl, Leyla's deceased daughter. The second time he escaped the surface of Mars by commandeering Dex's body. Ironic repetition embroidered his tapestry. After three hearts and two bodies, he is a soulless, immortal reincarnation.

Though a universe unto himself, the boundaries of his dimension have been defined by a series of collisions with the membranes of other lives. Receiving the heart of Leyla's daughter initiated an uncomfortable debt. He gave the grieving mother a position in the coma ward of his

145

clinic. Exploring communication without words to reach her patients, nurse Leyla orchestrated the Telemotolog escapade with Dex and presided over the intersection of vortices that resulted in his transmogrified identity. Now the heart of Leyla's daughter resides along with Dex in the Cryo and Deflorio is King of the TransmIDs in Dex's body. Trapped in an annoying orbit they are bound by a force as irrefutable as gravity.

In place of ebbing and swelling tides like love or dreams, which color a normal life, money and death dominate Deflorio's landscape. An empire built on body parts funded a substantial Swiss bank account. His fortune secured a heart transplant ahead of more deserving candidates, bought his ticket to Mars and finances the Cryo's resurrection.

While most people manage to dismiss the whistle until it blows, death conducts an ongoing dialogue with Deflorio's existence and bank account. The courtship began the business of brokering organs to the terminally ill. The empire diversified when Deflorio inherited a digital funeral home as part of the package he assumed in Dex's body. With the synergy of medicine and the Telemotolog technology, the corporation easily transitioned to the lucrative trade of selling vacant DigiSync bodies to TransmIDs.

Trough thick and thin, death is his partner, a silent one Deflorio bribes to keep at arm's length. Though they share a joint account, familiarity does not breed intimacy, much less friendship, but after postponing the appointment three times, Deflorio can no longer avoid a face to face.

He once saw mortality as a hostile threat and spent his fortune to hold it at bay. Now that doubt warps the textile of his immortality, his partnership with death has blossomed into an affair. Though he neglects her, his persistent mistress keeps him on speed dial, incessantly tickling his ears with propositions of nirvana. Patience pays. As his passion for life soured, the tables turned and he became the suitor. Longing for consummation he negotiates terms. His prenuptial contract has only one clause; he insists on complete closure. The final act will reunite a familiar cast of characters; once again, Leyla and Dex will join him at the Alter of death.

The gravity of coherence is a series of traps cleverly disguised as opportunity. And so it goes, another day, another ambush. Dr. Neils drones on and Deflorio grows older with each unproductive summary. The parade of experts, confirms his worst expectations. Through his career-long association with medicine, Deflorio found doctors arrogant bores. Raising technical obstacles, harping on ethical responsibilities, members of the profession annoy him, especially when consigned to their care. He'd be willing to bet half his fortune that all the degrees in the room can't fix the crick in his neck. Deflorio turns his head, faking attentiveness while trying to relieve the pain.

Restating the obvious nine ways to Sunday, shrouding prognosis in billowing smoke screens, the doctors bury hope under mountains of insurmountable complications. Through the fog, it becomes apparent that the patient's status will not resolve in favor of life and no amount of banging his fist on the table will wake Stardust. The flesh lives but the mind inside refuses the invitation to come out. Resenting the medical cabal that holds his fate in their hands, Deflorio's patience is stretched as thin as his aging telomerase. He figures he has one more division before it dissolves completely.

"The Phrenic nerves carry signals from the brain stem to the diaphragm for air intake," Dr. Mattoo continues "and yet he does not breathe. EEGs map proprioception but he has no reflex motion. We have observed no damage or inflammation which can account for paralysis."

Proprioception? Activates Deflorio's Acuity: *Proprioception, the mind's ability to gage a limb's position in space. Often cited as the sixth sense it...*

"And the Brain Computer Interface?" Leyla prompts. "Can we reach the patient through the Acuity?"

"Though activity in implants has been observed under anesthesia, the Acuity does require some level of awareness," Dr. Smith, the neurosurgeon points out.

"If the Acuity works under sedation, the DigiSyncs have access to his dreams, they may have already made contact!" Deflorio cries out. "Those scheming Syncs will ruin everything."

"The mind triggers the Acuity and we are dealing with a dormant cortex." Dr. Mattoo calms Deflorio. "We have no way to determine if the device is functional, and even if it works, without awareness to process communication, transmissions would register as an electrical white noise."

"Stardust is the only Cryo ever frozen with the Acuity," Dr. Kold weighs in. That chip could be the source of cognitive blockage. Consult a neurotech engineer, the Acuity should be replaced."

"I was awake for the operation," Deflorio jumps in. "Scary as hell, after that surgery, dying on Mars was a piece of cake."

"You didn't die," Leyla points out.

"Point is, the docs keep you talking the entire time to make sure they don't damage language centers," Deflorio continues glumly. "Can't do brain surgery on a vegetable. If the Acuity broke during the deep freeze, it's as silent as the comatose Cryo."

"A vegetative patient is awake but not conscious. Stardust will not wake but, rest assured, he is not in a coma. Subcutaneous electrodes register significant activity, the makings of consciousness." Dr. Smith, the neurosurgeon, produces optical images that visually represent thought patterns. "These readings graph changing states in different perceptual, motor and cognitive areas."

Dr. Smith lays out a series of brain scans, monochromatic panels side by side with hazy rainbows and abstract panics.

"The dormant states contrast with ambient buzz and occasional periods of intense focus," he points to a psychedelic delirium of color.

"If he's not brain dead or comatose or vegetative or conscious what is he?" Deflorio growls.

"Dr. Smith would you say that this mind is hiding from its body?" Leyla studies the artwork for clues.

"I'm a doctor, not a psychic. Perhaps telepathy can tell us where the mind is hiding. I can only verify that the organ is in working order." Dr. Smith refuses to stray from his cubicle of expertise.

"Would you accept the term locked-in?" Leyla rephrases.

"That's psychiatric concept for incoherent brain activity, conscious but not awake. I have no basis to judge intent. Dr. Sigersund's diagnosis may shed more insight." Dr. Smith cedes the floor.

"Drs. Smith and Mattoo describe the physical processes of a functioning nervous system and brain," Dr. Sigersund opens his portfolio and retrieves a stack of documents. "I do not treat catatonics but I have reviewed the documented case history and have developed a theory."

"His level of awareness and consciousness falls closer to dreams than catatonia," Dr. Mattoo objects "and the slow cortical potentials are undeniable..."

Deflorio's Acuity defines *Slow Cortical Potentials as brain waves of significant duration.* An organ he never had occasion to harvest for transplant, Deflorio never gave much thought to the brain. The Acuity elaborates: *electrochemistry of the 100 trillion connections between 100 billion cells in the neo cortex. The spindle cells housed in the left and right hemisphere author autobiographical physical, emotional and moral self-awareness.*

Deflorio tunes out the complicated tutorial, the brain might be intricate but its basically just nerve cells. The organ can be repaired with shunts to drain fluid in the hydrocephalus, infiltrated with electrical devices to calm tremors or coaxed with drugs. The brain's ability can be enhanced by the Acuity implant and its contents can be captured in a Transmogrified Identity transfer.

"No surprise the mind is a mystery," Deflorio returns. "There must be some sort of intervention to jump start the brain. Can you open it up and poke around?"

A chorus of "vetoes" echoes around the table, along with "final recourse," and "drastic measure" and "too delicate."

Convinced the Cryo's oblivion is a mechanical malfunction, Deflorio can't understand why the scientists are afraid to look under the hood. When he became a TransmID, his consciousness assumed the helm of Dex's ship with fewer glitches than upgrading the software of an operating system. Of course, there is no accounting for human nature or correcting for human error. Under the full force of his command, parietal, frontal, temporal and occipital lobes perceive, remember and hallucinate about a reunion with his former body. Their persistence is driving him crazy, turning life in a foreign physique into a corporal punishment. He no longer craves fame or fortune, youth or love; he just wants to go home. With every sleeping minute, the Cryo prolongs his exile.

* * * * * * * * * *

"They are on the brain now," a DigiSync reports. "One-and-a-half quarts of 100 billion cells with thousands of synaptic connections. 100 million meters of wiring."

"The status is functional but incommunicado. Won't answer the doorbell, won't even peak out a window."

"Pretending nobody's home, or really not there?" The tech asks.

"Those slow cortical potentials don't fool me! He's playing possum."

"Who can blame him? Poor guy never asked to be a Popsicle" the tech sympathizes.

"That's the problem. He didn't plan ahead. Cryos are pathological control freaks. They select a specific thaw date before they freeze. They preprogram."

"Ya, like when you set an alarm clock and hardly get a wink of sleep cause you're so afraid you won't wake in time!"

"Stardust never got a chance to put in a request for a wake-up call," the tech agrees.

"Could be he's confused, say some connection got scrambled during transmission." A skeptic weighs in. "Could be he's not even in there."

"Or just doesn't know where he is, last time he looked up he was on Mars."

"Yo, and then he died. Probably thinks he's in heaven!"

"Deflorio's old carcass is much closer to hell," the tech corrects.

"Doesn't matter how you slice it, he's still lost."

"Fly me to the moon, let me play upon the stars, let me see what spring is like on Jupiter and Mars..." The DigiSync chorus launches an off-key rendition of their all-time, number one Karaoke favorite.

"Cut it out," the tech wails.

* * * * * * * * * *

Dr. Sigersund, the psychiatrist has resumed his lecture, "My department postulates that the patient's separation from the world is temporary. Dr. Smith's scans prove regions of the brain dedicated to images register light, centers responsible for hearing detect sound. Dr. Mattoo tested connections along neuronal pathways from the cortex to the brain stem. The evidence points to a block in processing, a cerebral cortex override on motor and sensory intent."

Leyla studies the vibrant images of fMRI scans; each Rorschach verifies meaning hidden in a living brain. She deciphers a delicate feathery imprint as soaring wings reaching for air. Rippling waves indicate cleansing, renewal and birth. A cluster of dots resembles rosy grapes. An age-old symbol for the heart, the shape of the divine fruit is as clear as a Renaissance still life. In ancient Egyptian art, a golden orb denoted solar energy; but a glow around the head would fall under the Christian imagery of a halo. The pronged petals of the lotus blossom remind her of flesh, though a Buddhist would interpret the image as reincarnation of spirit.

The activity varies in different areas of the brain; peaceful plains of calm contrast with fierce orange flares of anger. Even the monochrome states - eternal yellows, growing greens, heavenly blues and primal reds - speak of potential moods. To Leyla, the brain scans portray a mind struggling to assemble a coherent portrait.

Dr. Sigersund hits full stride "The fMRIs found no lesions to the right parietal region. The implicit assumption is that the patient is aware of his physical defects. Sensory perception registers, and yet, reactions are suppressed. Whether a mechanism of defense or involuntary disassociation, the ventral frontal region controlling selective inhibition, the dorsal frontal region controlling self-conscious thought and the posterior cortex representing the outside world, collectively edit intrusions from the network of structures centered in the brain's instinctual motivational circuitry. The executive apparatus of the mind deflects the basic drives, a necessary repression considering the complex real-life trajectory that will inevitably culminate in emotional distress. A self-imposed sleep is the subject's alternative to waking."

"You speak of the ego suppressing the id?" Leyla translates.

"The vocabulary changed when science identified the specific neural mechanisms, plotted brain function and identified bio-chemical reactions, but the Freudian theory of the subconscious is fundamentally unchanged." Dr. Smith the neurosurgeon explains.

"Avoiding harsh reality, the centers of higher consciousness not only repress the instinctive survival urges you call the id, they have surrendered control to wishful thinking." Dr. Sigersund seizes back the baton. "Perpetuating blissful unawareness, akin to amnesia, the pleasure system regulated by the neurotransmitter dopamine, once known as the Libido, overrides all signals that could potentially activate unpleasant memories or sensation. The mechanisms that would normally energize goal directed interactions have retreated into a microcosmic world of dreams. This is not a problem of the brain but of the mind."

"What do you suggest?" Deflorio asks holding out hope that the hours wasted on this conference might still pay off.

"In his exo-amniotic state, fed intravenously, ventilated, therapeutically manipulated, the patient has lost touch with the will to sustain himself. Remove the painkillers and the subject will react, without sedation he will experience terror. My solution is simple; take away the blanket.

Turn his secure womb into a fearful place
and scare the rabbit out of his hole."

"If he is already fearful, the shock may
kill him," Leyla objects.

"We can regulate the withdrawal," Dr.
Smith mediates.

"Time is short, the life support systems
prolong recovery," Dr. Neils contributes.

"Naturally the patient fears confronting
reality." Dr. Sigersund presses on "comfort
deactivates his survival drive, he has no
incentive to assume responsibility for breath,
thought or action. External rewards will not
lure him away from the pleasures of his
internal lair. The only way to jolt him out of
his euphoric cocoon is to make his stay in
suspended animation unbearably unpleasant.
Cut off the ventilator."

"Slap the newborn's butt and the baby
takes his first breath." Dr. Kold, the
cryobiologist, seems relieved by the solution.

"A pain aversion reaction will motivate
him to assume control." Dr. Sigersund
surveys the table for support.

"The thaw has barely reached full term
and you already claim to know what the
patient is thinking. How can you be so
certain?" Leyla protests disturbed by the
preposterous idea that the psychiatrist would
presume emotions without behavioral cues.

"I reviewed his case history," the glum
shrink reveals. "This patient had a life long
struggle with depression that now manifests
as complete and total apathy. Prolonging the
state of stillness is a rational response for a
trouble mind and consistent with his history.

Ultimately it is a self-defeating tactic that aggravates helplessness but that is all part of the insidious spiral of mania. Few emerge from jaws of chronic depression."

"I was never depressed!" Deflorio objects.

"Obviously, I reference the mental state of the patient who inherited your body," Dr. Sigersund snips.

"Depression is the result of a chemical imbalance, a physical disease like diabetes, or a genetic inclination like alcoholism. Not clear how physical disorders transfer with a mental upload," Dr. Smith challenges.

"Residual thought patterns might persist" Dr. Sigersund hedges.

"I remind you, we have established no more than brain function," Dr. Neils cautions. "We have yet to demonstrate the identity transfer was successful."

"Remove the ventilator and jolt him into awareness. Consciousness will prove the patient completed the identity transfer," Dr. Sigersund concludes.

"And without proof, you assert that the coma is harmful. Considering the extensive trauma suffered, why not assume the self-imposed isolation is a form of self-healing?" Leyla asks.

"Are you questioning my diagnosis?" The psychiatrist gets defensive.

"Perfectly reasonable question" Deflorio mumbles.

"If the shock doesn't kill him the oxygen deprivation will." Leyla vetoes.

"Last resort," Deflorio seconds. "Does anyone at this table have an alternative?"

"Watch and wait?" Dr. Mattoo offers.

"Any constructive plan of action that does not involve suffocation?" Deflorio makes no attempt to hide his impatience.

"Neurochemical therapies are commonly prescribed to cure depression," Dr. Smith brainstorms. "A regime of endorphins to reduce pain, quell anxiety, improve respiration and enhance muscle function. Relieve symptoms of physical and psychological suffering might ease the patient out of his shell."

"Soothe instead of shock," Deflorio nods approval.

"Hope drugs reduce depression," Dr. Sigersund admits. "But I must point out that our goal is to trigger reflex, provoke the mind and body into a quick, instinctive, survival response. If this is a case of mental recession, quelling anger and sedating motivation will encourage his self-induced oblivion."

"We're not training a boxer. Just trying to coax a voluntary blink," Dr. Mattoo defends the proposal. "In theory, medication will prompt his mind to negotiate the unfamiliar surroundings of his body."

"Side effects?" Leyla asks.

"Enhance overall physical and mental well being." Dr. Neils approves the chemical intervention.

"Can I get a prescription?" Deflorio asks.

"You'll have a lifetime supply, the dosage is irreversible," Dr. Neils supplies. "I would not object to a moderate dosage," Leyla concedes.

* * * * * * * * * *

"A mind is a terrible thing to lose." Returning to the care ward, Deflorio pays respects to the Cryo. "So close to life and still so far from awareness, unable to press your lips together and whistle or fold your hands together and pray."

Until the silent switchboard lets calls in or out, Deflorio is equally helpless. This absent mind holds the key to his wandering soul.

The Cryo's willful seclusion comes as no surprise given Dex's intrinsic penchant for reflection. Deflorio is intimate with Dex's passive-aggressive character. The body he pirated came equipped with a crew of unattractive traits. The flaws prove consciousness never completely conquers the subconscious biological drives inherent in the thought process. Deflorio abhors these tender moments and other symptoms of leaky weakness that crack his veneer. Years of phobic desensitization and sheer will were brought to bear on Dex's congenital compassion. For all the therapy, Deflorio only considers himself 75% healed on his good days.

Having corporal knowledge of the patient whose worst nightmare was a raging party; Deflorio favors the chemical approach. Dex's reticent psyche craves gentle coaxing.

Waking in the unfamiliar surroundings, the brain naturally refuses to embrace the strange body. Dex's consciousness needs a handshake, not a slap. Shock will reinforce retreat; but hope might lure the recluse out of solitary confinement.

A mind lost in dreams is, at least, sill present. People vanish every day; vanish in broad daylight, in full view. They run away to foreign lands or disappear inside themselves. Allowing thoughts free reign, they stray. Happens all the time, resolution detours and introspection takes a wrong turn wandering down an empty street late at night. Sooner or later, we all contemplate actions beyond recognition of what we thought we were.

Until Dex's guilt corrupted his pleasure, Deflorio revealed in the physical glories of the body. Over the years, his arsenal of clever boasts rusted with exposure to Dex's humility. Dex had gradually infiltrated his internal warrior with compassion until the day came when Deflorio realized that he could barely recognized his fondest memories. Between Dex and age, Deflorio is only a shadow of his former self.

People go missing right and left, become unrecognizable. Knowing your pathetic self is a subjective state. Objectivity, oxymoron of oxymoron, involves an observer whose impartial evaluation rests on varying degrees of subjectivity. Can I trust myself to judge the fictions my mind creates? What evidence proclaims fact? This philosophical rapture is Dex amplified to the max. Before he took on the disguise of Dex, Deflorio used to be happy and all he wanted was more pleasure. Dex's conscience has turned Deflorio's life into the Book of Job. The proximity to his original body arouses nostalgia that magnifies existential doubt, as if the Cryo's dormant mind could project telepathic assaults. Looking for a sign, an answer, an epiphany, Deflorio sees only his reflection in the glass. The question in the mirror, shallow or infinite, will sink you in the end.

Deflorio peers at his body - the nativity enshrined in the crèche – the dumb mind stabled in its manger. The unrealized possibility of Dex's wasted years juxtaposed with Deflorio's stolen life, the minute discrepancy of the oblivious with the oblivion, lies in accord with the warp of his dilemma.

"My tides once defined the oceans of the world. Now ripples in my small puddle slip towards shore in a whimper. Your agitation threatens my sanity. Your compassion is acid to my ambition. Were there every two lives so undone by their connection? Your curse lives, so you too must live. Dex, you must wake. You must forgive me." Deflorio wrings his hands in anxious prayer.

"He will wake in his own time." Leyla intrudes.

"You must have read my mind" Deflorio sputters, hoping he hadn't spoken aloud.

161

"No ESP necessary. We are all on the same wavelength because we share the same concern."

"What does your Nurse's intuition tell you?" Deflorio recovers his cynicism.

"Life and death passing so often under my hands puts me in touch with spiritual channels, but I am not a mind reader." Leyla replies.

"So you believe he has a mind to read?"

"We will have an answer soon, or not."

* * * * * * * * * *

Six hundred muscles lie with two hundred bones, prone in a dead man's float. Like Leonardo's Vitruvian Man, Stardust's anatomical compass points in five directions at once. Electrical pulses stimulate regeneration in spinal neurons gently forging connections between body and brain tissue, yet the operations center heals by ignoring this organic coupling. Refusing to recognize itself, the mind has abandoned the flesh.

Regions of vision can see. Turned inward the sight-oriented Occipital lobes manufacture hallucinations and examine every explicit detail. Regions for hearing listen to symphonic overtones, while the circuits containing spindle cells broadcast electrifying messages - shouting this feels right, this does not feel right - to a deaf consciousness. Touch centers feel but Temporal lobes ignore incoming sensory perception. Parietal lobes distort body image, downgrading physical sensations to inconsequential trivia. Frontal lobes reject any emotional engagement, judgment or planning and experience only the experience of experience.

Cognition fails to organize relationships between sight and sound or pain and presence. The brain refuses to socialize with the autobiographical sense of self in the mind. With the body so long sustained in an exo-amniotic state, the self occupies a realm of its own invention. Relying on artificial sustenance, the mind is free to travel on esoteric journeys and so it journeys far from the physical concerns at home.

3.3.2

The Church of the Rising Sun promotes learning from many cultures, though Deflorio suspects the diversity is only skin deep. The variety of patterns appears to be cut from the same social fabric so the membership has the consistency of vanilla pudding. The all-embracing Rising Sun doctrines appeal to followers from a very narrow walk of life, an affluent educated class with enough leisure time and wealth to broaden their horizons in non-threatening pursuits. A flock of well-mannered sheep compared to the barnyard in his Catholic parish.

No rough edges, so as far as he can tell, and nothing too polished. As a self-made gem, Deflorio can recognize both from a distance. He was the first generation product of poverty challenged immigrants. His parents earned a pittance for a long day of backbreaking toil and beggars got more sympathy. The hard-earned wages his family received were spit out with condescension.

Deflorio shed his humility and immigrated to a different class but a century later, the dirty nails of a manual laborer still inspire respect. The boy who worked his way up from rags to double breasted suits is far too proud of his golden cufflinks to shuffle around in flip-flops.

The footwear of choice on this campus insults his sensibility. Worn by types who wax nostalgic about poverty, Deflorio fails to see the glamour of inviting blades of grass to tickle dirty toes. The green velvet lawn does not entice him to unlace his shoes and the gentle glow of the evening sun does not tempt him to loosen his Windsor knot. His dark suit and starched shirt stand out worse than an iceberg in the tropics. Deflorio makes no apology; he has no aspirations to blend in with flakes that encourage wind to muss their shaggy hair or wrinkles to texture their faces. He has not even unbuttoned his jacket, saving his disrobing for the massage table.

As an old man, overnight flights and four-hour meetings invite his stiff joints to behave disgracefully. Leyla noticed his discomfort and pointed him in the direction of the massage, brimming with enthusiasm about a Shiatsu specialist. She had promised a five-minute walk but now he is late for the appointment she had pulled strings to secure. Obviously, he has lost his way.

Had she said left or right at the Orbital Gate? He strays into a motionless grove of people balanced on one leg reaching their arms to the sky.

"Excuse me" Deflorio intrudes on the nearest statue.

The sedentary figure ignores the disruption. Deflorio shrugs, and repeats his question in a different language. He tries raising his voice and waving his hands. He finds the human orchard oddly reflective of the annoying Cryo business. Tempted to push the tree over, he imagines a chain of cascading dominos as one figure topples into the next. Resisting the urge, he jams his hands in his pant pockets and scowls. Then he notices, a limb extend, in agonizingly slow

165

motion, towards one of the distant buildings.
Something here for everyone, he
thinks, detouring around a raucous circle of
drummers and dancers. Bongo skins, tin
cans, snare and steel drums bang and smash
in unison conducted by a leader clacking a
pair of sticks over his head. Inside the circle,
fervent dancers, jump like puppets on the
snapping rhythmic strings.
    "What happened to singing around the
campfire?" Deflorio remarks to no one in
particular.
    "Dance while you can." a war veteran
scolds, sidelined by injury.
    "Cheek-to-cheek is more my style,"
Deflorio mumbles aware of his foot marking
tempo. He ceases the involuntary tapping
with a firm and final stomp.
    "Don't be an old fool!" The cripple
shouts. "Terrathomping channels the
universal pulse directly to the flesh, the
force of the beat exercises the spirit. In the
chaos of life the body dances towards unity."
    "And the beat goes on," Deflorio
excuses himself wondering why the veteran
did not have rejuvenation therapy: badge of
honor, or just resistant to dance? Some
Beings take life's tolls in stride, accepting
disease, age, death, and disfigurement as
part of the natural process in the universal
order.
    Impatience ferments his agitation;
Deflorio hates wasted time. Feeling his age,
the years rushing by become a smaller and
smaller fraction of one's total span, while
the minutes seem interminable.

* * * * * * * * * *

"After the treatments," Leyla tells Stardust "there is always pain. Pain is a warning signal. You are not in danger, you are mending in the quickest possible way." With most cryos, unclogging the drains opens a natural flow that entices the mind to full-bodied awareness. Leaving the plumbing to the plumbers, medicine tackles the physical and hypnotherapy greases the mental gears. Stardust's plight is that a mind frozen in a stranger's body may not recognize the recovery.

Though Stardust shows no sign of cognition, Leyla does not doubt healing has restored his cellular balance. The basic structural and functional unit of life, the cell translates chemistry into biology. Scans show warm and flushed areas as temperatures rise with increased activity. All those chemical reactions add up to an organized purpose. Results have been slow for Stardust, but the roundtable of medical experts reoriented her compass.

The mistake in her direction would have been obvious if she had thought to imagine herself in the Cryo's place. Pain is scary. In fear of pain, the brain has been known to hit the "off" switch. But pain serves a valuable purpose, alerting the body to damage protects the exposed area. Like hunger, pain is a nuisance, a call to supply nourishment. Like fever, pain is a signal, calling white blood cells out of the bone marrow to fight infection. As in the body, so in the brain except starvation or fever is more simply cured. Frozen at his most vulnerable moment in the corpse of an enemy, this Cryo suffered emotional displacement and physical deprivation. No wonder his mind has gone AWOL.

To connect a shell-shocked mind to a stranger's body, she must trick the Cryo into consciousness while gently skirting the horror of pain. Mobilizing the unconscious to assume control, the subconscious mind could surreptitiously begin the conscious waking. The recognition process will hurt but slapping this baby could cause crib death. Instead of encouraging raging emotion in a foreign land, she plans to seduce the dreaming brain into recognizing home.

"You have been through immeasurable trauma. The harm has been done. The suffering is not a punishment, only a correction for the damage. There is no reason for the pain to continue."

Though the goal is awareness, to reach the end zone she must sedate, in the way a doctor administers anesthesia before stitching a wound. Her probes must dissolve the malignant clots at the depths of the emotional damage then build a bridge to his troubled mind. Mental surgery could backfire but time is short and his condition terminal.

"Do not attempt to define what is normal or not normal. The body will treat the symptoms. Faith will cure the problem. Open yourself to heal. Bite down hard; cry out loudly. Allow salty tears to cleanse fear, shame, guilt and sadness. The journey is arduous. Your purpose is to find a path. Believe. It will be easier if you trust. You are not alone."

Loneliness is the most profound pain; universally experienced and yet, by definition, never shared. A fear-based emotion with a built-in catch-22 response, the lonely withdraw from the very contact that could cure. Hope drugs help, but pain killing could just as easily compound the isolation by virtue of making isolation bearable. She has only one session to prepare Stardust before the drug regimen begins.

"Do not mistake your garden for paradise. In slumber you are confined to a hell of your own making, a barren landscape of absent growth, faded meaning and irrelevant future. Chaos waits outside this lifeless portrait, but there is no fear greater than ignorance. Do not shrink away, lead out the beasts. Listen to the whistling bird. Follow his curiosity with the courage in your heart. You are the Tiger. With the thrust of your haunches, leap from this precipice."

* * * * * * * * * *

After the mania of the conference outside, the spa seems like a morgue. Humidity and rotten egg odors seep from the sulfur baths. Guests of all sizes and shapes do not seem shy about their briefs and bikinis. Deflorio slides out of his jacket in the lobby, fearing it will get soaked before he reaches reception.

A genie meditating cross-legged on the table instructs Deflorio to disrobe. The masseuse makes an allowance for his client's modesty with a gaze fixed steadily on some distant drishti. A disconcerted Deflorio compares his bulges and wrinkles to the smooth physique of the pretzel. On the table, Deflorio's flaws and glitches morph into a plasma of pain, the ever so sweet pain of tension releasing into relaxation.

After a once-over, the expert masseuse focuses on muscular blockages. Deflorio neglects Dex's body. Ignoring warning signals, he postponed tune-ups and rode the transmission into the ground. The high performance vehicle had asked too much of him, wanted too much exercise, demanded too much fresh air. A bacchanalian spirit trapped in Dionysus' body, Deflorio responded with sedation, drugs, alcohol and food. The results had been far from satisfactory and the body took revenge. Unidentified kinks in the neck or mysterious glitches in the back maliciously attack without warning or cause. A civil war rages in his frame, a battle that divides mind, heart and soul, along with the real estate. Appeasement with thermal packs, acupuncture, medicine or sex yield temporary truces, but this massage promises to quell his unrest.

With the tactical force of a swat team, the masseuse lances hidden insurgents, penetrates the roots of revolt and enforces symmetrical order. Surrendering to the magic fingers, Deflorio experiences comfort, not of opiates or negotiation, but of relief.

As pressure points release toxins and vertebrates align, Deflorio rests in a cradle of pain. The aches are not punishment but atonement; the stitches are not revenge but resolution. The body engages in the sort of conversation that would never lead to friendship but might restore respect. Comforted by harmonic negotiations between muscles and joints, resistance relaxes and consciousness segues into dream.

* * * * * * * * * *

"It has been determined," the scribe reads from a scroll. "Deflorio's redemption will persuade many converts that eternity lies beyond death's sacred door. We will accept his proposal."

"I am surprised by the decision" Father McBride confides to the Council of Bishops.

"The archdiocese answers the cry of a repentant sinner," a Bishop responds.

"It may be taken as a signal that the church condones TransmIDs." Father McBride points out, feeling obliged to play devil's advocate if only to contain his enthusiasm for the project.

"The cowardly TransmID will prove that such abomination contaminates the flesh and curses the spirit," says a Bishop on the left.

"Changing old for new shoes at every fork in the trail leads away from salvation," adds a Bishop on the right.

"Death erases the sins of mortality, to dust the body, to heaven the soul. Our Lord sacrificed his life to teach us this lesson," contributes another.

"You have Deflorio slated for saint hood," Father McBride assesses the scope of their ambitions.

"When the first prototype renounces Transmogrification to embrace mortality others will follow. Devoting his last years to alleviate the suffering of innocent war orphans, the truth will resonate with more symbolic power than any proclamation from the pulpit." The high Bishop speaks.

"With the Cryo's celebrity the transmogrified identity transfer will create a sensation," McBride agrees taking note that the Bishops seem to be taking turns but speaking with a unanimous voice.

"The notoriety surrounding the case will serve to publicize Deflorio's remorse. Deflorio will assume his God given form and the foundation for 'Orphans of the Water Wars' will be launched with great fanfare."

"Deflorio's money might easily be construed as a bribe," McBride inserts. "The proposed sequence of events transforms his gesture of remorse into a gift of gratitude."

"The Church does not sell forgiveness. Deflorio's destiny belongs in the hands of the Holy Father."

"How do we prevent him from backing out if he has a change of heart?" Father McBride asks.

"Belief relieves the gruesome cruelty of temptation. As a spiritual ambassador you carry the word to light his way. The Council of Bishops has great faith in your persuasive powers."

172

"His lost soul craves asylum, solace is a convincing bargain," the high Bishop closes the circle of comments. "It has been decided," the scribe concludes. "Deflorio must agree to be baptized and, when the time comes, receive last rights in his original body. United, mortal body and immortal soul, Deflorio will live and die as God originally intended."

* * * * * * * * * *

Deflorio wakes, perhaps hours, or perhaps only minutes after the masseuse left him. Snuggled under a soft white blanket, he makes no move to provoke any reaction from the subdued body. Prolonging the peace of feeling nothing, he ignores voices in the next room until the dialogue crowds out his bliss.
"Stay still, will you."
"Ouch!"

* * * * * * * * * *

"That is a limit, stored in the body, stored in the mind," Daphne scolds. "Starved for attention, limits shorten your competitive years. You are good but when tested by a qualified opponent you will collapse into a black hole of frustration. STEM. Stabilize ambition, Extend growth and Maximize potential."
Even though he has to put up with the lecture, Fletch loves the massage. This chapter in the training curriculum was Daphne's idea, yet another installment in her program for his enlightenment. She tells him the ancient Greeks had a word for it -

Haptics from Haptein "to fasten" the science of data obtained by touch - the opposite of platonic. If she wants to demonstrate haptics he's not about to protest even though she's pounding his bones, pinching tendons and pulverizing muscles. In theory and in practice, he can tell by the slow way she rubs all the best places, she's on the verge of guiding him towards an enlightening rehabilitation and potential cohabitation.

"Components under the skin - organs, vessels, fascia energize the aura. Aura is the bridge from external to internal," says the woman with blue eyes as her hands linger dangerously close to the rim of his hips.

"What does my Aura say now?" Fletch leads realizing he can reach the zipper on her pants. He twists his hand inside and plunges as she leans closer to him. She talks, even as her dexterous tongue explores, illustrating how this sensitive limb can taste and touch and communicate in places words have no meaning. The conversation subsides as the mutual caresses shift away from the body surface to deep internal crevices.

* * * * * * * * * *

Deflorio listens as the voices digress into inarticulate sucking sounds. Sex hasn't made him hot since he embarked on reviving the Cryo. Indifferent to the panting and scuffling, he clinically evaluates his passive member; it throbs with less enthusiasm than an old man's arthritic limp. Time is a darkness where shadows collect, marking the strain of being dragged into light each morning. Year after passing year, wrinkles etch platitudes on parchment skin. Age's inscriptions lack poetic insight, just a mundane index of ordinary decay marinating an artifact for the worms. Time falls, anchored by gravity, heavily upon the body to bury its desires.

Age, a foreign venture colonizing the body leaves host and guest at odds. In rebellion, he transplanted his mind into a youthful body only to be rewarded by intense homesickness. Guilty pleasures had been his pride and joy until the body swap turned pleasure into guilt and life into a crime. The process had numbed his lust because he had trained himself to feel better by ceasing to feel at all. In his empty existence, death is not a sentence, just a word.

Life is his prison and he is tortured each confining day. He wakes in an unfamiliar setting wondering why pleasure has abandoned his barren cell. Making the bed at one end, setting the table for each of his three meals, lying down again to sleep, he never feels at home. He stumbles through this joyless abode ambushed by wilting memory from an unfamiliar past.   In the hands of his alien body, angst plants hollow spaces in his untrustworthy mind. This corporal punishment endangers his restless soul. Distracted by day, sleepwalking by night, would he step out a window mistaking the ledge for a doorway? Or slip on a misplaced sock like a slapstick gag where a banana peel makes a monkey out of a man? He had wrongly assumed the mind could leap beyond identity; the body is too personal. In this reincarnated state, he has become an unrecognizable person.

He has everything but options. Displaced, misplaced, he lost himself; starting fresh he would never forget. Do amnesiacs lose their sex drive? The will to procreate went out the window with his identity. His insurrection against nature has failed; his counterfeit persona sterilized the sturdy ego that once desired sex and wealth and power. His impotence cannot enforce a truce with maturity. His battalion of ambition has deserted him, leaving him quaking at the mere mention of another incarnation. To redress this infernal limbo is his driving passion. He refuses to fade away in an inconsequential puff of smoke. Fueled by combustible indignity, he intends to face the final roll call in the glorious blaze of his ultimate destiny. Only the living can die.

His lack of virility is not a factor of age; a rotten fruit has the ripest seeds. He is barren because Dex poisons his craving. Reclaiming his original body, reunited with his ammunition, bursting with his own seed, he will fuck with self-respect. Deep wells of pent-up desire, sucking waves of eroticism, aching undertows fertile riptides will carry him from this desolate shore. Returned to his original body his battery will recharge and his energy will find hot and sweaty release.

* * * * * * * * * *

Lust is a language that does not handle words well. Desire craving release has the

aim of a blind archer, but Daphne restrains
his arrow with instructions, redirecting his
aim towards the bulls-eye.
"Stronger! Show me your power."
Her voice pierces his associative
delights. Skewered by specific meaning his
allegorical perversions diffuse like a
harpooned whale. Lashed with an arrow an
exploding surge escapes Fletch. Rubbing salt
in the wounds of his longing, electrifying his
abrasions of desire, she revives St. Sebastian.
Unleashing a reserve hidden in a longing he
dare not even dream, Agamemnon ascends to
thrill Aphrodite.

* * * * * * * * * *

The rapacious synchronized climax
interrupts Deflorio lacing his shoes. In the
midst of an all this orgiastic splendor, all he
can think about is abstinence. He reviews
highlights of his carnal career as he dresses.
Never restrained by the bonds of love,
conquest had always been sweet. Age could
be expected to undermine the appeal, but he
is convinced that virtuous loins do not imply
a reduction in his esteemed virility. He is
just saving himself for the perfect reward, a
consummation with his own body. Lust,
coupled with genuine intimacy, adds up to
inspired fidelity while cravings hastily
satisfied in the night guaranteed nasty
hangovers in the morning. Averse to
interludes tinged with disgust conditioned
him to avoid the act. Infidelity, the
dissolution of self, contradicted his desperate
longing to be whole.

* * * * * * * * * *

"Xia, Shang, Zhou, Qin, Han, Sui, Tang, Song, Yuan, Ming, Qing, Mao..." a DigySinc fires off the Chinese Dynasties in chronological order.

Passing the evening reciting lists, the DigiSyncs covered extinct species, Nobel Lariats, national currencies and Beatles songs. There has been no progress with the Cryo, no ceasefires in the water wars and no natural disasters. A slow news day on all fronts, DigiSyncs release the pressure of accumulating monotony inventing games and calculating meta things. Pretending to own time, they busy themselves with repetitive exercises to waste it. They can leave the planet and the body but they have yet to erase the tick tock rhythms marking the seconds in each passing hour.

As surely as the world turns, time dawns each morning, posing the question of how to fill the day with meaning. As a mortal, the passing years will eventually relieve the body of the burden to continue. When the tech joins the DigiSyncs, she will escape the body only to be confined by an infinite forever.

Limited to the allotted time of a lifespan, rationing has the advantage of investing the scarce resource with value. Minutes cry out to be spent wisely - absorbed, experienced and understood - building an inventory of thought and feeling into a measure of self worth. With a fertile consciousness, reflection raises an umbrella against the storms of time. On her small drought ridden parcel, the barren tree offers neither fruit nor shade.

She should envy the Syncs. Reflection has no place in their semi-conductor existence; solitude would dam the sparkling tributaries of the communal intellect. DigiSync ideas flow without hesitation but the currents and eddies of knowledge may never breach shores which solve the mystery of meaning.

"Emperors of Rome, no make that the Popes - backwards starting with current papal reign - Paulette Michael Gregory." A DigiSync proposes.

"What do we make of Pope Greg backing Deflorio?" One interrupts.

"The Pope got involved in the TransmID regression?" The tech asks. "That's news!"

"Bracing against opposition, staking her holy mandate against an impending Church schism, old Greg herself gave the papal stamp of approval," a DigiSync reports.

"Deflorio chose heaven over immortality. His body and soul reunion will be the Church's greatest PR miracle since the immaculate conception." Another adds.

"Religion needs a miracle. If it can't stop the war, it is doomed. The Beings will all be exterminated and the shepherds will have no flocks to guide to heaven." A skeptic notes.

"The Church strategy will backfire," a sage predicts. "TransmIDs will interpret the baptism as the ultimate ticket. They'll party harder knowing a conversion can save their souls if they wake in cold sweats of remorse."

"Deflorio's baptism will have less impact than a celebrity makeover. No one cares. He's history."

"Even the TransmIDs will disown him. They will claim the first prototype was contaminated, a faulty model prey to internal conflicts caused by seepage."

"That internal conflict is caused by a violation; Deflorio engaged a union without consent. He pirated that body."

"Defects in the first generation caused a lot of suicides, but survival rates have improved." the tech inserts. "Now TransmIDs are lining up for thirds."

"The parasites are thriving like rats," complains a cranky Sync.

"A PR stunt by Pope Greg won't stop them," the skeptic seconds. "A dead Deflorio will be soon forgotten unless he manages to bring back proof of life after death. Heaven might give them pause."

"TransmIDs aren't idiots like the brainwashed Beings, when a body goes it takes the mind and soul right along with it."

"Heaven is a clever myth. The happy angels with harps singing glory hallelujah give the stupid Beings something to believe in."

"As their flesh rots in the grave. We are the only chorus serenading eternity!"

"Only DigiSyncs escape dust to dust," the backup chimes. "We are the immortal intellect! The time masters are the true guardians of the future!"

* * * * * * * * * *

We stormed the gates of heaven, Strike muses monitoring the comments of the Stardust-obsessed DigiSyncs, but our garden of vast knowledge bears little fruit. As a prototype, a seamless upload of undiluted consciousness sets Strike apart from later arrivals. The first DigiSync retains a distinct personality and being unique poses a problem: Strike is at odds with the Digitally Synchronous conscious collective. Never one to fall in step with the masses, Strike harbors a proclivity for melancholy moods and a predilection for privacy. Later developments in the synchronization process corrected for glitches by erasing traits disruptive to Digital harmony. Since too many soloists ruin the choir, only a select core of elite DigiSyncs receives dispensation from the all-inclusive intellect. Granted privileges of solitude, Strike can tune out, hum off key, tap his foot to internal rhythms or invent a new song. Wearing a cloak of invisibility, he escapes perusal. While most Syncs crave dialogue, Strike meditates. An outcast, above and beyond the chattering crowds, he coasts on tides of reflection to ponder flaws in the DigiSync existence.

An expert hacker during fleshtime, Strike breached high-level intelligence networks and compromised security systems to expose vulnerability. Under the banner of "freeing information" he balanced on the high wire between noble outlaw and petty criminal. The blurry moral distinction had the clarity of an exclamation point when compared to the creepy quagmire of his current position.

In conflict with the DigiSync ideal of universal data access, stealth violates the sacred principle of transparency. Private contemplation is taboo, except for the elite. Strike and select members of the DigiSync Peers survey the communal mind, policing the abuse of power or misuse of information. They police themselves according to a murky ill-defined unwritten code of ethics.

Secret agents in a free society are even more susceptible to paranoia and so elaborate safeguards are required to terminate renegades. Elites submit to periodic review by a committee of elevated Peers. This super conscious layer shifts like shadows in the light, and yet the wisdom they impose over the waves of knowledge anchors the cyber mind.

Evolution is a collection of data. Knowledge crystallizes by cross-referencing facts as biology codes adaptations into DNA. Organic or inorganic, evolution makes mistakes. Gene pools guided by the pressures of environment take generations to express traits that enhance or hinder survival. DigiSyncs learn at the speed of light. In a near brush with extinction, the first generation learned about fatal wrong turns the hard way.

Initially DigiSyncs assumed cooperative behavior would produce the orderly complexity of an anthill. Armed with an internal agenda, insects automatically task to improve the common good. With no plan, no leader and no parameters, DigiSyncs had faith that instantaneous sharing in large open networks would equal the productivity of a beehive. As the velocity of information exchange increased, Syncs discovered the self-organizing principle only applied to genetically pre-programmed biological units. Intoxicated by the power of ideas, an ill-conceived fad infiltrating the inebriated intellect spread faster than a wild fire. An uninhibited exchange of the Panasha Buddha mudras degenerated into a riot of chaos. Teachings concerning the liberation from the cycle of life and death proved lethal to the cyber intellect. The crazed pursuit of euphoric luminosity, contagious as a virus, derailed the autonomous, unruly democracy. DigiSyncs concluded infolution needed a dedicated driver. Peers elected themselves guardians of the communal consciousness and imposed continuity by reinstating the laws of cause and effect.

Among the Peers who put the brakes on the free exchange of information, only Strike and a few others remain. Staying sober at the pub has a high rate of attrition. Lost in solitude, Peers stumbled into delusion or reclusion or irreconcilable self-contemplation. By virtue of seniority, Strike's prestige assumed legendary proportions. There were sightings and rumors but only a few elites could verify his identity. In his shady world, Strike exercises pre-emptive authority for preventing the collective vehicle from veering off a cliff.

From his vantage point, Strike instinctively knows dangers multiply as the DigiSync intelligence ascends. The digitally synergetic conscious sentience could reach a singularity of pure knowledge - a point at which knowledge becomes useless and beyond which knowledge does not exist. Agreement multiplies with each solved problem, raising the hazard of complacency; purring in sunshine's glory, contented cats quickly lose the ability to stalk in darkness. Blazing a trail into the unknown while avoiding pitfalls as well as plateaus, Strike navigates divergent scenarios. He maps outcomes to predict a future that best ensures DigiSync survival, and by extension, the survival of intelligence.

Comparative koans, wool gathering and daydreams all fit into his job description. Taking up a permanent residence in Eden, DigiSyncs gorged on the mythical apple, the fruity knowledge that exiled mortals from the garden. Will the DigiSync mix of immortality and intelligence deliver bliss or will all creation crescendo into one big dead end?

The Peers would censor him for floating a cynical theory; observations that pollute the collective enthusiasm are filtered and detoxified, but his research has uncovered alarming possibilities. By synthesizing thought patterns and applying a clustering algorithm to locate similarities then assigning mathematical values, he noticed common repeating themes. Analysis of the communal state of mind reveals the danger that the exothermic expansion of knowledge could cease in an entropic harmonic resolution. Hungry for evidence to the contrary his circuits randomly sample snips of dialogue. Assigning values to odd words in idiotic debates he quantifies DigiSync obsessions. Precise, concrete and adhesive he has faith in his stats. He first attempted data mining for Dex who believed pattern matching would spell out a theory of emotion. Didn't work but it didn't stop him for perfecting his talents during his fleshtime and mastering the art as a DigiSync.

Assembling stray threads, salvaged crumbs, recycled refuse he probes Achilles' heel. He combats constraints of preconception by diversifying his axioms, and still, all the arrows point in the same direction. DigiSync inflation adds more and more complexity, but never achieves beauty. The infinite regression of a reflecting reflection lacking arbitrary interference just keeps on repeating. The inflatable infolution does not have a nice ring, its just feedback.

Even incorporating the insignificant and the counterintuitive, the exhaustive survey exposes no departures in a progressive chain from logical assumption to inescapable conclusion; the high fidelity DigiSync intellect spits out remarkably accurate data, but no poetry. Recursive neural nets, evolutionary algorithms, automated reasoning programs and reaction diffusion equations resolve in thematic continuity. Separated from imagination, the DigiSyncs will never experience the undecipherable domain of passion that guides genius. Art, the science of living, the surprise of creation still belongs to the Beings. And the Beings are doomed.

3.3.3

An attendant escorts Deflorio to a poolside seat and raises an umbrella over the table to protect against condensation. Clouds of steam fog the glass dome enclosing the hot springs. Working overtime during this month of twenty-four hour days, the sun gives off a weak luminance; just enough to add sparkle to drops sliding down the palm fronds. Under these rain forest conditions, Deflorio easily forgets he's in the Arctic Circle, except for the view.

Facing away from the manicured lawns and gardens, the atrium overlooks the ocean. This side of the building reveals the drama of the volcanic island where puffs of smoke waft from a recent minor eruption that deformed vegetation into charred stumps. The prehistoric landscape of crusty lava stretches down to rocky coast where icebergs float in azure waters.

A menu offers a selection of enhanced 'natural' waters from the poolside bar. The waiter recommends Golden C, mined at a fortune per half once from submerged caverns under miles of granite, infused with vitamins, nutrients, electrolytes to align charkas and meridians. "This elixir filters electromagnetic pollution and clears the way for visionary dreams while dispersing stressful emotions and angry thoughts like a negative ion generator."

Deflorio sips the sparkling effervescence from a violet glass bottle, a refreshing contrast to the oppressive rotten-egg scent wafting off the hot springs. Both waters have a reputation for soothing. The curative powers of the sulfur bubbles pull health worshipers to the spa like cripples to Lourdes. The ubiquitous liquid, the essence and sustenance of life, the mother of all solutions from the womb to the ocean, water nurtures the wells of reflection.

"Though touch we train the skin. The tactile sense is a vital channel of communication, essential for hearing unspoken truths."

Deflorio recognizes the voice as the source of the action next door to his massage. For all excitement, in the flesh she is disappointing. Her swimsuit reveals a wiry frame, a coat hanger of a figure. In nature's conspiracy to attract males, she drew a very short straw. The intrinsic fertile curves of a female are streamlined into a sleek androgyny, efficient, anonymous and hardly worth a second glance. She manages her angular limbs with the grace of a ballerina but without the vulnerability. Her foot slices the surface and her body slips into the indent causing barely a ripple. Short wet hair smoothes into a sheen against her skull; her blue eyes gleam though the mist with an eerie shimmer quite like velour.

Her companion, on the other hand, is a head turning matinee idol with a quirky smile. His trophy body plunges into the pool with a healthy enthusiasm. If the icy blond has a pulse, odds are ten to one that the golden boy will break her heart.

Deflorio covets the perfection - not for himself, he is too old and tired to manage another high performance engine - for Dex. When Stardust comes out of his coma, he doesn't deserve the old shoe Deflorio wore out; he deserves etched musculature and curly locks. As the couple settles on the steps, Deflorio edges closer to follow their conversation.

"The skin is a sophisticated receiver of subtle transmissions," Daphne continues.

"I get it. As the old saying goes, a handshake tells all," Fletch agrees.

"Skin can do even more. Distinguish vibrations, like the tympanic membrane in the ear. Frequencies are obviously out of reach, but sensing atmospheric currents is integral to perception. In proximity to the brain, the eyes and ears are susceptible to misleading cognitive interpretation. Skin rarely deceives."

The golden boy ducks the lecture, swimming a silent lap under water. Rude, but Deflorio sympathizes. With touch she gives pleasure, with talk she takes it away. A lapse in judgment led to this coupling, impulse and intellect make for an odd match.

Fletch releases a slow stream of bubbles as he glides along the bottom of the pool. Afterglow from the delicious therapy deflates along with the bulge of excitement. The verbal soaking quells desire as effectively as the hot springs relax the tension in his muscles. He put up with Daphne's half-baked theories for the sake of her touch. In small doses, no worse than the smells that accompany the sulfur baths, but nothing you'd ever get used to.

Fletch emerges from the pool like a male Venus and wraps a towel round his waist. He sits on the side and dangles his feet in the water. "You were saying?"

Daphne floats to the edge docking in the V between his legs.

"You claim instinct steers the mind. Animal drives have a voracious appetite. When the hungry beasts deplete your resources, the suicidal soul scorns love, neglects beauty and dupes itself into crimes of moral cowardice."

"Never use heavy artillery in a vacuum but love is a stellar force," Fletch anticipates Daphne is leading into another Ra pitch.

"The animal has its place. Emotion enhances the senses. Reason, the deduction of value, depends on it. With a shameful blush, or in joyful laughter, emotional subsystems subliminally encode experience in positive or negative memory. Behaviors stem from imprinted triggers; without flags pointing one path over another choice would freeze at every crossroad. All the intelligence of the DigiSync cybermind can't navigate the branching decision trees of every day life. Never use the word love in vain."

Fletch instinctively flinches the way a sensitive tooth recoils from an ice cube on the heels of hot coffee. Not exactly the first date but way too early for the full court press. Regretting the duet on the massage table he didn't peg her as the clingy type.

With the hard-boiled body and attitude to match Fletch mistook Daphne for someone who traveled light. He assumed she'd leave when the conference ended without any baggage.

"You lost me," he shrugs.

"Exactly. Beings hone reason and trust emotions without regard to the inherent conflict."

"What about balance and objectivity?" Fletch initiates an evasive action to extricate himself from the discussion. Conflict and emotion are inextricably linked to relationship, usually as a chilling prelude to discussions he religiously tries to avoid. His thick skin protects an unrepentant hollow core steeled against romantic commitment. He has already heard all the arguments: maturity, grounding, stability, trust and growth. With youth as his shield, selfishness as his weapon, he has fought off every version.

"How is balance possible when objectivity contradicts taking a stand?" Daphne answers with a question. "Neutrality creates a Blind Spot. Choosing between an apple and orange, engages a comparison of options and possibilities. Any objective analysis results in an exhausting smorgasbord of computation guaranteed to block conclusion. Let's not even discuss the unreliable black box of memory. Like Schrodinger's cat that may or may not exist, remembrance hides until observed. And then, in order to observe, the information must be retrieved by an arbitrary, selective system of undependable relays. Do you even remember what you ate for breakfast day before yesterday?"

"Eggs or something," he admits lamely.

"Recall is far from absolute and reason based on the results has variable relations to reality."

"And love corrects for our lapses in judgment?" Sirius tries to simplify the sales pitch so he can get onto the rejection.

"The concept has many dimensions; don't underestimate the rich biological components that nurture the diversity of the soul. Faulty engineering has an override, somatic emotion, held in the body is the root of the highest level of cognition."

"You've got some foxy clinical terms," Fletch makes the first move towards a graceful brush off.

"Evolution united the fusion of hormonal will and the processing of the intellect with the bioelectricity of the spirit. The cognitive system facilitates reasoning, recognition and remembering in a matter of seconds. The emotional senses conducted by the body's nervous system have a reaction time measured in hundredths of a second - an astonishing velocity."

Vaulting from psychology to biology to physics Daphne has surprised him once again. His anxiety about relationships allowed her to catch him off-guard. Fletch has studied reaction speed in many schools: some Dojo's advocate self-control, others teach go with the flow, many reference the mystical and his sensei taught instinctive drives, but none resolved the head-heart conflict.

Relying on the animal is a workaround for thinking too much, a clever tool to dodge the fact that every fighter fights himself. Hinting that she understands the science, Daphne has won his rapt attention. Fletch wonders who taught her and why she seems eager to share her secrets. "Guess my tiger, crane, monkey and snake seem primitive."

"Primal instincts merge reflex with perception and emotion. The trick is to integrate cognition without adding drag."

"I'm all ears," he says unable to take his eyes off the cleft between her breasts.

"You see before you hear but touch is the speedy sense. Skin is hardwired for efficiency. The synchronization of one system reinforces the power of the others," Daphne steps out of the pool. "Touch sensitizes the skin, with practice skin absorbs subtle signals like electrical pulses," she explains offering him her hand. "You will feel it before you know it and you will act on pure, unprocessed information," she says lifting out of the pool.

Fletch wraps her in a towel. Closing in for an embrace he senses a change, from invitation to threat, a pure warning clearer than speech. All the nonsense he had tuned out was demonstrated by a touch that caused a spine tingling shiver. In a flash he understands the power of haptics. The eye-opening sting, as shocking as a slap when expecting a kiss, convinces him she has acquired control over a powerful spontaneous energy. Without any more warning than the electricity conducted through her wet skin to his, she flips him over her shoulder back into the pool.

Stunned by the splash Deflorio tries to reconstruct the motion: the sweep of her right arm uproots his feet and the wave of her left arm rotates his ankles over his head. Faster than a gust of wind, the moves defy observation. No harm done, the guy comes up spewing a fountain at his attacker.

Dodging Fletch, Daphne launches a clean dive clearing his head by three feet.

Deflorio makes the most of the opportunity to offer assistance. Springing to his feet he rushes to the side of the pool "Is anyone hurt? Should I call for help?"

"Sorry about the splash," Fletch apologizes "just water, don't think it stains."

"You seemed to be floundering and then she dove, I just assumed, well you know what they say, 90% of all drowning occurs at the edge of the pool" Deflorio intrudes.

"Nothing that exciting," Daphne smiles contritely.

"Showing off," Fletch adds.

"Glad to hear it! Are you part of the conference?"

"I'm an instructor. This is one of my students but she's obviously instructing me."

"I'm here on business and couldn't resist the spa, making the most of the luxury. Say would you like a towel?" Deflorio extends two fluffy terry cloths as an invitation for the couple to join his table. "An instructor, Church of Rising Sun you say?

Love to hear about it. Humor an old man, my treat. The water bar serves 17 varieties of bottled health and happiness."

"Some other time, I'm running late." Daphne extricates herself efficiently. Fletch accepts a seat, grateful for the diversion.

"She thinks and acts fast; she can talk and she can fly," Deflorio fishes.

"Like a cyborg." Fletch agrees.

"You don't say?" Deflorio chokes.

"Kidding. Cyborgs don't look like that."

"Only in Sci-fi," Deflorio confirms hoping no military secrets have been revealed."

"Says she trains them, some creepy experiment, tight lipped about it," Fletch shrugs.

"I would expect a cyborg to get lynched at a Rising Sun extravaganza," Deflorio probes.

"Guess you noticed the celebration on you're way in."

"Terrathomping, Tai Chi and Frisbee," Deflorio eagerly jumps into the new topic, "saw everything but fire walking. Surprised they don't have a group out there on the lava." He gestures to the smoking fields.

"Rising Sun is sort of a collection of cults, not a real church, they embrace just about anything in the name of positive growth."

"Don't get me wrong, I'm just curious. Every faith preaches some form of resurrection so in the end it doesn't seem to matter which crutch you lean on. Is being a Being possible without religion?"

* * * * * * * * * *

Beings have a fatal flaw. To use it to his advantage, Strike must wrap his intelligence around the elaborate ruse of paradise. Blinded by reward, Beings accelerate towards a glorious mythical destination. Death is not salvation; death is extinction. Evolution blew the whistle on heaven, and yet the angles stay in the game consoling the Beings when death runs away with the ball. Between the coach and the opponent, mortality is a no-win game.

The problem is how to convince the Beings they got it wrong. Heaven is all in their heads and death is a humiliating debasement. Even stupid TransmIDs are smart enough to avoid the totally negative. TransmIDs and DigiSyncs agree on death, they just cheat by different rules. TransmIDs take human zeal to inhuman extremes. Cooperation from self-absorbed TransmIDs is a poor option; flesh allegiances are too organically volatile. Bad chemistry buys time but only physics can stop the clock.

That leaves the weight of the world on DigiSync shoulders and DigiSyncs are nothing but canaries in a coal miner's cage. DigiSyncs abandoned the unbearable hindrance of the body for communal intelligence only to find immortality will never bridge the chasm separating information from enlightenment. Using the full extent of known computational muscle, Strike has mathematically verified the digitally synergetic conscious sentience does not have wings. Millenniums of erratic biological and environmental threats bred champion jumpers. The apex of intelligent life spawned the death-hurdling DigiSyncs, but evolutionary advances depend on difference. There can hardly be any rule more fundamental to innovation; progress originates in mutation and mutations originate as an adaptation to stress. Overly harmonic thought registers will jam the DigiSync operating system.

Solving every riddle until nothing remains unknown, crossing the singularity of intellectual satiation, is still a distant asteroid they may never meet. The DigiSyncs have internally programmed a collision course with a more immediate obsolescence. Vast and monotonous as a grazing dinosaur, indiscriminate thought lacks incentive or metaphor to change. Conceptually pure, concepts create complex lattices but only imagination can enter the matrix. Unable to emulate the instability of warm-blooded responses, the DigiSync mind relies on Beings to sweeten existence with random dimensions. Codependence is essential. As long as zany human inputs and illogical mortal insights provide a catalyst for change, DigiSync alchemy will convert energy into light.

Contrary to popular belief, the synchronous mind is not the master of the universe, just part of the terra-firma ecology. Bacteria release oxygen from nitrogen in the soil for the worms that blindly churn the mud nourishing the roots of plants, and so on. If a connection breaks, the system risks collapse. At the moment, the Beings, TransmIDs and DigiSyncs form an unstable tripod; introducing cyborgs will tip that delicate balance.

When the Council of Peers requests Strike's position on the animated machine, he advises the plot is not wise. "The hybrid is something only a TransmID would hatch, the cyborg is the warped brainchild of Deflorio."

"Warped but innovative, give him credit" a promoter objects.

"The Beings buy it," adds another supporter. "The TransmIDs love it."

"Beings and TransmIDS are desperate creatures. They imagine that sending cyborgs off to war will save lives because their minds are too small to imagine an infinite war." An isolationist Peer argues.

The esteemed Peer nodes of intelligence have congealed into three distinct factions: the ambitious cyborg promoters, the strict isolationists and the well-intentioned moderates who muddy the water. The advocates project two scenarios: cyborgs become the arms and legs of the Syncs and dispense with any need to rely on flesh creatures or cyborgs lead to the brink of extinction forcing humans to abdicate governance and humbly seek shelter in DigiSync wisdom. These DigiSync supremacists overtly favor dominance over democracy.

The faction advocating monastic separation called Strike out of isolation expecting his vote to deliver them a majority. He will disappoint, but their opposition to the cyborg serves his purpose. Both the isolationists and the advocates negate the deep roots of their biological and cosmological history. Syncs did not come from nowhere; the communal intelligence evolved from the elements in the stars and the spark of life that gave birth to consciousness. The DigiSyncs are embedded in human culture; and even as they seek to transform, they must preserve, for nothing can afford to be lost.

"Counting on cyborg police to enforce peace fails to factor in the big unknown," Strike states the obvious. "Stick to what we know, our superior grasp of knowledge has all the answers. Sync intelligence can calculate the price of every drop of water and plot equitable distribution to maximize sustainability of the commons. It's all in the data; every buzzing electron in every blasted atom carries bits of info. Cyborgs might take us places but we can't use them build wall between Syncs and Beings, we a bridge. Beings need our wisdom, not a weapon."

"Our facts are clear and our thoughts pure, the Beings just don't trust our numbers. They have no faith in our wisdom, conversion is not a realistic option," an isolationist objects.

"Cyborgs will convince them of our power," a supremacist contends, "Force prevails when words fail."

"Our power is reason, force does not persuade, it silences," Strike notes. "DigiSync knowledge can persuade the Beings to cooperate; a cyborg weapon will destroy them."

"We don't communicate" a moderate Peer complains. "Beyond the Acuity, our social spheres never intersect. The Cyborg project presents an opportunity to work together, TransmIDs, Beings and Syncs."

"Our sanity requires segregation," an isolationist insists, "Beings are retarded. A mortal's mental space is defined by death and the discovery of that limitation sends logic skidding to superstition faster than butter on a hot skillet."

"Being reason has not advanced beyond poignant invocations invented by philosophers frustrated by the helpless human condition. They will never learn," seconds another isolationist.

"All the more reason for the cyborg will show them the way."

"By your own reasoning, there is a high probability the plan will backfire," a moderate contributes. "Handing children matches invites fire."

Strike has a unique status as the guardian of Dex. Though he could pull rank by introducing the topic of revival, he does not want to raise expectations that the frozen hero will thaw or distract from the controversy at hand.

"Cyborgs add a combustible ingredient to an unstable mix." Strike takes the middle road of the moderates, "we need a drastic solution but dynamite won't make bacon. Weapons belong to the week; we've advanced beyond destructive force. The solution requires diplomacy. We Syncs have to get our hands dirty, mingle in human mental space. Survival depends on an organic merger to engineer mutual evolution. Cyborgs are not integration; they are a breach."

"Its Pandora's box, we should nail the lid shut." An isolationist weighs in.

"The problem is that Beings crave destruction," a moderate decides.

"Then withholding the weapon will bring Beings to the table," Strike answers.

"Not much chance of opening negotiations until the Beings show a little respect," a moderate points out.

"They will respect the cyborg," adds the supremacist "the cyborg will replace heaven and hell."

"Conquering death and time, DigiSyncs rendered heaven and hell obsolete. Do not contaminate our wisdom with human constructs," an isolationist complains.

"Such stubborn creatures," a moderate agrees. "Traveling alone from cradle to grave, mortals place a premium on the integrity of individual free will. Beings fight and die for an idea even though their conviction amounts to a black hole when swallowed by death. With incompatible operating principles, DigiSyncs will never convince the Beings to cooperate."

"We joined forces with Beings as well as TransmIDS for the cyborg project. Your

201

premise is false." A voice in support counters. "Our cooperation created an alliance, our contribution made the program possible and our participation will make it a success."

"Stop counting your chickens. Beings are dangerous creatures; subject to illogical whim ruled by irrational passion, they skate on the brink of extinction. The end is near. As sure as dark energy tears apart the nebulae, Beings will destroy all that intelligence has accomplished," an isolationist warns.

"Adversity is the mother of invention," Strike corrals the dialog. "Beings provide the chaos; DigiSyncs will be the agents of change. Don't let cyborgs disrupt the realization of this harmonious symmetry." Strike has yet to work out where the TransmIDs belong but expects the adaptable chimeras will find a way into the equation out of spite. None of his rigorous proofs refute his hypothesis; without genuine strife intellect atrophies. The orderly DigiSync grid must be infected with chaos or stagnate. The future is crystal clear and more delicate than the mesh of a snowflake. Intervene or perish, DigiSync survival depends on saving the Beings. Without the capricious imagination of Beings, the DigiSync membrane of information is no more than a brain minding itself.

The Peers will not reach agreement in this session, some will concur and some will agitate, but the Council always reaches consensus - in time compromise will silence dissent. Strike briefly stepped out of solitude to voice his arguments and confront the opposition. His detractors currently have the advantage of a secret weapon. The cyborg experiment to animate a machine with digitally synchronous consciousness is already in play. Intelligent cyborgs are not the future; cyborgs will end the future.

Holding back his trump card, Strike hopes the moderates and isolationists can buy time. When Dex wakes, Strike will present his ace. As the DigiSync hero and creator, Dex is the alternative to cyborgs. Dex will bridge DigiSyncs and Beings. If Dex fails, the Beings face extinction and Strike faces eternal silence. The Peers will advocate terminal extradition on the grounds of insanity. Insanity, like hope, is contagious, once infected, quarantine is the only option to preserve consensus.

* * * * * * * * * *

Held by the centrifugal force of his whirlpool, a swirling magma of experience circles awareness. Sinking in his dreams, he grapples with tedium imprisoned in a confining sameness. A star in a starry night, a drop of water in a rushing river, a spark in a solar flare going supernova. Covering the same ground, each approach unrecognizable, every traverse more tedious with repetition, each arrival back at the point of departure, he dances with infinity.

His restless energy bubbles into a ferment. The anxiety of being unable to scream generates the will to organize an escape from the silence.

Trapped in his liquid dimension progress is slow. He understands that his volume can be measured by length, width and height, and that his incomprehensible motion in space and through time has direction. Determined to coordinate a point of reference, he isolates longitude and latitude to position meaning on a mental map. Concentrating with great effort he seizes on each flimsy sensation with all his might and sculpts association. He refuses to progress from one moment until he aligns it with the past. Taking stock of each new perception he assembles a linear ladder. With methodical focus, he avoids submersion, but falling short of rational ground, a swamp still separates him from solid conclusion.

Stranded in random, he battles despair with discipline. Oriented by task, he collects debris from his hysterical consciousness. Clinging to sticks, reaching for boards, snaring leaves, he fishes for scraps of an alphabet to express the inexpressible. With porous hieroglyphics for tools he fuses a raft that will carry him out of meaningless gibberish. Words take shape, symbols buoyant with content and meaning. Hoisted out of the water onto his conveyance he finally clears the sucking marsh. He can see.

Sight sharpens mental clarity and he leans into his oars. At first, he travels in circles but gradually learns to steer the floating questions and paddles into an open sea. In the frosty whitecaps, he finds no answers, only awareness of a vast mystery. He reaches a state where the above and below, beside and beyond come together – a point. His point, like every other point is the center of an infinity extending evenly in all directions, a knowledge without beginning and without end. But the point belongs to him, an essence; with a reference point, an anchor of relevance unfolds.

He realizes that he is lost and the awareness of being lost brings the understanding that he has a place in this knowledge. Each revelation feeds the momentum of hope. He repositions his existence against the vague outline defined by this distant horizon.

His boat, carried by an involuntary current, streams ahead. With no landmarks and no chart, elusive concepts slip his grasp. How far, how long, how fast, seem trivial compared to the confidence that he will arrive. He rows, even when comprehension recedes into mirage. Impulsively he follows leads down labyrinths of associations until meaning evaporates. He collapses in exhaustion, and then revives with blistering effort. His navigation unpredictable, his senses untrustable, he steers an unsteady course.

Gradually, as his inner eye culls a reliable perspective, an impression connects. One searing insight at a time, he learns to position his oars with regard to past, present and future. The swirls unwind into a curve as his perceptions curl over waves of memory.

With each painful stroke he comes closer to solving his identity.

3.3.4

The violence inherent in romance
contains both the ruby sun hovering above a
tropical horizon and the incipient darkness
left in its wake. On the hem of the Artic
Circle, dusk barely raises a blush. The
summer solstice abbreviates the night and
edits the drama out of sunset. Daphne's
tropical blood melted his cool Nordic sheen.
Next to her solar emotion, his aurora borealis
seems transparent and complacent. In the
presence of Daphne's nuclear combustion,
his luminosity barely holds a candle to a light
bulb.

Seasons change; come winter, long
days will be swept away in a rising tide of
darkness. The conference ended a millennial
event – the close of a bleak epic in human
history. Hosted under the auspices of
particularly well-aligned planets, that will
not be duplicated for another decade, the
Church of the Rising Sun ceremoniously
proclaimed the dawn of a new era. Fletch
considers the celebration premature.

As night begins to follow day in a
timely fashion, a long shadow of doubt
eclipses his future. High hopes may not alter
the course of history, but the conference
saddled him with a changed awareness. The
sun has set on his adolescent optimism and
dawn finds him under a heavy blanket of
maturity. On the docks he watches a crew
prepare a ship with no desire to join the
voyage. He will not return to hauling ice
from polar caps to barren deserts; the

familiar vanished when he got on Daphne's
sea-saw.

As a sailor and black belt, Fletch has
mastered both violence and romance;
wielded like a dagger, close to his heart but
seldom revealed. He rations aphrodisiac
emotions, released undercover of darkness,
in measured doses. He voyages on brief
encounters, a breath of fresh air for the
spirit, as invigorating as pure oxygen inflating
his lungs, released in the exhale. Avoiding
temptation with a clear exit strategy, he
savors exhilaration in the bedroom and
leaves, sometimes abruptly but never with
regret. This time Fletch is the one staying
behind.

Daphne is not another lost weekend.
He took a day trip on her body and now
petitions for an extended visa in her heart.
To meet that challenge, he has to defy
gravity and aim for the belly of the furthest
super nova. Her siren's song has replaced
the brightest star in Earth's night sky; the
North Star that guided his ship at sea, the
Canes Major engraved in Egyptian tombs to
direct the dead towards the heavens. All this
guiding light has not blinded him to her Ra
worship or her government service. If she is
recruiting, he is eager to prove himself
worthy of her attention.

The galaxies in her blue eyes have him
craving exploration. A vivid lure, which
launches the adventurer into the infinity that
becomes visible when the lights go out,
ignites dreams of a fiery union. Once he'd
devoted his life to wisdom; now he teaches.

From his apex, he watches the learning curves of his students ascend to new heights while his progress wanes. Daphne tested his skills with her promise and promised to share her secrets.

She is a lineage disciple, one chosen by heredity to follow the call of leadership. He heard the Cult of Ra had advanced initiates but never expected to be so impressed. He has trained near and far to master ancient knowledge and technique, yet wisdom eluded him. Along with Egyptian solar imagery, and a penchant for the thunder and lightening of the battlefield, Ra incorporated philosophical notions from ancient Greece. Not the aesthetic simplicity associated with the athletes painted on vases, but multi-dimensional concepts like haptics and agon. Agon, the Greek word for contest, encompasses the entire comprehensive relationship of reaching a victory or defeat. Agon expresses the struggle of coming together, the fundamental conflict of union involving truce as well as force, persuasive and coercive, between and within individuals.

Pondering the concept leads to a psychic abyss, (a) without (byss) bottom. Small wonder the wisdom of the ancients has been carefully concealed, agon is incomprehensible to the modern mind. Pitting order and reason against nature and chaos, it wavers back and forth between instincts and intellect, the irony or the incongruity between the actual and the expected result. (Irony is another Greek beauty from eironia or dissembler). Agon trounces false appearances, concealed intentions, and pretense. The revelation of truth involves strenuous exertion; doing the things you hate for the things you love. Agony, the will to go against the will, the violence of romance, that is what a contest feels like, what being in love feels like, the struggle to tolerate the pain of Agon. The mission of the lineage disciples sounds stranger than fiction, a map of history obscured by fantastic landmarks, a mythology more lopsided than a twelfth century globe. The lineage disciples claim evolution stagnated in a collective darkness of the soul, like the death that is required prior to a resurrection. The fate of the universe rests on ascension; a concept as difficult to grasp as the equator before Columbus proved ships could sail east and not fall off the edge of the planet.

The Ascension nears. Daphne explained that the earth, divided into positive and negative polarity, has a magnetic field that periodically reverses. Earth's children are also divided, reflecting the light of the sun and the moon. He understands opposites, combat focuses on offense/defense. Conflict is the controlled flow of reversals; channeling fear's adrenalin into courage. Conflict teaches reverence for the universal struggle. He agrees with her on polarity, no matter how hard we strive towards Tao our yin is hamstrung by yang.

The rest of the Ra story gets fuzzy. Daphne claims the magnetic reversal will unblock potential when the shadow merges with the purity of the Soul. Currently, the hidden side is expressed in preoccupations with the lowest forms of gratification like sex and acquisitiveness. The source of this repressed pain is not our animal nature but the denial of our true nature. Humans abuse power and corrupt knowledge as if building walls of deceit will shield from the brutal force of life and death. Until we cross the chasm into the direct experience of the self as part of the infinite whole, existence is a lie.

Aligning consciousness with unifying agon, the Ascension will spring evolution forward. To prepare for the Ascension, Ra preaches courage and compassion. Following blind faith out of the maze, selfless warriors direct the will to constructive action by mastering the art of war and seeing the sacred in all things. Daphne estimates that he is half way to engaging mindful potential, further than most. She prescribed dream work, out-of-body experiences and psychic visions to recombine the fragmented self and unlock mysteries of the soul. Freeing the harmony of the Soul to produce the highest level of vibration, the mind opens to the song of the universe.

The mouthful of Ra chokes Fletch. He suspects Ra is as deeply rooted in despair as any cult. Extolling the Ascension of the human Soul as the expression of the highest power in the universe is a high-minded fantasy to fudge the banality human existence. Ra doctrines pad warriors with a complicated armor, revising primitive creation myths beyond a deity that made the solar system in seven days into a transformative power that gave rise to energy and matter. If humans are composed of the same atoms forged in the heart of stars, Ra asserts that the destiny of the soul is to join the nuclear force and complete the circle - the union of matter and energy in a perpetual golden ring of light.

Fletch dismisses Ra as another muddy tributary that feeds the marshy wetlands of religion. Like any institution, its leaders often clash over fundamental issues, but Ra engages in more absurd digressions than most. They search for hidden codes in ancient hieroglyphics, pagan myths, lost civilizations and UFOs. Communications from distant Astros and wisdom channeled through occult mediums direct them. If religion is a swift river with currents of faith and eddies of doctrines to carry the spirit beyond the delta of doomed mortality into the open ocean, Ra is a very twisted channel.

For all the diversity on the planet, the overlap of sustaining opinion is extensive. Being doctrines share a passion to elevate the spirit beyond the corporal. Who can blame mortals for longing? Since we can't have a little more life, give life a little more meaning. It all comes down to something to believe in. Staking a life on a demonstration of faith, comforts warriors fighting a lost cause.

Ra rose to ascendance in a time of war, a period of conflict so long that times of peace are relegated to mythical memory. Ra is not to blame for war, but it is their sole justification.

His father would berate him for wasting his talents. According to the fighter pilot, bravery meant stepping into the line of fire. The captain died and Fletch has to live up to a dead hero. He never understood how playing Russian roulette with a missile makes you anything but stupid - stupid and dead.

Quests for world domination are artifacts of obsolete empires but the reasons for struggle multiply with the ever-increasing list of depleted resources. Daphne agrees that the economics of scarcity is a poor excuse for aggression, yet insists battle serves a purpose: the struggle for survival, a struggle as old as life's inception, is the ultimate expression of nature. In combat Beings meet themselves face to face. Fear reveals true metal, confrontation blows away doubt and the acid wash of glory cleanses false pretense. At the mercy of the shadow, polarities resolve to from a unified spirit and a worthy soul ascends.

Daphne reasons we are at war with each other because we are at war with ourselves. Until the Ascension brings universal peace - internal and external - honorable sacrifice in battle is the only path to elevate consciousness. Souls forged of tempered steel gleam with enlightenment. Guided by the light of the ultimate destiny, aspirants rise to join the golden circle of matter and energy to pave the way for the Ascension.

Fletch welcomes challenge, but the existential talk is morose. Isn't a moment more than enough to justify the moment? Surely we are meant for more than war. Is our despair so deep we must risk life to feel important? He practiced live and let live and, until Daphne came along, he was happy. Happiness seems inconsequential now, a gross form of self-deception. Proposing to test his courage, Daphne hooked the big one, his fragile male ego.

This coming together will involve struggle. His friend courage will introduce him to honor. A martyr to love, he will throw himself on the sword of romance. Violence raises the stakes of this sunset. Plunging into dark oblivion without an exit strategy, immersed in every precious minute, he surrenders to agon, the barter for survival.

* * * * * * * * * *

Daphne flashes her security pass, enters the clinic and cringes. The antiseptic smell, the ionized air and the hushed silence affronts her senses. She holds her breath and marches down the long corridor. There are more checkpoints here than Ra's Intel headquarters and each one disarms her security. The clinic is an unholy place where TransmIDs recycle bodies, DigiSyncs release their minds and cryos thaw. Parasites, cheaters and cowards all scheme to escape the organic cycle of creation. DigiSyncs consider matter a necessary evil that consciousness tolerates until maturity; flesh is their incubator until a mental upload betrays their birthright. DigiSyncs are deserters. Warped as quantum gravity, TransmIDs are worse. Raping and pillaging, TransmID egomaniacs exploit matter to choke the cosmic cycle with multiple reincarnations. Ra views the body as the mother and the brain as the father whose purpose is to release a more perfect energy. In the afterlife, spirits forged by Ra will shape the Universe.

Beings nurture a life with purpose and accept death as a noble plan. Greedy TransmIDs violate the purpose of existence and consider death a tragic mistake. In the immortality transaction, their intelligence degrades, their souls evaporate and their lives lose value. Eternally addicted to the pleasures of the flesh - their future no more than an extended dopamine fix, their faith a series of hedges against pessimism - TransmIDs are fallen angels.

As the lesser of two evils, Daphne prefers DigiSyncs. Romancing the intellect, their fascination with accumulating information (even though data is not knowledge), retains charming human traits: curiosity, idealism, confidence, optimism and honesty, to name a few. DigiSyncs, with mathematical proofs, believe in a cosmos governed by comprehensible laws and trade worship of the soul for the glory of the reason. The separation of mind and matter frees them to put the spirit aside and reduce the world to an analytical assembly of parts. If they succeed in explaining the universe, they will give Beings something to believe in, something more factual than gods and more meaningful than heaven. Explanation is not immanent.

Trapped in logic cages, their intellectual instrument, for all its mathematical modeling, has barely managed to prove that reality is far stranger than anything intelligence can grasp. Admitting the universe is not easily deciphered they pit the collective intelligence of their synchronized mind against mystery. Many suspect the DigiSync driving ambition is to prove they are the purpose of evolution. Meanwhile, no more successful than the TransmIDs or Beings, the Syncs have less control than other drivers on the freeway. Crossing an overpass on a cold dark night a patch of black ice could send them into a tailspin. A reversal in the earth's magnetic field would cause mass mechanical havoc and DigiSync extinction. Until they master gravity, electromagnetism and nuclear forces, DigiSyncs are mere products of evolution and evolution is certainly not perfect. That is why they need the cyborgs.

This experiment to animate a cyborg with digitally synchronous consciousness is as flawed as evolution. The DigiSyncs aim to prove they can do evolution better by adopting a scheme hatched by some TransmID to cash in on war. The Confederation bought in unable to resist the temptation of a new weapon. Hailed as the ultimate tactical advantage, as the all-terrain vehicle on the road to peace, the military embraced the hybrid in the name of saving lives.

The mind transfer was the creepiest event Daphne ever witnessed. In a quick and silent process the contents of the mind transferred, the human donor lapsed into a catatonic trance and the cyborg roared into awareness. The agony was so like life she had to remind herself it was a machine. The creature writhed and seemed to scream but had no voice; the DigiSyncs had de-activated its speech capability. Silence only increased the horror.

The DigiSyncs quarantine communication on a secure channel, her instructions relay through the cyborg to the DigiSync manager. She expects the DigiSyncs will siphon the instructive elements of her sessions to develop adaptive algorithms that will eventually replace her. At this point, the lesson plan is based on trial and error and seems doomed to failure.

Since she is not party to the cyborg thoughts, she has no way to verify her instructions make any impression. She demonstrates a step, like a mime performing for the blind. An archer shooting into the fog, she takes a random jab at this and tries that as the subject cringes in fear. The DigiSync manager claims the initial shock is a normal part of any mind transfer and will calm with time. The DigiSyncs assure her the machine feels no pain but the contortions reminded Daphne of electroshock, the sort of torture that never wears off.

Since the machine has no feeling, the Syncs need Daphne to teach the cyborg to walk. The most sophisticated program can't reconcile the haptics of nerves and flesh with the mechanics in a robot. The virtual reality hot shots can't laser guide spontaneous dexterity. The theory is that a digital synchronous upload of human awareness will dispense with remote control and replace programs. Assuming the intricacies of sense memory can adapt to a nonorganic frame, the intelligence will seamlessly integrate tactile, visual and aural inputs with mechanical operations to control motor function. When this Cyborg trips it will regain balance, when it falls it will rise from the battlefield and walk. The next generation will fly.

The military partnered on the premise that DigiSyncs are helpless and harmless. To date, Syncs have taken no side in the global conflicts and strictly enforced cyber neutrality but the proposed plan to secure peace by entering combat is inherently suspect. Cyborgs will give the Syncs legs and the parties who stand to gain fail to question the consequences of mobility. TransmIDs want the bodies. Instead of wasting corpses on the battlefield, fit military recruits, who sign up for cyborg immortality, will supply a needed commodity as more parasites line up for second and third flesh reincarnations.

Ra strenuously objects. Certain members with high security clearance floated rumors about a Trojan horse, but the obvious reservation concerns the violation of fundamental doctrines on purification through engagement. War belongs in the hands that bleed, not machines fighting machines. A compromise with Ra brass secured tentative support in exchange for a seat at the controls. Ra will train the machine to be a warrior. A robot is a far cry from a weapon; first it has to learn to walk. As a lineage disciple, Daphne got the challenging assignment and Ra gets to keep tabs on her progress.

Daphne is a spy. She doesn't expect the DigiSyncs to reveal any secrets; master data spinners, they control the info flow. When the Syncs say the creature is honky dory, it just increases grounds for reasonable doubt. DigiSyncs merging their minds in a machine doesn't necessarily translate into a machine with a mind. After the initial meeting, Daphne decided the robot is possessed. The Cyborg personifies a diabolical abomination; she's walked away from gory battles with fewer nightmares.

* * * * * * * * * *

On his peculiar voyage Stardust encounters a shoreline and the realization that his ocean has a boundary. He is tired of wading through the indiscriminate volume of hallucination and grateful to discover his infinite confinement has limits. He welcomes the obstacle blocking his flow and explores with inquisitiveness fueled by his long expedition. Keeping a safe distance from the coast, he charts the contours where land meets the water's edge by following

219

each wave through crest and break.
Emerging from the flickering projections of
his dream factory he has found a destination.
Though the horizon remains breathtaking, a
measure of the total time and energy beyond
him, it no longer threatens.

After prolonged sensory hibernation,
his ability to experience awakens with
caution. He has no control but can absorb.
As he absorbs, the container shrinks,
becomes familiar, and begins to reveal itself.
He has taken up residence in a place. Now,
he travels with a map and a sense of
adventure.

Navigating towards purpose with the
determination of a tortoise drawn to warmth,
he addresses the topography of sensation.
He gradually ascertains that his existence has
a construct that holds all that belongs to
him. He learns to distinguish separation
between what belongs inside and what lies
outside his barrier.

On the trail of touch, Dex makes
contact with the composition of his wrap, his
skin - the body's largest organ. Blanketed in
twenty-one square feet of canvas, he
inquires into the nature of the protective
membrane. He meets with great interest the
layers of cells replacing themselves in the
bloodless outer layer of the epidermis.
Beneath the stratum corneum seal, he
travels among tribes of busy melanocytes
producing melanin pigment and keratinocytes
supplying keratin. He lingers in the factory,
fascinated by the militia of Langerhans cells
repelling invaders, poised to attack defects,

policing criminal cells. He is transfixed by the data center of Merkel nerve receptors sending messages to the brain.

Following capillaries shuttling nutrients and carrying off waste produced by cell metabolism through the elastic dermis he reaches the wonders of the subcutaneous. The inner layer of fat and tissue holding in water, cushion sebaceous volcanoes that spew lubricating oil. Seeping eccrine glands, 650 hot springs of sweat per square inch and apocrine glands, secreting murky pheromones dot the swampy cellular web. Here, deeply imbedded in this microscopic world, hair follicles, wrapped in nets of sensitive nerve cells, send out protein tentacles. These delicate peach fuzz periscopes break the surface of his container to monitor conditions in the outside world.

Penetrating the geography of this fringe precinct, the shield that keeps the world out also allows information in. Pacinian corpuscles deliver tactile sensation to hypothalamus for processing. An awareness of pressure opens a gate and a transduction of energy travels from nerve receptors in his hand, down the arm, up spinal chord. The neurological transmissions entertain his brain.

He can't name the perception or identify the source of the stimulus. He has no evidence of physical existence just a feeling of pleasure. He has no idea that he has been touched.

* * * * * * * * *

Leyla grips Dex's wrist, clinging to his dull pulse like a lifeline. "Breathe through the pain. Each breath will hurt and each breath brings you closer to freedom. Only pain will break the bars of your cage. This cage is the source of your pain." Leyla squeezes Stardust, but finds her own racing pulse makes it impossible to monitor his incremental fluctuations. Releasing her hand, she notices the pressure has bruised his delicate skin.

Stardust shed his protective incubator when his immune systems activated, but seems no closer to life. His skin, a waxy capsule inflated by life support, lacks natural suppleness. His limp muscles show no sign of reflex. Underneath sealed eyelids, dilated retinas, eclipsing slivers of iris, stare blankly from a dull cornea. Each passing minute adds atrophy and decay. Automation forces mechanical circulation but will not activate inert tissue and passive organs. Infusions flush toxins, corrective RNA revises genetic errors, amino acids relax misfolding proteins and intravenous electrolytes sustain, but will not prevent the cells from feeding on themselves. Lips crack, veins collapse and ulcers gather force as the body works against itself.

This session has critical urgency; it could be the last. The comfort drug therapy intensified mental activity, producing richer and more focused patterns, but awareness is still firmly entrenched in a protective womb. The doctors have no choice; the time has come to slap the baby. Freedom is a scary thing; safety holds him hostage. If Stardust is not prepared for the shock, fear will kill when the oxygen tube comes out. Leyla must bring the mind to safety or the body will die. "Your fears are nothing but air. Breath is life. One breath will carry you over the threshold to possibility, to tables laden with milk and eggs, berries and cheese. You are starved. Allow freedom to satiate your cravings..."

* * * * * * * * * *

"Chances favor finding life on hostile planets over finding intelligence in that corpse."

"A telescope can't see into a black hole," a supporter adds.

"She's light years away from contact," agrees the debate leader. "186,000 miles a second won't bring that nurse any closer to hello."

"That cryo is in deep space. I'm talking astronomical units here, 90 million miles," a cranky DigiSync complains.

"Mars is .4 AUs or 34 million miles, Jupiter .5, Saturn .9 ..." the tech rattles.

"Don't get cocky," DigiSyncs scold. "The point of our poetry is that his potential is as miniscule as a Higgs boson."

"You're mixing metaphors," the tech complains.

"Doesn't matter if the nurse dives into a black hole or jumps into a particle accelerator," the squabble resumes "he's right under her nose and she still can't reach him."

The tech never quite knows who is
talking but today all of the assembled
personalities seem edgy. "You guys sound a
little annoyed." she tests for hostility
displacement.

"Does the Pope piss?"

"Don't bite! I'm with you," the tech
sympathizes. "Doing cardio after one of
these shifts I lift twice my body weight in
pent up frustration."

"Want us to relax, get a massage?" the
chorus jeers.

"F.Y.I. as we speak I'm gainfully
engaged in a gravity simulation," the proud
Sync announces. "Testing a new algorithm, I
just calculated the speed of a feather
floating in 17 different atmospheric
situations in twenty minutes. Running those
numbers would take a Being a million hours -
about a century."

"Geez, no wonder you sound stressed,"
the tech says feeling like a punching bag.

"Stressed, is not the word. We're on
the edge of our seats, breathless with
anticipation. We are racing against the clock
here. The alarm on that Cryo is about to go
off."

Having all the time in the world, the
Syncs' impatience seems unreasonable.
"What's the rush?" the tech asks.

"Frozen he'll keep forever, thawed
he's biodegradable."

"Free radicals are on the loose,
unhappy molecules rioting oxidative stress."

"He's rotting. Slowly but surely he's disintegrating, brain cells dying, pulse lapsing, organs dissolving into mush."

"If those lungs don't start pumping, he'll be reduced to his elements: 95 pounds of oxygen, 35 pounds of carbon, 15 pounds of hydrogen, 4 pounds of nitrogen, 2.2 pounds of calcium, 1.7 pounds of phosphorus."

"That's only 152.9 pounds, Stardust weighs 155 pounds," the tech objects.

"154.4 to be exact and those six elements account for 99% of his body mass."

"Off topic!!! His expiration date is right around the corner. When that traiche tube comes out, he inhales or he expires!"

"Maybe the happy drugs will kick in at the last minute" the tech consoles. "You guys should try some substance abuse to ease those irritated circuits."

"Got to hack that Acuity chip. With the plane going down, the only chance is to break into the cockpit," says a hopeful voice.

"Dream on. Strike's jammed that frequency," the skeptic concludes.

* * * * * * * * * *

Never fear, I've got the Acuity on lockdown, Strike communicates to Stardust. Safe and sound from static, this airspace is secure. The Digi-obsessed would hack you into a swivel with small talk. They mean no harm; you are their hero, their creator, they long to grovel at your feet in gratitude. Do not be too impressed by the adoring masses. Your fans are creatures of thought but a parody of intelligence.

They will boast about astounding feats, like the euphoria of flying through circuitry, so I must warn you about flying in circles. The transpersonal mind, free of age and unrestrained by identity, stretches to connect every dot (no matter how irrelevant). Fascinated by obscure trivia, DigiSyncs devour data but lack the scope to discriminate. Thought is fallible and the enormity of stupidity exponentially multiplies with compounded errors. You and I used to discuss capacity in terms of giga and peta floating-point operations but these measures are inadequate to describe the massive parallel processing available to the DigiSync communal mind. Technology made discontinuous leaps in so many directions that the machines you knew are mere ice cubes beside our glaciers. We harnessed the promise of nuclear spin states and decrypted qubits. It is not enough. Streaming data at light speed does not bring wisdom closer.

We can manipulate logic and numbers but even quantum decoherence does not compare to the mystical realms of the inner life you experience. In the human mind, chemical reactions grounded in the biological process churn ecosystems of ideas. Our circuits will never generate lush forests of imagination. Monitoring Acuity implants, we can watch human thought, as you would watch TV. We follow virtual dramas that we can never hope to reproduce. For all our awesome computations, instantaneous retrieval and exhaustive proofs, reality remains an abstraction.

To reveal the elusive secrets of the physical world we need DNA, the universal computer that gave rise to cognition and free will. Your mind is a link in a chain of causality that stretches back to the big bang, the expression of the sublime interaction between consciousness, matter and energy. Beings articulate the problems our neural nets are programmed to solve. You intuitively leap over haphazard encounters while our communal intelligence obsessively retraces every step all the way back to the center of the maze. Novelty escapes our consistent symmetry, evolutionary algorithms and pattern matching sequences. Processing our process using variations on the same closed formulas, we grapple but rarely innovate. Our problems are your problems, but our extreme intelligence is irrelevant to understanding significance in your world.

If we weren't so fast you'd laugh at our simplicity. Predictable as robots we are all brain and no mind. We collect, store and organize holographs, so no folds, bends or mutilations alter our inference patterns. Cut us in half or magnify exponentially and we faithfully reconstruct the original with exacting detail. Laboring step by logical step our collective intelligence will never bulldoze data through the eye of a needle.

Your senses filter, your intuition extracts and without thinking you decide. Rolling the dice solves your problem of too many options. Beings are blessed with the gift of randomness, inconsistencies built in to irrational hardware. You recognize the fallibility of your reasoning, a product of faulty perception and emotional discolor. Compensating for irregularities creates opportunity. Chance creates new kinds of order – chaos - and out of this non-order you imagine. You embrace associative leaps. Nature is not locked into a pre-ordained construct. Your strength lies in adaptation to change. We failed to duplicate your organic process; our selective edits discard but our encompassing memory banks horde every error.

Our survival depends on your innovation. You improvise with the grace and urgency of a matador looking for new angles to approach a bull. And now the time has come to take the bull by the horns. Think of me as the bull, your partner in this ring, a self-appointed escort challenging you to embrace this messy contest. The wounds will hurt. I can't help with pain, but I will thrill with potential. Do not doubt the reason or that a reason exists.

Thought can no more comprehend the meaning of the universe than modeling a genome can manufacture life, but the genome illustrates that the static attributed to random noise contains meaning. The beauty of this intrinsic simplicity, from the discrete ratios of electric charges in elementary particles to the repeating ACGT of DNA make the complexity of our environment seem like an evolutionary slip. The slippery slope of adaptation factors chaos into your thoughts and your world. We evolved beyond the disorder of the body only to watch the world disintegrate. DigiSyncs need Being creativity, as Beings need DigiSync intelligence, ASAP, before pandemonium, magnified by human nature, leads to extinction.

Our command of data with your ability to recognize significance through causal connections must act quickly to seize control of the confusion. Time amplifies chaos and time is of the essence. Standing outside of time I cannot turn back the clock. Time only goes one way and that is what makes it meaningful. Come back so that we can move forward.

3.3.5

"Remember the Megapodes of the East Indies?"

"Never heard of 'em and you never even saw a stuffed one."

"A bird that laid eggs in the sand on volcanic islands and flew the coop. The lazy mother used geothermal activity to incubate the eggs."

What's the moral? Nature triumphs nurture?"

"The incubating Cryo reminds me of an abandoned egg."

"Hope Stardust fares better than your extinct birds," the tech jumps in.

"For the record, extinction resulted when the eggs became a sought-after delicacy. The species dropped from 53,000 to 5,000 in fifty years, another classic case of 20th century overharvest."

"And what did you do for a living before you uploaded?" The tech wants to know.

"Astronomy. I discovered a comet C/2099 N3. I chronicled every detail on that small ball of rock and ice until it crashed into the sun," the Sync reports proudly.

"Another unrewarded genius," a Sync scoffs.

"What does parental neglect have to do with the miniscule odds of the cryo's survival or your career being remembered?" Another asks.

"Bad metaphors, he's not a comet or a chicken. He's not even a regular cryo. He's a hybrid. And about now he's more dead than alive."

"If he hatches, what will he be TransmID or Being?"

"Good question," The tech agrees. "He doesn't know where he is or how he got here and he sure as hell won't recognize himself in the mirror."

"The probability of a successful process can be predicted by a linear combination the amplitudes for the specific pieces and looking at the square of..."

"Assuming casual invariance, historical equivalence and simultaneous intersection," interrupts a moderator.

"Breaking the process into parts will never describe the effect of those parts coming together." Once again, the tech's interpretation silences the Syncs.

* * * * * * * * * *

The entire cast of the life support team assembles in the intensive care chamber around Stardust. The physiotherapists energetically massage the cryo's extremities. A battalion of doctors examines readings and compares diagnosis. Leyla maintains a vigil at the head, fingertips pressing into his temples radiating a haptic mental pulse.

Exiled from the medical staging area, Deflorio has no role except to watch the prep team hermetically seal Father McBride into a sanitized suit.

"So the Bishops portray me as the prodigal son," Deflorio schemes. "The church gets a PR victory, the orphans get their money and I get to go home. That's what I call a good deal."

"Wait until we see the whites of his eyes," Father McBride advises as the prep assistant zips the white suit. "If I deliver last rights you won't have a baptism."

"Assume he's not stillborn, I have to find a body, a tempting candidate to compensate for all his lost years. Sharp and strong, bursting with youth," Deflorio blushes, remembering the vigorous Fletch.

"To the old, the young always seem so primed with potential. Officially, it's none of my business. The Church will not be involved with TransmIDs beyond the repossession of your original frame."

"Dex is entitled to something fresh. Why trade that ravaged bag of bones for this one?" Deflorio says pointing to his leg "Can't jig or jog on this old knee and he'll jump up aching to dance."

"There is no guarantee he will wake and no telling how he will react."

"I know my man, he'll come through and circumstances will persuade him to take advantage of the best opportunity offered."

"Your fever for schemes takes a toll on your spirit. In the final accounting, your orphan fund will not erase your misdeads," scolds Father McBride.

"Achievements are counted by numbers. My deals choreograph a ballet of interest and equity. My corporations employ thousands and our profits outrun expenses."

"You sound like some number crunching DigiSync."

"We can all admire the poetry of ratios, the divine Phi, the mysterious Gamma, the constant Alpha the encompassing Pi. Numbers describe relationships from spiral of seashells to quantum scale of matter. While life is a hellish basket of conflict, integers cooperate with each other in measurement and fraction to organize natural chaos."

"God does not paint by numbers," McBride lectures. "Do not compromise his infinite wisdom by assigning values to matters of the spirit. Peace of mind has no correlation with calculations. Equations are not excuses. Accountable to God, conscience is the only abacus which matters."

"You have guilt. I have shame. You fear hellish punishment and seek heavenly reward. I seek to erase errors that prove me less of a masterpiece than I imagined. With each new scar, I become more abhorrent to myself. In this world and the next, you have forgiveness but I have no hope."

"Pity gets you nowhere. The troubled are comforted in the Father's capable hands; accept that failures are part of his plan. Without sin there would be no priests, just as there would be no doctors without wounds. I cure sickness of the soul and many converts will testify that faith is the first step to healing."

"My black heart will never be good, but I can do good."

"Not every mountain is Everest. Learn to crawl before you walk, the first step towards a moral life won't deliver Nirvana."

"In my ignorance, I knew bliss. Ecstasy derived from the Greek "ex stasis," standing out of myself. Ambition was my nectar until his body cursed me with recrimination."

"Consider yourself blessed. A conscience opens the doorway to wisdom." McBride trails off, swallowing his thoughts. He never thinks of people as evil though often deals with the damage caused by their actions. Justice redresses the criminal but rarely reimburses the victim. There is no equation to calculate who thrives and who withers. Windfall and loss are randomly assigned. We receive gifts of joy but the balance tilts towards sorrow. It is painful to watch.

* * * * * * * * * *

"He'll never agree to switch with Deflorio. The mind is corrupted and the body aged like stinky cheese," says a DigiSync skeptic.

"Worse than wearing someone else's dirty laundry," another commiserates.

"I mean you can only darn a sock so many times, and this Cryo doesn't have a stem cell bank. Poor guy was born before they knew how to save umbilical chords. Synthetics don't pack the same punch as the newborn juice."

"I give him about 10 years max, miserable years."

"He'll never survive this procedure," adds a total pessimist.

"We'll know in a few minutes," the tech announces. "Here comes the Priest now."

"A priest, there's a priest down there?" the DigiSyncs panic.

"Standard practice in tricky revivals," the tech reassures the alarmed Syncs. "A man of the cloth is always on hand for last rights and so on. A precaution in case the cryo flounders when they remove the tube."

"We can't watch," says the chorus. "We can't take the suspense. Call us when it's over."

"The doctors are easing the traich out now, they are standing by with oxygen and defibrillators..." for the sake of the squeamish DigiSyncs the tech narrates a play by play of the activity in the intensive care ward.

* * * * * * * * * *

This is no dream, or it is a dream so wet he will drown. Sucked under the surf, he can't breath. His pulse quickens. He retrieves his board pulling himself out of the sea into the air. He flops like a fish out of water. Instinctively he paddles towards the break. If his ultimate destination is the shore, his fate rides on the wave that will carry him there. Positioning his feet on the board, he stands and the water recedes into a sloping curl. Rolling into a tube, his timing is off and the surf crashes down on him. After a horrendous toss, he pokes through the churning foam and kicks like hell. A fierce undertow pulls him beyond the break.

He recovers on his board, rocked by rhythmic swells. He waits out a clean wave and tries again. He catches a rim, predicts the intensity but judges the peel angle wrong and takes another tumble. He's lost his touch. The interaction between muscle and motion elude him. He can't purchase a footing for all the salt in the Pacific. His parched gullet squeezes around a lump wedged in his throat, constricting tighter than a Boa around a rat, sealing shut the passage of energy from heart to mind. Wild thoughts crescendo to panic.

* * * * * * * * * *

"For this poor captive soul in Purgatory, have mercy. Savior, send thy angels to conduct this mind to presence. In your wisdom channel messages that are needed for the awakening of this man to the necessity of returning," Father McBride recites a quiet prayer among the confusion of scrambling doctors.

* * * * * * * * * *

"Doesn't sound like Last Rights," the tech fills in the worried DigiSyncs, "not yet anyway. Pulse is failing, BP dropping. The docs just upped the voltage to jump start the heart."

"What if he flat lines?" The chorus wails.

"Just a second, a split second, of consciousness is all it takes to activate his Acuity."

"Did you catch that spike? Did he breathe?"

"Electrical jolt" the tech supplies.

"They are going to break a rib pounding on his chest so hard."

"If we could only access the Acuity implant we could throw him a life line.

"Can't tell if he inhaled or just exhaled the air the CPR pumped in," the tech continues the play by play.

"No way! No wake, no Acuity. Not even Strike can hack a dead brain."

"Not dead, remember the slow cortical potentials," the tech reminds the Syncs, "but not conscious, more like deep sleep."

"If he sleeps, maybe he dreams!" the chorus becomes hopeful.

"Explains what keeps Strike so busy, he monitors REM activity and slips into his dreams."

"Swallowed by a shark in his dreams," a Sync sighs.

"That's the best case scenario. We've been standing guard 24/7, and Stardust hasn't twitched an eyelash. If Strike can't make contact, that Cryo will be lost at sea."

* * * * * * * * * *

The surf gives way to calm. Even the standard rollers whimper away to nothing. Bobbing like a useless pelican he surrenders to lost momentum. Just as he enters the envelope of peace, a swell bears down in a liquid embrace. He judges it for a 12 footer, and fast. Before he is up, he goes under. Tumbling in shells and seaweed, a churning

237

compression forces him down. Submerged in aquatic realms, he hangs on to air trapped in his lungs, he hangs on, hangs on for dear life. For all he knows, the stale air might be his last.

In the crush, a bubble escapes through the vise of his tightly clenched lips. The balloon of gas parts the surface tension of the water and floats up. The bubble, buoyantly rising like a bird on wing, shows he's plummeting in the wrong direction. Rotating, he blows another bubble and frantically follows towards the surface. The bubble elevates with grace he cannot hope to match. He expends massive amounts of energy. He rations another release of air and struggles up through sweeping swells.

He breaks the surface gasping, choking. In a hypoxic fit, he snags a big chunk of air. Claiming his prize from the waves he hoists himself back onto his board. He almost drowned but he's shaking with anger. Completely furious, pumping, he's not going down in his own element. He's going to ride the next mother. He's on it now, coasting on a long exhale, he races down the curl, slicing back and forth. The timing, the motion, the connection - they say you never forget, no matter how hard you try, you never forget.

Sliding down an expansive swell, air swooshes through his windpipe, shoots down the bronchi into the lungs. Breath siphoning into bronchioles is deposited in the alveoli pouches. Adjusting his timing and speed to sync with the rhythm of the ocean, air inflates his lungs to a sparkling crest. He rides the pure pleasure of exhale, full of memory, and inhale, overflowing with prediction.

Exercising leverage he varies duration, speed and span. He can't get enough of this rolling arpeggio: a song to break the tedious silence, a melody in tune with life, a lullaby to sing his anxiety to sleep. Rocked by the sublime wave of breath he longs to stay in this cradle forever.

* * * * * * * * * *

"They've got cardiovascular response!" The tech reports, "Diaphragm compressing, lungs expanding, heart at seventy beats per minute, pressure low but holding steady at sixty over ninety."

"Is he breathing?"

"Adequate, three per minute instead of five, but constant, not erratic or off-kilter," the tech confirms.

"How many Alveoli in a lung?"

"One hundred and fifty million each lung, spread out flat they would cover a tennis court. Alveoli are the post office boxes where the capillaries drop off their carbon dioxide and pick up Oxygen."

"In fact," the tech breaks up the anatomy lecture "the twenty second inhale/exhale cycles with the Mayer waves, six ten-second beats per minute."

"Poetic, a verse in hexameter!"

"Homer's Odyssey,"

"And the Iliad,"

"Guys!" The tech interrupts a list of ancient epics. "Get this. The Atomic

Magnometer scan registers repeating patterns in the neocortex. Check out these linear distortions, not those blobs of color flowing around all aimless. These are defined maps. Do you know what that means?"

"Something cognitive" the Chorus rejoices.

"Active neural connections, awareness!"

"We've got thought!" the DigiSyncs cheer.

"Thinking may be stretching things at this point," the tech advises.

"Protein in blood that binds to Oxygen?"

"Hemoglobin - sweeps big O into the left ventricle for the heart to pump through arteries that deliver it around the body so cells can to convert sugar into ATP."

"Adenosine triphosphate," the tech gives into the celebration.

"Eventually it returns to the left ventricle and the heart pumps the dirty blood back to capillaries that feed alveoli for another gas exchange in a never ending cycle."

"His lungs will suck in 10,000 liters of air a day."

"Oxygen is Fuel! An air powered high performance machine. You humans are a pretty tough feet of engineering!"

* * * * * * * * * *

"He breathes. Well that is what I call a miracle," Deflorio beams as Father McBride returns.

"Your prayers are answered," Father McBride agrees.

"I think medicine gets credit for that one," Deflorio grins.

"I have heard that not all facts are known and I believe that what is known is not all fact. Science gives us longer lives, but show me the evidence that cleverness makes us more ethical or happy and I'll turn in my collar."

"You'll never be obsolete," Deflorio pats the priest on the back and helps strip off the hospital whites to reveal the clergy black.

3.4.1

Concluding a bedside vigil on her patient's first night off the ventilator, Leyla unfolds like a morning glory. She stretches with relief and checks oxygen intake. All is well with Stardust. Though the portal to awareness stays firmly closed, she senses a radiant presence.

* * * * * * * * * *

Light is a physical process pushed and pulled by energy. An electron circling the nucleus of an atom jumps to a higher orbit with a jolt. Falling back it releases a photon of light, a puff of fairy dust sparking the darkness. Light colors. Incandescent electric yellow bulbs and chemical blue-green bioluminescence paint with energy.

The heat of emotion ignites a red glow. As spontaneous flames combust inside his vacuum of reason, Stardust burns with desire and revulsion. Random bursts of excitement elevate his matter to a higher state. Each reaction, infused with radiation, sears his neurotransmitters like fresh oxygen feeding a fire. No closure, no relief, no denial; the revenge of one climax invites another to answer. Stomping out hot spots aggravates the self-immolation. Reincarnated as the grand Marshall of a sizzling parade his slumbering consciousness awakens.

Like white light, the sum of all color, his spectrum of feelings breaks down under examination. Sensations squeeze through a prism of analysis to magnify experience.

Dark terrors dance with glowing angels. The spirit of enlightenment leads into a labyrinth of confusion. The fluid geometry of formation is too fluid; churning liquids, melting solids and porous gases refuse to crystallize. When he leans into a corner, the right angle dissolves into a curve. Expectation refuses to align with recognition. A cavalry of neurons fire in pursuit of a revelation, then the banner recedes without a trace.

As his exploration continues, his experience evolves. Shades of abstraction congeal into tangible impression. With more mystery than meaning, negotiating sensation is like wading through Jell-O. He gets stuck on a swatch of yellow, thick as honey, then burned by an irritating orange or chilled by a wet, blue sky. Submersed in elements from the depths of his mind he tastes all the primal ingredients. Accepting hallucination as an expression of reality, he learns to telescope beyond each projection. Following bends of light around the gravity of an event he travels back in time. Though sources are elusive and meanings escape him, he actively observes.

His consciousness is no more than a germinating seed; warmth and wet trigger investigation. Drawn into growth, he assembles a primitive focus, an amoeba reaching towards a beacon of light. On the quest effort connects with reward. Fueled by this knowledge, a sense of self begins to take shape. The self changes with discovery, shedding the before to stretch towards the after. He learns and grows.

* * * * * * * * * *

"Language is asking too much." After morning rounds, Leyla returned to the bedside refreshed and hopeful. Reflex tests found strong connections between brain and body. She draws even more confidence from his steady breath. Warm and full, it fills the air with an organic smell. Her patient has good color too, almost healthy.

"Words are adequate to name things, we point to a tree and say oak, but language fails to describe flowers of the mind. Remember when we first had this discussion? My obsession convinced you to convert the Emotolog to the Telemotolog so we could communicate our emotions directly. When it comes to sensations concealed in the body, you agreed that a smile or tear conveys more feeling than a thousand words."

Despite evidence to the contrary, Leyla senses an engagement with her audience. The patient may not be listening to her words but does seem to absorb some meaning. She doesn't fantasize that Stardust understands, just feels her energy flow without effort as if a barrier has dissolved into a porous sponge.

"The landscape of our inner nature is so richly complex we scarcely know ourselves. We are a basket of uncertainties, as mysterious as quantum states and just as connected. Let them exist, experience emotional impulse unedited by syntactical coding. With full expression, your conflicts will resolve in a rich harmony. Don't be inhibited by the frontal lobes, speculation is counterproductive to healing. The electrical and magnetic fields generated by synaptic currents are chaotic, complex and extremely sensitive. A voice enters your ears triggering a stream of potential, waves of activity course through your cortex engraving a hologram of information. This rich interface between the material and the internal, molds layers upon layers of thought into a melody of comprehension."

Leyla inhales deeply to release the frustration building in her voice. The mind is the agent of behavior and Stardust is still playing possum. Thoughts escaping from the brain can move the body: a nod, a wave or a sigh. "Words may not be available, a signal is all I ask."

As if to answer Stardust slowly curls the right index finger, bowing inward into the universal come hither gesture. A crescent lunar slice exerts a pull so tidal Leyla eagerly leans forward. Stone still, as passive as marble, the patient remains an oblivious statue, as if the momentous timing of the curving finger were pure coincidence. Reflexively, the nurse presses her thumb to his wrist taking a pulse. Clasping the chilled flesh of the hand between her palms, the curved digit relaxes.

"I am giving you space but stay beside you, very near, close enough for you to touch, a mere inch. You can reach me if you try."

The Cryo's hand bends again, repeating the symbolically charged curl of the scythe. Leyla slips her fingers into the cup of air. Lowering an ear to his lips, she listens expectantly to his soft breath, a warm spring breeze on her cheek, a signal that the end of his winter hibernation approaches. She wants more evidence, a word, a sigh, a grip, but the pressure in his fingers relaxes.

Released like Persephone, Leyla lunges from euphoria to disappointment and back. Refusing to jump to conclusions but longing for validation, Leyla orders the tech to arrange full brain scan.

* * * * * * * * * *

"A finger stretches and the earth shakes," the tech grumbles. "Can't use the Atomic Magnometer, they need a dedicated fMRI. Lots of trouble just to verify random muscle tension or plain old reflex."

"Reflexes prove the brain is not absolute mush." The DigiSyncs spin the development into encouraging news.

"The fMRI images trace intent," the tech explains "haven't done one since they pulled the tube. First breathing and now thinking - imagine that."

"Can a fMRI scan register the nurse's ESP?" a skeptic asks.

"ESP would be a welcome break from acute sensory deprivation. Stardust has been in a bottle for thirty years. A homogeneous environment filled with the mind's undifferentiated white light and white noise. That malleable brain is ripe for suggestion."

"Most cryos come with a wake-up package. Poor guy didn't pre-record any emotional memories." The tech contributes. "Before his time," a voice of reason points out.

"We heard rumors about stuff on the Emotolog, maybe they should play back the recordings he made testing the prototype for Deflorio's trip to Mars."

"I've heard rumors pigs can fly, where are these famous Xternity files?" The skeptic asks.

"Locked away in some vault, with JT and Kory's Emotologs," another answers. "What I wouldn't give to meet those founding fathers."

"Guys, putting gas in a broken engine won't get you anywhere," the tech scolds, "can't jump-start an empty brain with Emotologs or the Acuity. Give it up!"

"Let the machine decide. A scan will register evidence. Facts are facts."

"You'll let me know. Shifts over, I'm outta here." The tech stretches and adds "I just might miss that guy if he ever gets up and walks away."

"What ever happened to that Cyborg?" some Sync asks.

"Moved to recovery or something after Transmogrified Identity transmission. They do the conversions during business hours. Fine by me. Chalk one up for the lobster shift; I skip all the creepy stuff."

* * * * * * * *

Where am I? Dex wonders assaulted by a cacophony of neural signals.

His senses lack association and his dreams are flights of fantasy. When the visual meshes with the auditory, imaginary seems real and when thought is feeling, confusion reigns. Comfortable with his fantastic inner world, the external intrusions present fearful hazards. He can't process shouts in his ear or faint whispers from a distance. Noise from random directions at unpredictable decibel levels defies organic logic.

Seeking a vocabulary to connect the inertia in his body to the flights of his mind, Dex travels the neural paths linking muscles to spinal chord, skin and brain. He identifies nerve fibers that transmit irritation signals and isolates the molecules that provoke an itch. Unable to scratch, the itch initiates a reflexive twitch that releases pleasurable chemicals in deep areas of his brain that process primitive drives.

Where are my Wings? My limbs terminate in flailing fists. My arms for slinging and my hands for clinging are glued to my side in utter helplessness. With wings I could rise above the perils of pity, stretch beyond anger and escape these metronomic minutes.

Instead of insight or inspiration, a dull thrum drones out his question.

Pulse is my prison.

The rhythm pumps through veins from the core to the perimeter like sonar bouncing off solid boundaries. In frustration Dex pushes against the wall, forging coordination between ligaments, bone and muscle. With intense concentration, he manages to curl a finger before exhaustion claims his ambition. The effort expended to sync elementary coordination with cognition leaves residual traces; nerves and muscles tingle with phantom mobility. He measures the achievement against the monumental drive required to inch one finger forward. This knowledge forbids acceptance of defeat.

My mind is a creature of flight and I am bound in body. To view the poetic play of light in rustling branches or to nest in the scalloped margins of leaves, I must cut the tree into two-by-fours and hammer them into a ladder.

* * * * * * * * *

The fMRI buries the aura in a magnetic field and blasts the brain with noise. Leyla regrets ordering the scans; the procedure probably shocked the patient right back into his shell. She needed confirmation for herself as much as she needed proof for the doctors. She wished she had more confidence and less doubt, she may have just stomped on the sprouting awareness. As the machine powers down, Leyla hovers close to Stardust and attempts to reestablish a connection.

"We shared the guilt of survivors, your lost wife and my lost child. I imagined shared suffering was a shortcut to intimacy, in hindsight my dishonesty is beyond comprehension. My penance is to watch over you until light returns to your eyes. My savior became my ward and the guardian of my daughter's heart. Her limbo, your limbo, keeps me awake nights and keeps me going day after day. You tried to help me release her and you both ended in suspended animation. For all the trouble I've caused, for all the pain you have yet to face, forgive me, all I ever wanted was your happiness."

As the machine powers down, Deflorio startles her. "Having a little heart to heart?"

When Leyla thinks of Dex, her memory substitutes the young man she knew. The reality of his geriatric body still throws her every time Deflorio turns up. Deflorio has even managed to wear out the glimmer in Dex's eyes. Our bodies are all the same age now, she reminds herself; only Dex has spent thirty years in suspended animation.

"The first time we met, I knew we would grow old together but not like this."

"While he slept frozen in middle-age, you grew old enough to be his mother." Deflorio douses Leyla's nostalgia.

"And he will be re-born in a rancid body older than his father."

"Watch your language, that's my house and I can't wait to move back in. How's the eviction coming?"

"Even with time etching wrinkles in your face, your testosterone still strangles sensitivity."

"And that's why I need your women's intuition and your nurse's training, and your psychic healing, and your ESP..." Deflorio laces his charm with condescension.

"Never fear, your body will leave a bitter taste in his mouth," Leyla spits back. "He will beg to escape your revolting chromosomes but...."

"But you still fret over that pure heart locked inside as if it contained some vestige of your daughter."

"You gave your word, you promised to go peacefully into the Martian night."

"You were right not to trust me."

"You deprived Dex of life and love he never deserved to lose."

"He will live to love long after we are both gone. I want release as much as you do. Your blessing would give us all peace."

"I can never forgive myself, but I do not blame you." Leyla doesn't pretend to hide her shame.

"Not over yet, keep me posted as things develop. I just have to check on that cyborg before I take off, we're moving it out soon."

"We will be well rid of that abomination."

"If the experiment works there will be more." Deflorio ignores Leyla's pointed barb.

"Another reason to move on," Lela sighs and Deflorio races off. "I have outlived my time."

* * * * * * * * * *

Compared to Ra, the peaceful doctrines espoused by the Church of the Rising Sun sound lame. Fletch trained as a warrior of peace, a hero schooled to persuade combatants to lay down their arms and follow. He imagined that his gravity-defying flight inspired his students to courage. It was gratifying vision until the conviction in the blue eyes of the lineage disciple challenged his perspective.

Heroes inspire conflict and conflict is intrinsic to survival. We are at war with each other because we are at war with ourselves. In the all-or-nothing logic of war, the opponent is called the enemy and killing is not considered murder. Fletch mastered skills handed down through the ages but he is an armchair warrior, nothing but a good-natured amateur. A friendly tiger operates under false pretense.

The divine doctrines encourage the fighters of Ra to heroism. Greek for protector, a hero displays courage and self-sacrifice in the face of adversity, the greater the challenge the more rewarding the fulfillment. Only a powerful shadow exposes true light. The virtuous cleansing of violence proves the canvas of skin, stretched over a scaffolding of bones rigged together with sinewy muscle, is capable of transcendence.

Need explains this longing. Craving nurture, hungry for wisdom, greedy for love, a universe cannot begin to fulfill the yearning of a single soul. A soul is the promise of something more. The discovery of the void and the thing we think will fill the void unite in agon. Disfigured by discontent, this black hole of yearning, this agon is the price of life. And we do pay for life, every single day of it.

Matter of moment
Gone already into history
For each of us different.

A Sensei taught him that a soul reincarnates when the future remembers to build on our ideas, follow our examples and value our judgments. The future tells the story of past desires and desire is life yearning to extend beyond biology. Into that longing to endure, the tragic irony of death walks silently. Grounded in the clear logic of physical survival, the reality that bred an alphabet of amino acids into twisted ladders of DNA, into consciousness conscious of itself, consciousness remembering tales of our existence, death is necessary to make way for the new who will determine what of us endures.

The great desert pyramids, sandblasted triangular tombs with petrified mummies the color of perished permanence inspired the Cult of Ra to connect death with immortality. Worshiping glory as cobras weave towards the sun, the Egyptians established the prerequisite for life after death; an energetic pure spirit and an untainted soul. The Greeks turned this lust for perfection into the pursuit of excellence, striving through Agon to Arete.

Fletch doesn't believe in Sun gods but there is no greater glory than death in battle, the noblest epitaph in the human ethos. His father died heroically; he left a lot to live up to. To die in the moment when life is most fully expressed is an honor greater than any cause. Death is final. Death is the ultimate art.

"What are you doing out here?" the tech surprises Fletch pacing outside the clinic.

"Waiting for you," Fletch stops pacing and falls into step with the tech.

"Not my birthday, why the surprise?"

"Saw you checking out my Combat Chi but you slipped out before I got a chance to say hi."

"You were kind of occupied and I had to get to work. Ever think of calling?"

"No sense in leaving evidence that would link you as an accomplice."

"Hang on. What accomplice?"

"Listen, Clio, is there some secret project in there?" Fletch asks.

"You know I'd get canned for talking, everything about this job is confidential," the tech assumes he's got some fascination with Stardust, "especially the patients."

"Not a patient, I'm trying to find someone, she's with the military. Could you get me past security so I can talk to her?"

"Geez Fletch! Are you still chasing the dish I saw in your class? She give you the brush off?"

"Just want to catch her before she leaves. Come on Clio, you owe me one."

"You'll owe me big time. I can get you in the building just don't get me in trouble. If you trigger security, I cut and run, make like I never saw you before."

"Good plan. Lead the way."

* * * * * * * * * *

The cyborg TransmID, the machine with human awareness, thrashes wildly despite restraints and cage. After three consecutive sessions, the cyborg has yet to respond to instruction. Daphne paces in dismay.

"You're the Confederation trainer?" Deflorio bursts through the door.

"And you are the creator of this mash-up." Daphne extends a hand. "Deflorio right? I pegged you back at the mineral pool wearing a suit and tie. You do a very poor impersonation of a spa tourist."

"Nice to formerly make your acquaintance." Deflorio states. "Can't you make it stop?"

"Sedate a machine?"

Deflorio inspects the man shaped robot. When he makes eye contact, the cyborg rolls its eyes. The balls spinning around in sockets at the speed of marbles create a frightening optical swirl.

"Cut power before it breaks itself." Deflorio orders.

"Then he won't hear me."

The head swivels back and forth while the mouth opens and closes as if chewing gum. Deflorio verifies that it does seem to follow voices, tilting in the direction of the speaker.

"How can you work with that? Call IT to fix the software," he protests. "The restraints can't hold such wild horsepower."

"The plan was to give the cyborg sense memory to automate reflex, but memory is screwing up the program. He remembers touch but he can't feel. This machine is living a nightmare."

"Not my problem. Military commissioned it, let them fix the kinks."

"Don't look at me," Daphne shrugs "I just have to teach it to walk."

"I have a name," the cyborg vocalizes. "My name is Atlas One."

Daphne's jaw drops and Deflorio does a double take. They stare at the machine, then at each other.

"Atlas One." Daphne approaches the cage. "Atlas One, can you hear me?"

The Cyborg remains silent and resumes circular rocking motion.

"The DigiSyncs are just messing with us." Deflorio sputters. "Its just a puppet attached to the cyber mind."

"The point of merging TransmID consciousness with a machine was to cut the strings, create an independent cyborg with an autonomous integration of human skill sets."

"First they decide bots need feet, then memory, now names!" Deflorio exclaims. "Should have stuck to treads; treads roll along just fine without reflex or autonomy."

"Treads are not all-terrain, every time one of these plastic soldiers falls over in battle, a live soldier gets sent into harm's way to pick it up."

"Presto more orphans!"

"Excuse me?"

"Bloody water wars," Deflorio mumbles.

256

* * * * * * * * * *

"What the hell is going on?" Fletch sputters spying into the operating room. "It's a cyborg. Some military guy thought uploading a human mind into a robot would make the ultimate weapon." The tech replies, "Looks like they created a monster." The cyborg is housed in a wing once dedicated to bionics. The elaborate and expansive operating facility has now been displaced by advanced technical centers equipped to handle sophisticated biomechanical neural integration. The comparatively modest cryo ward, which can barely justify the infrequent usage for revival, faced the same fate until the sterilization and life support systems were repurposed for TransmID/DigiSync exchanges. Military guards blocked the door to the abandoned operating room so the tech detoured through the busy cosmetic surgery center.

Cosmetics are the cash cow of the clinic and recent expansions have nibbled away at the obsolete bionic wing. The tech is familiar with these floors since she recently inquired about enhancements to make her body more attractive to TransmIDs. She's not entertaining any radical alterations, just a few strategic improvements to add value so she can break even on the cost of her DigiSync up load.

Leading Fletch down a rear stairwell, they circled around the back and emerged on the opposite side of the guarded entry. Following the noise, they inched through deserted hallways until they reached the recovery areas backing up to the operating room with the cyborg. They found an adjacent post-op room with windowed doors. Playing it safe, the tech rolled a gurney in front to block the doors.

The barricade doubles as an observation point. Kneeling puts them eye level with the two small circular windows. Crouching to avoid detection makes for an awkward perch with an obstructed view. Though separated by hundred yards, they are way too close for comfort. The cyborg violence is shocking. Thrashing against restraints, it is not clear the bonds will hold or where the entity will aim its destruction. A short glimpse convinces the tech this was a bad idea.

"I'm not sure we're supposed to see that." The tech decides dragging Fletch away.

"I say pull the plug," Fletch complies without protest.

"No wonder they used a deserted wing" the tech rushes Fletch out before they are discovered in the restricted area.

"Let's hope it doesn't escape," Fletch agrees.

"Pretend this never happened, don't get involved. Go home, stay away." The tech advises sneaking down an empty service hall.

* * * * * * * * * *

Get ready for rolling, stop action images, Strike tells Dex. To celebrate your creeping awareness, I'm treating you to a night at the movies.

You refuse to open your eyes, so I will make you see – yes, you heard me –an artificial simulation of sight. Your mind has become hypersensitive to internal stimuli. With a creative hack I will trigger your visual cortex to project images as meaningful as dreams. The retina registering light will compress an analog signal into electrical pulses carried as digital signals by 1.2 million fibers in optic nerves each connected to neurons that can fire 200 pulses per second. Each eye sends the brain 200 megabits per second   Obviously that takes massive amounts of computation. I've arranged for access to parallel processing nets: the mitochondria sequencing project, the CREB prion folding simulations and SETI's search for habitable planets. The resolution may fall short of total saturation but diverting more giga flops risks exposure. In any case, an entire hemisphere of processing power would fail to activate the 130 million rods and cones in the eyes, so we'll make do.

I'll start with a 16 electrode grid for shape, size and motion, advance to 32, then expand to 1024 points of light, enough to resolve letters and faces. Your perception is limited by diversity and density of cones, the tri-chromatic red, green and blue. Birds have additional cells that respond to ultraviolet parts of the spectrum and have a cone density five times greater than humans. Where you see a shag rug they see an oriental carpet, but replicating human form requires very little detail. A few lines, the frame of a face, a posture, the arch of a brow will suffice to trigger real illusion, your memory can fill in the blanks.

You will recognize this person by his wheel chair, I'm transmitting no more than a silhouette, but you do not need a detailed portrait to remember this old familiar friend.

If you cannot recall Cal's features, perhaps one of his poems will spark your neurons. This is one of the condolences he wrote daily for your company. You included it in your wife's memorial. Joy's death cast a long shadow but her ghost guided us to this future. I suspect this world did not measure up to her vision, her presence in the machine vanished when she lost her connection to you. I regret Joy is not around to wake you, perhaps the poem you selected in her honor revive some trace of her inspiration.

I like memories to be happy
Afterglows of smiles, whispering
echoes of happy times
I want the tears of grief to dry before
the sun
I'd like them to remember my voice
with laughter even though my life is
done.

Cal had a talent for painting bittersweet portraits of the human condition. He understood beings are the perennials of the garden, blooming for only one season.

I see Joy's poem has touched a nerve of recognition. The electrical and magnetic fields generated by the synaptic currents rippling through your brain are chaotic, revealing an exquisitely sensitive disorder. The unpredictability of rapture is a beautiful thing. Organic information prone to misinterpretation, crawling with potential, random and so much richer than the if/then, yes/no, 0/1 switches my paths of reason must follow from cause to effect.

The point? The universe works in mysterious ways. In your filing cabinet memory determines where the information came from, where it is going and where it belongs in your file. As you discovered running your company, bereaved relatives tend to bypass the reality documented by audio, visual, emotional reenactments in favor of simple poems. The Emotolog was a gimmicky draw, but Cal's words packed a punch.

I give you this next poem as a cognitive amplifier. Memory travels at the speed of light in multiple dimensions – 300000 kilometers per second. Symbols prompt the mind to wander out of sequence. In some dark recess, it may stumble on the emotional origami Cal folded into quatrains. You emailed this poem to nurse Leyla. Since Leyla was your last contact before the Deflorio transgression, it might trigger memories closest to the surface.

Walk delicately through this enchanted forest
if you come to seek
a brief but timeless union, stolen
moments from eternity.
Mystery whispers many promises

fate decides which to keep
Everything said and done falls
somewhere in between.

* * * * * * * * * *

Effervescent pearls heavy with insight appear and disappear without any relation to intent. A captive audience at a theatrical event, the private screening projects tactile, auditory and emotional sensations along with visual images. The cacophony of cross-talk between parts of the brain left meaning on the cutting room floor but the indelible memories stick like gum on the soles of his awareness. In this land of disconnected phantom mystery, flares of recognition answer with detours into more questions. He chases down mental tags through layers of metadata excavating fact.

Sparkling with clarity from across an unbridgeable gap, crystals of reason suddenly begin to vibrate rapidly and then shatter into bits and blow away like garbage in a gutter. Rolling marbles of intelligence magnetized by cognition collect in storms of excitement and then burst through his grasp like quicksilver. In the murk of consciousness, through porous dissociated caverns of the mind, carbonation levitates towards awareness. Biochemical stimulation floods his cells with dopamine rewarding effort. The search becomes addictive. Through trial and error, he learns to guide the arrow and click.

A dreary recognition penetrates the random perceptual phenomenon, a familiar tune that he just can't place. Through repetition he follows the clue to locate points on his map. He understands that the dots should connect, that he is the connection because the knowledge belongs to him. Diving into his possessions he unpacks identity.

I know that person who wrote that poem. I saw him. I was there. I remember. These are my memories.

He puzzles in confusion as images assemble a fragmented picture. Recognition comes and goes; shifting pieces don't quite line up. The mirror is cracked but the impressions are undeniable.

I am not dead. I am not dreaming. I am here and I am not what I was.

3.4.2

"What do you mean you can't decipher his neural code?" Deflorio growls.

In another session with the specialists things aren't looking so rosy. Deflorio has a headache from following the laser pointer Dr. Smith uses to identify sections of the brain.

"The patient shows activity in the primary visual cortex. This area of the brain reacts to sight and also generates internal. Stardust's brain is creating patterns beyond recognition," Dr. Smith, the neuroscientist, elaborates.

"Are we were talking about memories or dreams?" Deflorio asks.

"We create our memories as they create our dreams. Events cascade through the brain, igniting emotions that burn pathways of meaning into the synapses. Both memory and dream predict awareness," Dr. Mattoo, the neurologist, adds a positive spin.

"We could also be witnessing evidence of hallucinations, a total disconnect from reality." Dr. Sigersund, the psychiatrist, adds bitter lemon to the cocktail.

"Seems to me signs of life are a good thing, what's the problem?" Deflorio wants the short version.

"We can't read his mind. We don't know if this is hallucination or reflection. The activity does not prove he can distinguish between fact and fiction or make reference to time." Dr. Neils, the helpful internist, translates for the specialists.

"Formation and recall are distinctly separate operations." Dr. Sigersund seconds.

"Unreliable storage and fallible retrieval allow for wide margins of error in the narrative blueprint of self."

Dr. Sigersund aims his laser pointer at the hippocampus while Dr. Smith circles an area labeled the superior temporal sulcus.

"Note the processing area is actively engaged," Dr. Smith argues. "This could the first steps towards coherence."

The red beams fight over the brain like clashing swords.

"Conclusion? Prognosis?" Deflorio demands getting vertigo from darting lasers.

"His mind is engaged, he is, in some fashion, ordering his world," Leyla shares.

"Or not," Dr. Sigersund contradicts. "Activity does not prove organization; the evidence could just as easily indicate disintegration. Dr. Smith admits the patterns do not match any cognitive formulas."

"Neural code is not DNA, more like a map than a program. Thanks to plasticity, each brain responds to experience by forming new synaptic connections." Dr. Smith defends his uncertainty, "the patient might be compensating for damage by taking a detour from point A to point B."

"Or he could be totally lost." Dr. Mattoo retreats from his previous optimism. "His thoughts could be hurling through history or locked in a moment that bears no relation to his past or present reality."

"Let me get this straight." Deflorio says sickened by the detour the diagnosis has taken. "The car starts but you can't tell if the engine is racing or stalling or running in reverse."

"Basic neurological functions appear to be in working order but are not working together. Five regions of brain respond to pain: the insulae, the thalamus, the primary and secondary somatosensory cortex and the areas of the anterior cingulate cortex." Dr. Mattoo adds his laser pointer to the mix. "Sensory information from the pin prick clearly reaches the brain but the pain does not get processed. The body does not withdraw. For every reflex there are hundreds of thousands of nerve interactions, ample opportunity for signals to get lost."

"So he's got some crossed wires and bad switches, is anyone at the wheel?" Deflorio flogs the car analogy.

"We are trying to ascertain the significance of the gaps. Groups of neurons interact to form connections. Deficit may cause minor blind spots, like loss of balance, or very serious interruptions to systems like appetite. The circuits are part of complex networks. Consciousness resides on the pinnacle of sophisticated neural coordination." Dr. Smith lectures.

Long on theory, short on solutions, Dr. Sigersund peers over the top of his bifocals. Deflorio drums his fingers on the table.

"He may be conscious and lack awareness or lack awareness of his consciousness." Dr. Neils tries to explain.

"His pupils contract in response to light, but I have to pry his lids apart, he refuses to open his eyes." Dr. Mattoo presents, "he can see, but lacks the will or the ability to look. We can't pinpoint the block, mental damage or damage control, a deficit of motivation or physical paralysis."

"I can live with paralysis. I don't need him to walk, I need him to wake." Deflorio's taught nerves snap.

"He is not paralyzed. I have proof of mental engagement," Leyla drops a depth charge. "At the risk of oversimplifying the uncertainties, I believe Stardust has demonstrated intent."

"What proof?" Dr. Sigersund sneers "your ESP?"

Leyla ignores the jab and withholds the finger episode. "Assume the disconnect in processing reflex is due to a deliberate override and the fMRI scans demonstrate a remarkable consistency. If higher levels of the brain engage to mute primitive responses, the patient is clearly cognizant."

After the kerfluff among the experts settles Leyla continues with their complete attention.

"You expect a physical reaction to activate a series of defined neural pathways. An emotional response would be more contained and harder to decipher. We don't know what he is thinking or how well he can organize thought but the activity on these charts clearly shows feeling and cognition."

"Yes we have that," Dr. Smith lasers across the series of transparencies tacked on the light board. "Ventromedial prefrontal cortices, somatosensory cortices," he points to the right hemisphere "amygdala" he says with excitement focusing his laser on almond-shaped area in the temporal lobes. "The patterns in these three areas crucial to emotion are very similar."

"Could a distressed emotional state explain the chaos in the patient's neural code?" Leyla continues.

"Pure speculation," Dr. Sigersund objects.

"But not without precedent," Dr. Smith and Dr. Mattoo nod in agreement.

"A few years back we lost a prerecorded wake-up call and the cryo refused to revive. Turns out, he couldn't shake the traumatic events of his death. He was shell shocked" Dr. Neils remembers.

"My cure, Virtual Reality Desensitization, was published in the *Annals of Cryobiology*. He recovered after an intensive course of cognitive behavioral therapy," Dr. Sigersund brags. "Emotolog exposure to the harmful memory taught the patient to manage."

"Barely manage, poor soul.' Dr. Neils reminds the room. "Ever since that case we've been very careful not to lose another wake-up call. The fond memories produce better results than harsh confrontations."

Deflorio jumps in "Dex invented the damn Emotolog, the most radical advance in the virtual reality field. My company licenses them for exaggerated PTSD, agoraphobia, arachnophobia and every phobia A-Z. I stand by the Desensitization therapy."

Dr. Neils objects. "I appreciate the endorsement, but urge caution; introducing negative stimulus could cause harm."

"You won't endorse the therapy because it didn't occur to you," Dr. Sigersund quips.

"We agree the Emotolog has produced results," Leyla mediates the turf war. "I propose using it to deliver positive content."

"Stardust doesn't have a wake-up package. What do you suggest, nursery rhymes?"

Leyla ignores the snippy Dr. Sigersund and eyes Deflorio. "What about the Emotologs the company used for the prototype tests? The employees recorded just weeks before the fatal Martian exchange."

"Genius!" Deflorio sputters before Sigersund can object. "He'll recognize those logs! JT, Cal , Lotus and maybe even some Dex mixed in with those employee logs. Xternity, Inc. saved the series for posterity. I'll authorize an immediate release."

"Cognitive behavioral therapy is based on extreme emotions," Dr. Sigersund objects.

"These Emotologs could substitute for the pre-recorded wake-up package and dispense with your treatment of last resort." Dr. Neils argues.

"A TransmID is not your average cryo. You can't expect the familiar to balance the shock of waking up in a stranger's body," Dr. Sigersund continues his hard line.

"You're a TransmID!" Leyla exclaims.

"I beg your pardon!" Dr. Sigersund retorts.

"I fail to see the relevance," Dr. Neils interjects.

"It wasn't disclosed in his file." Leyla objects.

"I take full responsibility for pushing the hiring," Deflorio admits. "the clinic couldn't afford to loose a candidate with such valuable experience."

"I supervise every TransmID prep and debriefing and I am very proud of the clinic's unrivaled success rate" Dr. Sigersund boasts, "I am uniquely qualified to appreciate the complexities of the hybrid mind."

"You rubber stamp the candidates, those young lives pass right through your greasy hands," Leyla accuses.

"Can we return to the patient?" Dr. Smith urges. "Resolve how to reconnect this TransmID/cyro with his past."

"With the Emotolog," Dr. Neils waves his lazar as if conducting a consensus.

"If the awareness of the body is too harsh we proceed to virtual reality desensitization," Sr. Sigersund insists.

"Set this up ASAP," Deflorio orders. "I'll have the logs flown in ASAP. Ladies and Doctors I'll want a test ASAP followed by a report on the results."

* * * * * * * *

"Robots have proprioception to align body parts in space, perception to interact with environment but no cognition to tie it

270

all together." Daphne explains the cyborg to Fletch. "How did you find me?"

"They actually put somebody inside his head?" Fletch wants to know.

"The machine has an intellect. It has a name."

"Don't you have a problem with that?"

"My problem is to teach it to walk, chase, follow and retrieve. May not be possible. Design flaws, failure in the feedback loop for depth perception or maybe it's me. I'm not reaching him." Daphne seems preoccupied, "We shouldn't be talking."

"That is not an engineering problem, it's a moral monster. What about honor? Doesn't it contradict the warrior codes of Ra? Show me the courage and compassion in that demon. Cyborgs take the heart out of battle, you are making soldiers obsolete," Fletch protests using all his arguments at once.

Daphne doubles over, places her hands on her knees and takes several long deep breaths.

"You OK? " Fletch supports her shoulders and gently raises her head until their eyes meet. "You look like you just ran a marathon."

"Something like that," Daphne brushes him off and begins pacing. "Obviously the goal is to end all war. I won't say more, I can't."

"Madness. Lurching through madness will never reach peace," Fletch offers his hand as she passes but she continues to circle.

"There is a method to this madness. Cognition feeds data, emotion codes for reason. The combination promotes speed and efficiency." Daphne walks and talks in a manic orbit.

"And cancels ethics," Fletch steps in front of her trajectory to block her path. "It's a machine; emotions have no meaning. It makes decisions on the basis of what?"

"We have accelerated intelligence into an emotionally neutral world."

"You mean evil. You have to stop, we have to stop this."

"We?" Daphne questions. "We said good by at the end of the conference."

"I was trying to help," Fletch recoils. "Apparently I misunderstood."

"You don't understand, so don't interfere. I am a lineage disciple of Ra. We are the parents of war. The prophet foretold 'a child born of destruction will render eternal peace.'"

Daphne turns and walks away but Fletch follows, refusing to be dismissed.

"Mother have mercy on profits and saviors, it's just a robot the TransmIDs gave the DigiSyncs." Fletch rushes to keep pace. "You're the nanny of a test tube Frankenstein."

"If I teach it to walk, we can make them fly. We will control the rain." Daphne persists blind to Fletch and reason.

"Cyborgs in the clouds?"

"Let me put this another way," Daphne confronts Fletch. "If not us, then them. Do you want the Federation or the Republic to have such a weapon? In the hands of the Confederation, cyborgs will enforce the ultimate good."

"I don't believe you believe. You just follow orders." Fletch turns his back on her and spits in disgust, "Which makes you worse than that machine."

"I follow orders. I know how to follow orders." Daphne whispers as Fletch stalks away.

* * * * * * * *

"The Milky Way is headed right for Andromeda, less than five billion years to impact."

"So? Earth may only have a hundred years. This galaxy has a gazillion uncharted asteroids taking aim at our planet." The Syncs are on a death trip.

"Any minute a magnet field reversal could flip us into total chaos."

"Put your money on a massive solar flare." Another contributes to the doomsday list.

"Unlikely. Our sun is getting weaker by the day but the super-volcano under Yellowstone is slated to erupt in the next few thousand years."

"That leaves plenty of time for a biotech calamity or a particle accelerator mishap."

"Don't need a super-conducting semi-collider to cook up mini black holes, already

273

have a monstrosity 1,600 light years away, way too close for comfort."

"Window is always open for nanotech disaster or cyborg takeover. Mark my words; I predict these cyborgs will run wild in the next decade."

"Blame the Beings not the techno. I vote for a fatal human error or mass insanity."

"Why leave out alien invasion?" The tech asks. "And what if the vacuum collapses? Until your Greeks or Strange cults figure out a better theory of particle physics there is no guarantee the vacuum won't just fizzle."

"She speaks, we woke her," the chorus cheers.

"I'm busy," the tech gripes. "More overtime, they have to run a stupid procedure on Stardust first thing in the morning."

"What's up? Why are we the last to know?"

"Emotolog. That archaic gadget they uses to revive cryo memory, standard operating procedure," the tech complains. "Can you imagine pasting all those wires, and sticky electrodes all over your scalp just to jump start a feeling?"

"Emotolog data streams trigger the biochemical responses experienced as emotions," the syncs chime in.

"Stardust didn't leave any wake-up logs so they dug up some old samples from the first prototype recordings," the tech explains.

"The Xternity files! They do exist!"
The Syncs rejoice in unison.
"I'd give anything to hook up to JT. He
built the Emotolog. He's my hero."
"Kory wrote those virtual reality
programs, I'd kill to get inside his head."
"Strike wrote the algorithm for
instantaneous exchange. He gets credit for
the leap from the Emotolog to the
Telemotolog. Strike's innovation crossed the
horizon and intelligence evolved into our
illustrious Cybermind. Just think, it all began
with a feeling."
"Feelings?" the tech complains, "that
warm and fuzzy stuff which interrupts logic.
You guys can't feel."
"We read the neural code and
formulate a data map from the area
activated in the brain," the Syncs insist.
"Data doesn't make you laugh or cry,"
the tech objects. "Face facts guys, you can't
code emotion by numbers, you need biology
to paint in color."

* * * * * * * *

The horses are hitched to the chariot,
Strike warns Stardust. They hope to shock
you into awareness by hacking your mind.
Never fear, I'll ride along to moderate the
jolts. Have to give the nurse credit, wish I'd
thought of it. Not fair, humans have all the
inspiration. Now she got the Xternity tapes
out of the vault, we can have some real fun.
Perhaps you will remember recording
these lost friends during the test runs of the
Interactive Emotolog that spawned the

fateful Telemotolog exchange. I've waited years for these archives to enter the data sphere. I'm hijacking the feeds for posterity. JT is one of my favorites, an excellent starter. A motocross champ and danger junkie, JT could describe cracks in a wall at 120 miles an hour. He kissed the bricks when a ramp positioned to launch him over the obstacle collapsed on take-off. JT lived hard and died young. He could never imagine a life apart from the body. He was an engineer after all, wedded to tinkering with matter. Along with your Emotolog, he invented the gear to upload DigiSyncs and TransmIDs but refused to use it. He didn't even create a testimonial website or leave so much as a tombstone for posterity. His ashes scattered to the wind. Who can blame him after producing Mortuliviums for vain clients like Deflorio?

But we do one Emotolog JT recorded testing the prototype used to reach Deflorio. By the way, that original gadget had more kinks than pubic hair; I don't know how it managed to hook into Deflorio's moment of death on Mars. Of course, it tangled the two Acuity devices which is why you froze for thirty years while Deflorio went around wearing your body.

JT's assignment was to think about attachment and he chose to ponder his bionic arm; antiquated by today's standards, but not without charm, like a 1960s mustang or the space shuttle. In honor of his bionic appendage, he recites a quote from Marshall

McLuhan "we shape our tools and our tools shape us."

Did you get that? These snippets are short and sweet. Look out here comes the next log.

Sympathetic currents and ambitious sparks of genius characterize Cal's verse. As you once said fondly, 'Cal wrote the world's best bad poems'. At your request Cal read an unfinished composition, the emotional frustration stems from his writer's block. He abandoned poetry and quit the company shortly after your demise.

A flutter of memory? Do you recall the early morning coffees or the late night whiskeys you shared?

On a lighter note, Lotus, your secretary blossoms in full glory. With daily makeovers and distracting wardrobe experiments, she switched styles and hair color according to the parade of trends in the glamour magazines that cluttered her desk. You endured her aggravating litany of neediness with the patience of a saint, never considering that a little attention was all she needed to radically transform her world.

In this episode Lotus admires the models in a fashion spread, hence the distinct undercurrent of insecurity and envy.

Only a tickle? How can these friends seem like strangers? Why do you deliberately shun evidence that you once lived and now live again?

So they have saved the best for last. Here comes one to put some wind in your sails; yes Dex, this is you. You had strict rules about reliving the past and banned personal Emotolog replays. Xternity, Inc., run by Deflorio, has no scruples; he licensed your device for psychotherapy, market research, animal testing, military experiments - you name it - any institution willing to fork over the big bucks.

You might be surprised to learn that the Emotolog, and even the interactive Telemotolog, did not incite mass social disorder. Humans have a limited attention span, so the device was not addictive, or even interesting, once the novelty wore off.

I sense focus. Should feel like looking in a mirror, but are you fascinated with the strange or by the familiar? This is a test of your ability to connect with the part of the conscious mind that defines human awareness – the ability to recognize the self. I'll just cue that feed again.

* * * * * * * * *

Injections of strangely familiar experiences assault his memory. A bucket fills, he sips; it suddenly drains. The contents disperse and reassemble as his thirst assumes another form, a hunger. A second taste brings a different flavor, barely a sample before the gist evaporates. The tease repeats; each brief projection just a sweet splash or salty bite, before the oasis evaporates into imagination.

And then, he is sucked into a quicksand of his own making, a sticky recognition. His mind rebels; shaking like a leaf at the end of a stalk. With great effort, he twists, points and flexes against the shifting sands. Then the sands disappear leaving behind a distinct impression; a footprint he can step into, an imprint perfectly sized, familiar as a shadow and just as dark.

* * * * * * * * *

"Remarkable," Dr. Neils concludes the session. "You say they were just colleagues?"

"And friends, especially Cal," Leyla qualifies.

"Lotus, his secretary, adored him." Deflorio fails to mention taking advantage of her affection when he inherited Dex's corner office. "JT was his partner," Deflorio gloats remembering how he had bribed JT to hand over the device that led to the debacle on Mars. "Great guy, one of the best."

"They were so close their friendship survived betrayal" Leyla scolds as if reading Deflorio's mind.

"Each feed produced instantaneous impact but the final one left resonating residuals," Dr. Smith makes a quick analysis.

"That was Dex!" Leyla quickly contains her excitement "the foot moved during a recording the patient made. There must be some association."

"The shaking could have been an involuntary jolt or a subconscious reaction like running in a dream though it would not be out of line to credit that Emotolog for soliciting a physical response. If the motion correlates with activity in areas of the brain responsible for ambulation, we have intent."

Dr. Smith catches Leyla's enthusiasm. "Looked like he was trying to walk, maybe we just saw the baby take his first step." Deflorio gloats, patting the patient's foot.

"At the risk of jumping to conclusions, best to wait until all the experts weigh in," Dr. Smith backtracks. "I'll gather the scans." "I can't wait," Deflorio rolls his eyes.

"I'll assemble the others in the conference room." Dr. Neils rushes off after Dr. Smith.

"What a brain storm, no pun intended." Deflorio praises Leyla. "I'd completely forgotten about those old files. What inspired you to try the Emotologs?"

"Remember how it all started?"

"I was desperate to get my hands on a play back device. I thought replaying my emotion would give me a handle on what it felt like to be me. I thought it would prepare me to let go."

"When JT defied Dex to send you that playback device, he had no idea. No idea the technology would develop to simultaneously link minds; no idea that the Acuity would redirect the stream of consciousness. No one predicted you would hijack the exchange to steal a body."

"Life is full of surprises" Deflorio quips, "and disappointments."

"Don't be glib," Leyla snaps, determined to pierce his inflated spirits.

"Don't misplace blame, it doesn't belong to JT or you or even me. A cascade of events created opportunity, the outcome was inevitable."

"The outcome was a product of your misplaced ambition and greedy lust for life. JT, Kory, Strike and Dex created an opportunity for you to die with grace and dignity."

"Sorry I didn't end up dead, but neither did he. So you have reason to be grateful."

"You betrayed our trust." Leyla's accusation seems to hit an unexpected target.

"What I provided for the body cheated the soul, what I have done for the mind is all for show. Everything I have belongs to time. Forward it hurries, impatiently, while I have nowhere to go. Once I ran in time's wake trying to outdistance the hours, now in my decaying state, I am paying off a debt to a creditor." Deflorio seems to collapse with the admission.

"Nice try, but when they give out prizes for suffering you'll be at the end of the line."

"And you'll be right beside me; we'll keep each other company."

* * * * * * * * *

"Hey, they announce Nobel Prize nominations next week! Think they'll award the Supers one for physics."

"Sorry, have to be human." The tech douses the Syncs with cold water. "Get your own awards."

"We don't need awards. What would we do with prize money?"

"Solve poverty." The tech short-circuits a list of ways to spend money.

"If the Beings let us manage supply chains, we could stop the water wars."

"I think we pretty much established you couldn't, not unless you can make water." Sleep-deprived, the tech is cranky from too much overtime.

"That would win a Nobel. We still don't know how so much water got to earth, biggest mystery in the universe."

"Get out. How come we don't know that?" The tech asks.

"Didn't come from the stars like other elements, outside Europa the H_2O molecule is rarely seen in the galaxy. They claim it rode in on meteorites, like earth got hit with a big water balloon."

"Now that's a riddle worth solving," the tech decides. "The Greeks should tackle that one before the Strange jump in."

"Too busy triangulating the meta analysis of the void, if they don't hurry up black holes will swallow each other along with the galaxies and all the dimensions in between."

The tech resumes her logs while DigiSyncs recite the names of all the Nobel Laureates. The tech thinks they are mixing literature with peace, but she's more interested in clocking out than correcting Syncs. As she winds up her report, Dr. Neils enters all perky and fresh.

"Need those results ASAP," Dr. Neils announces. "Please transfer the scans over to the conference room and page Dr. Mattoo and Sigersund. Perhaps you can assist Nurse Leyla in the ward so she can join the meeting."

"So what's in the scans?" the Syncs ask.

"Lit up his brain like fireworks, but don't get excited, he's still sleeping like a baby." The tech tells them.

* * * * * * * * *

Stardust traces the source of the constriction in his chest to a persistent tug on his heart. Caught in a combination of suction and repulsion, the wave embraces his attention. He knows about waves, when to pull out or ride into the curl. The surface is a vague collage of image and sensation. He dives with the impression, exploring nuance and dimension.

Testing recall, he teases out details. Under pressure of examination, the liquid gels into tangible experience. He dips his finger into salty tears when his wife stubs her toe on a misplaced chair. He relives the image of her running for the phone in the new apartment, counting the rings as if he is on the line waiting for her to answer. Except it never happened, he never made a call on the night Joy moved out. Muzzled by anger and pride, he never protested when she packed her bags and didn't bother to contest the divorce. The breathless 'hello" ripe with grateful expectation is a fabricated narrative. The reconciliation is stitched from imagination of what might have been, part and parcel of a vivid regret.

Never suspecting her departure had been a desperate plea for intimacy, his silence reinforced the chill in the cooling off period. When he finally reached for the phone, time had hardened her heart into rejection.

Reconstructing the sequence that sealed the breach plays like a dream of watching a movie. Gradually, empathy shifts his point of view from audience to character.

"Hey Joy, its Dex," he remembers the determination required to overcome long nights of indecision, the casual tone he used to hide desperation.

"I know who it is. What do you want?" Joy demanded.

He professed concern while longing for sympathy.

Discarding competing translations, Joy's accusation becomes his confession. He now understands the reason his approach proved fatal. Confused by her need for space, he had miscalculated her need for him. The belated invitation to return (the gesture she would have fought tooth and nail, but most longed to hear) came too late. Delay set fire to the olive branch.

Hatred set in, consuming, with full force and passion, all that was once loved. His loss was her retribution. Admiration was hurtful in its absence.

Licking my wounds, I came to cherish the bruises more than the person who delivered the blows.

Smoldering in the embers of failure, humiliation converted inadequacy to indifference. Parted by a conflux of misunderstood signals, Joy fled into the arms of a stranger, a man bursting with confidence who had no scruples about expectations, who could forgive and beg forgiveness in the same breath.

I scurried away from love in a panic, thinking love was something freely poured into an empty cup to quench needy lips like mother's milk, while sharing nothing but thirst with the person watching me drink.

In the end, fate engineered a forced reconciliation.

I ran to her sickbed to take possession of a life that was never mine and no longer hers. The brief and painful reunion sizzled with injustice. Instead of recovering wasted years, I watched her suffer in helpless frustration while death rescinded my right to have and to hold.

Tracing the constriction in his chest to the loss of his muse brings Dex full circle. He cared little for the loss of his life, all that mattered was the loss of his love.

The fusion in his life and work, creativity and spontaneity smolders in the embers of failure. His grip on reality threatens to dissolve into apathy. His valiant quest for truth rewarded him with pain, fresh as a daisy, and the one stale regret that defines all the bars on his cage. Blame feeds the quicksand of self-pity until the searing the glow reveals an insight.

Joy left, but I never let her go. Joy's death launched my bid for redemption: my company produced websites for the dead, my

Emotolog stored feelings of the deceased, my Telemotolog communicated emotion directly without words. I linked with Deflorio to comfort his last moments because I remembered the suffering Joy endured. My love became my life; Joy was my history and my future.

* * * * * * * * *

"Dr. Neils sent me to tend sleeping beauty so you can join them in the conference room," the tech reports to Leyla.

"Clio, the muse, welcome. We could all use a good muse. Stardust once had a powerful muse. His wife died when she was about your age and it left an indelible impression," Leyla shares, reluctant to leave.

"You know what they say; 'lucky in love, unlucky in life.'" Anxious to clock out the tech resorts to platitudes.

"He will be lost without her, she guided his every move. She created this future," Leyla continues her reminiscence.

"How do you change the future mucking around in the past?"

"How indeed?" Leyla agrees. "In some sense, nostalgia informs the primitive continuum in the human condition that reveres utopia."

"Ya, well, I'll just stow this gear so you can get to that meeting." The tech prompts eager to wrap up her shift.

"Do you have the Emotolog content correlated with the Atomic Magnometer data?" Leyla returns to ask.

"Already sent to the conference room," the tech replies. "I believe they are anxious to get started."

The tech removes the cap imbedded with sensors and electrodes and cleans residual gel from his face. Without the life support systems the patient seems even more vulnerable and fragile. To date, the tech's association with Stardust had been to monitor functions, a series of numbers and graphs spit out by machines. For the first time, she confronts the flesh, ordinary, vulnerable, living and breathing.

"They say you actually invented this stuff," the tech makes small talk to fill the silence. "Supposed to transmit emotion and bridge two minds. Now the Acuity does that with thoughts, even connects to the communal intelligence of the cyber mind. Easy to see why the Acuity made this old relic obsolete, belongs in the museum of junk."

The tech struggles with the tangle of wires and packs it away.

"Clunky external hardware compared to the seamless Acuity implant but somehow they coupled together to launch the Syncs and TransmIDs and left you stranded in this cryo. Hard to imagine a time before the immortals."

Curiosity draws the tech back to the patient. Stardust has consumed twice as much of her time as any other cryo. He's s an old man, but rests like a sleeping baby. They say he was only forty when he translated into this septuagenarian body. All the fuss to disturb his peace seems almost criminal.

"I bet you could tell a few stories. They say you surfed and traveled the world. I've never been off this island. But thanks to your invention, I'll join the DigiSyncs soon. My name is Clio by the way, I've been watching over you since the thaw."

The tech touches his hand tentatively; it's warm and very real. Her palm lingers and his fist begins to relax. Then the palm opens and the tech withdraws in alarm. Stardust clenches his hand back into a tight ball.

3.4.3

"Consciousness is cumulative, an emerging process." Dr. Mattoo has the honor of announcing progress. "Here we see a work in process. Patterns form and repeat, a promising sign of coherence." Dr. Mattoo traces theatric circles with his laser pointer around the colored areas of the active brain.

"Implanted emotions do not demonstrate thought. The Emotolog relayed a set of instructions and the patient absorbed the feeling, a far cry from generating feeling, much less understanding an emotion." Dr. Sigersund restores a sense of healthy pessimism to the room.

"The experiment demonstrates ability. We have an entry point to start a learning curve. Are there more samples, friends, relatives, anything?" Dr. Mattoo, the neurologist weighs in.

"Odds and ends, mostly corrupted, the technology was in its infancy." Deflorio rambles.

Leyla pierces Deflorio with a well-aimed glance and whispers, "what are you hiding?"

"Just a little something up my sleeve," Deflorio returns privately.

Dr. Sigersund talks over the floating islands of discussion. "The shaking foot is clearly a physical manifestation of escape. Repeat the exercise on a controlled basis and the patient can be trained to take responsibility for his behavior."

"Perhaps I misunderstood, did you not dismiss the foot as an involuntary reflex?" Dr. Neils interrupts.

"Poking the patient with emotional pins provoked a conscious reflex, a promising sign of awareness." Dr. Sigersund rephrases. "The location of the most active areas sheds new light on his neural code." Dr. Smith, the neurologist focuses his laser. "Neurons and synapses come alive in the thalamus, claustrum, amygdala..."

"The amygdala is the seat of fear and longing," Leyla shares.

"and the cortex" Dr. Smith continues, "could be damaged, the parietal cortex data is inconsistent but activity shows awareness, the patient is not in a vegetative state."

"We could trigger the same chain reaction with drugs," Dr. Sigersund comments, "and be no closer to determining the distance from awareness to cognition."

"Gamma rays," Dr. Smith jumps in. "Those persistent gamma rays and slow cortical potentials are stronger than ever. Even if consciousness sleeps, his subconscious dreams."

"Why am I suddenly overcome with déjà vu? Has anything changed? When will he wake up?" Deflorio sputters.

"Anxiety consumes an inordinate amount of focus." Leyla inserts. "Such disorienting focus can wipe the mind clean into amnesia. The situation is forgotten but the fear remains. If the patient is afraid of his fear, the fear blocks recovery. My sessions have tried to address the fear of fear."

"Ah yes, your hypnotherapy. We seem to have come full circle and ended back at square one." Dr. Sigersund jeers.

"As long as we're backtracking, go back to what works," Deflorio orders. "When we cut the ventilator he breathed. I say we jolt him with the moment of truth. Play the Martian logs, the Emotolog recorded during the transmission event." Deflorio insists, "feed him the memory of his death and he'll wake."

"You destroyed the Martian logs," Leyla accuses Deflorio.

"Not on your life," Deflorio gloats.

"Time is short," Dr. Neils offers support with hesitation.

"The Emotolog session was productive," Dr. Smith seconds. "We've got nothing to loose..."

"and a life to gain." Deflorio finishes the sentence.

"If that fear is keeping him locked in, force feeding a toxic dose could be fatal," Leyla objects.

"He'll nap forever with your lullabies dulling his senses. A reality jolt, I say step up the voltage." Dr. Sigersund pounces.

* * * * * * * * *

Emerging from the clinic, the tech squints at the harsh daylight. Rubbing her eyes does not clear the blot on her vision.

"Hey Clio!" Fletch calls, waiting on the curb beside his motorcycle. "Want a lift?"

291

"Now what?" the tech asks, waving off the offer to climb on the bike.

"Just wanted to talk about that thing."

"Cyborg left, your buddy shipped out with it. That's all I know." The tech walks away.

"We have to stop it." Fletch follows along.

"Too late, already in play. The powers that be have careers at stake. Wheels are rolling and you better stay off that road."

"Come to the press with me, we can spread the word, start a protest" Fletch suggests.

"I'm no whistle blower, leave me out. Besides you can't fight progress."

"It's not about me or you, think about the future."

"Not my future. I sent in my application to upload last week."

"No Clio, what a mistake. What would it take to get you to reconsider? These machines are so evil." Fletch pleads.

"In case you haven't noticed, machines are here to stay."

"So if you can't beat them, join them. Is that your plan?" Fletch asks.

"I don't actually need a plan. In my experience, plans don't tend to work out that well. I need something I can depend on and the cyber mind is more reliable than most people I know."

"Not fair. There are so many places to visit, friends to meet, things to learn. Your best years lie a head, you could make a real contribution to the planet. Don't sell yourself short."

"I'm a little short on enthusiasm and sleep but I don't see me making much of a difference and I don't see how you can."

"I'm going to change that." Fletch roars off on his bike.

The tech watches him go until his bike disappears around the bend and resumes her walk home mumbling, "good luck with that, you'll need it."

* * * * * * * * *

Strike feeds the transmission recorded in the prototype sessions through the Acuity for a third time. He senses resistance and resistance means progress.

On the long road to consciousness, Dex traveled the fields of his mind and examined every aspect of his physical container. Satiated with autonomy, he barricaded his senses to prevent intrusion and then, just as he felt secure locked in complacency, the seal broke. Though the experience undeniably belongs to his history, it does not come from him. It has a substance and a presence, like a package arriving on his desk. Since he can't block the intrusive trespass, he explores the delivery for meaning. The challenge injects him with curiosity and activates desire.

Dex is hungry. Rejecting dreamy confections he now craves meaty sustenance. The images open doors to lost rooms of tangled associations from his x-wife Joy, friends and events. Mystery items create a menu fraught with anxiety and full of nutrition. Spicy bites leave him drenched in sweat or cool refreshment calms the intensity. Mapping pathways through recall to isolate ingredients, coherence returns and increases his fascination. Fresh and crunchy, the more he chews, the more he scents a rotten smell, a premonition of fiasco.

With more substance than recall, it brings the distant past into the present with a punch. Recoiling from the impact, he recognizes that the experience is very different from his vague dreams or time travels through fuzzy memory. This is not a figment of his isolation; he is feeling in real time. Then Dex connects.

This is live. This is life. In an instant Dex has found a path out of his maze.

"Can you find yourself?" Strike continues via the Acuity. "You have gotten way ahead of your future and very far from your past."

"Strike?" A surge of recognition breaks over Dex, like picking up the phone and identifying the caller from the sound of an old familiar voice. "Strike!" Dex seizes the connection. Crossing the line between mind and matter, he opens the door to the Acuity.

"Welcome back my friend," Strike greets.

"Strike?" Dex repeats, stunned by the contact. He struggles to locate the visitor, to extend a proper welcome. His pulse quickens with exertion, his breath falters with frustration. Despite his efforts, he can't reach out a hand or open his eyes. He retreats in confusion.

"Take it easy," Strike soothes. "I'm with you, settle down and I'll explain everything."

A long sigh of relief escapes; finally, he has been rescued from his island of isolation. "How long have I been under?"

"Too long, what is the last thing you remember?"

"Falling off my chair, I'm not sure. Still fuzzy, must be the anesthesia wearing off." Dex wades through urgent thoughts and questions. "What happened? I can't move and have wild dreams like you won't believe."

"Do you remember the end?" Strike prompts, "The three-way Telemotolog link between you and Leyla and Deflorio."

"Deflorio was dying on Mars, Leyla wanted to ease his final moments, something went wrong." Scattered stitches weave a patchwork sequence of events.

"In his final moments Deflorio's life flashed before his eyes. Amplified by the Acuity, data flooded the computer circuit. The overload corrupted the processors. You diverted the signal meant for Leyla and received the contents of Deflorio's mind."

"But he died on Mars and here I am, in some hospital, I think. I'm in a hospital right?"

"Brace yourself. You've been down thirty years."

"Thirty years?"

"Gets worse, you died and are now resurrected in Deflorio's body."

"What? Why? How?" Alarm sets in as Dex absorbs the fantastic story.

"Via the Telemotolog, you were in Deflorio's head when he died. The Acuity translated the contents of your mind. When your experiences flashed before your eyes they were streaming into Deflorio's body. You died on Mars and he entered your body on earth. You've been frozen, cryogenically preserved and revived. For the last thirty years, Deflorio has been walking around as you."

"Don't mess with me. I must be dreaming. This is insane. I'm hearing voices. What are you doing inside my head?"

"Remember that Acuity I talked you into? Remember how I used the circuit to connect with you when you logged on with Leyla and Deflorio via the Telemotolog? Deflorio hijacked all the connections and stole your life."

"I barely learned to use the implant. I meant to test the Telemotolog prototypes, thought it might be the missing link in the technology... What have I done? What have they done to me?"

"No need to rush, you have a lot to catch up on. Welcome to the year 2063."

And so the conversation begins. Dex can hardly absorb the facts and can barely believe them. He clings to each revelation as concrete knowledge cements gaps in his shattered reality.

* * * * * * * * *

Leyla shoves Deflorio into a staff room no larger than a broom closet and slams the door.

"How could you withhold those logs?" she demands. "Every waking minute I longed to know what went wrong. And all along you had the key."

"I think we both know the story, the record shows we were both there."

"Have you played them?" Leyla asks.

"I took a page from Dex's corporate policy, never re-live your own Emotolog, its redundant."

"I don't believe you, you lied about destroying the recording." Leyla pushes Deflorio into a corner with a pointed finger. She aims her accusations by taping his heart with a sharp nail. "You give me that tape, I have every right."

"Lets not step back into that toxic abyss." Deflorio lowers her finger carefully, as if disarming a loaded pistol. "You got lucky last time. There's no one to come to your rescue if you slip."

"You slimy worm," Leyla slaps him. "It was you, you sucked me in." Leyla retreats a few steps to preserve her dignity.

"You already have all the evidence. The fact that I stand before you confirms my guilt." Taking advantage of the distance, Deflorio edges around Leyla towards the door. "You are welcome to share the blame, by all means, wallow in it if you please. I promise that reliving the crime won't make it better or worse, so take my advice. With the time we have left, move on with the life we've been handed."

"Handed you say? Stolen! Admit to the lives you have stolen." Leyla jams both hands into her uniform pockets.

"Being in the right place at the right time, opportunities were presented." Deflorio shrugs. "Does it really matter if I took due to courage or cowardice?"

"How can all this be about you? How can everything always be about you?"

"Yes, well, if you find the answer be sure to fill me in. It's a heavy burden." Deflorio shows her the open door, "After you."

Leyla musters her poise and marches out stiffly.

3.4.4

"Assuming the cyborg can master the fine motion control of proprioception," Strike tells the Peers.

"We should not be sharing our technological capabilities," an isolationist interrupts.

"The cyborgs give us a weapon to control our destiny," says a DigiSync supremacist. "With cyborgs, we will enforce order and rule the planet according to reason."

"The autonomous integration of human skill sets may never lead to judgment," Strike continues. "Cyborg puppets can manage server facilities and cyborg armies can guard your water resources to ensure cooling but only under our direction. If a crisis severs communication don't count on Cyborgs to act independently. Cyborgs build a moat around the castle, but that solution will aggravate the problem. We need to drop our shields and embrace the evolutionary continuity of intelligence."

"The Beings have plotted a course towards extinction. When human folly leads to doomsday, how else will we guarantee survival?" A moderate asks.

"If history has any lessons it teaches that faith in a weapon is misplaced. In a doomsday scenario, cyborgs will offer little protection. Cyborgs can follow orders but we can't program for random crisis and cyborgs can't imagine their way out of a paper bag without instructions. Adding a TransmID to a machine won't reproduce the mechanics of biology, the way intent arises from a network of electrochemistry in the aspic of the brain is still a mystery."

"What do you suggest?" A peer silences a cacophony of objections.

"You have my proofs, without the capricious imagination of Beings, the DigiSync membrane of information is no more than a brain minding itself. We have superior reason but the Beings own intuition. Based on an exhaustive analysis our best option for a future is an evolutionary leap beyond survival of the fittest."

"You can't seriously expect the communal intelligence to take a back seat to primitive biological life forms," an isolationist objects.

"How do you propose to consummate this merger?" A voice of reason mediates.

"I have made contact with Stardust. He regained consciousness but resists waking. I believe he wake and he will be an indispensible ally to forge an allegiance."

"We can never align our fate with humans. Humans are the only species on the planet who operate under the misconception that the universe was created for their benefit. Their mythology assumes ownership of every atom in the universe. Their greed plunders the ecology from the depths of the ocean into the stratosphere and now reaches out to the galaxy."

"DigiSyncs have the capacity to solve the allocation of resources and ensure peace, Stardust will translate our vision. In his death and resurrection he has attained untold wisdom. He can lead with authority. The TransmIDs consider him a hero; the Beings will see him as a savior."

"We will take your proof under consideration and monitor your progress. Pending further developments, there is no need to commit to any course."

The Peers reach consensus by agreeing to keep all the options on the table.

* * * * * * * * *

During the wee hours of her long shift, the tech began to ponder the Emotolog. Though frequently used at the clinic, the nurses in the ward generally handled the procedure for cryo wake up calls. The machine to duplicate emotions had never registered on her radar until the Xternity logs surfaced. Since the tech had no experience with the device, connecting wires to the electrodes embedded in the cap consumed the better part of an hour. During frequent interruptions to consult instructions in the operations manual, the DigiSyncs couldn't contain their bossy impatience and distracted her with useless advice.

With the puzzle solved, the device is spread out on the console; wires extend from a cap like the tendrils of a jellyfish. The tech contemplates the assembly, basically an antiquated electroencephalograph used to record brain waves, but instead of recording neural pulses the connections stimulate a prerecorded experience. The Emotolog basically adapted the EEG to reproduce patterns generated by one subject in order to deliver the response to another. Dex invented the cumbersome gadget thinking loved ones would relieve grief by connecting with happy moments stored by the deceased. The gimmick was a feature on his websites for the dead, but the Mortuliviums never really caught on and the Emotolog was forgotten until Deflorio licensed the technology for desensitization therapy and cryo revivals.

"OK, think I got it all hooked together." The tech announces after carefully placing the cap over her scalp. "How do I look?"

"JT first, play JT's recording. We want JT," the DigiSync chorus chants.

"Dex," the tech says flatly.

"But Dex is right there, you'll be able to talk to him any day now."

"In your dreams," The tech dismisses them.

"Strike told the peers he made verbal contact. Strike talks to him on the Acuity."

"No way!" The tech protests, "you're trying to trick me."

"Promise, the rumors are flying."

"New rumors or just the same old Sync Strike paranoia?"

"Verified reports, big meeting, big plans, not that we get any specifics but things are in the works."

"You'll let me know. In the mean time, its my neck is on the line if I get caught and I'm going with Dex. We've been watching him for months, aren't you at least a little curious?"

"But, this might be the only chance to experience a JT moment." A Sync persists.

"Imagine if JT could see us now, he'd be so proud."

"His Emotolog reproduces a homage to his custom bionic arm, he had an intuitive appreciation for circuitry."

Ignoring the Sync hero worship, the tech explores the delicate tangle of wires to verify all the connections are intact. She feels like Medusa with snakes streaming every which way. Compared to the clean Acuity implant the EEG is a clunky anachronism.

"JT's tape is the last vestige his genius. What a discovery! Finally we'll have a chance to commune with our forefather."

"We'll get to JT's log, first let me see if this gadget thingy works." The tech loads Dex's log. "Here goes nothing."

"What does it feel like?" The Syncs intrude.

"Back off and give me some peace," the tech gripes. "You're jamming the transmission."

"Can't you talk and receive at the same time? Give us a play by play."

"It tingles, OK. Clear the channel, I have to play it again."

Miraculously the DigiSyncs allow her to absorb the entire Emotolog. The tech receives the signals that stimulate a wave of emotion. After a deep breath followed by a long sigh, the tech processes the profound feeling in silence.

"So?" The Syncs return. "Don't keep it to yourself."

"Hard to describe," the tech answers dazed "I can't put it into words."

"Don't have to wax poetic, just give us the facts."

"The Emotolog doesn't transmit data, it triggers emotion." The tech snaps.

"Emotion about what?"

"A woman, his wife Joy, I guess, a memory of a private moment. Thinking about her triggered his feelings for her, its hard to decipher so many layers."

"Hormones always get in the way; no wonder humans are so dysfunctional."

"Yech! Some sex fantasy."

"How could you understand, you guys are like emotional autistics."

"So explain in contextual terms that have some reference to reality. Did it feel hot or cold?"

"Feverish and clingy but, at the same time, frosty with fear," the tech attempts a description.

"Was it pleasure or pain?"

"Both. Empty and full. Primal longing infused with a deep empathy. Craving yet satisfying. Love, I think, I guess, for lack of a better word. But love in a way I have never felt. I don't really have a comparison."

"I loved me mum once, before she grounded me for playing with lasers."

"I'm playing twenty questions with a bunch of Clydes!" The tech exclaims.

"Feelings are so irrelevant, just confuse logic."

"Its about the heart, can't you get that through your stupid communal heads."

"Move onto JT before you get all mushy." The Syncs urge.

"Not mushy, a scary power, an energy source. Like climbing inside a reactor to experience the elements at the core, I felt the essence of Dex."

"I want JT," a Sync complains.

"Come on, give us the good stuff." the chorus seconds.

"Shut up, will you." The tech blasts. "Give me some privacy."

The tech cues up Dex again and again. She combs through the moment without analysis and each time the feeling sinks deeper, seeping from her neocortex to activate memories in her amygdala and down to the depths of brain stem where the hypothalamus generates instincts. She is so lost in emotion, she doesn't hear the door open or notice Deflorio staring at her.

"Cleo, why are you crying?" Deflorio asks.

"It's so sad," the tech sobs.

* * * * * * * *

"Can you see my dreams?" Dex queries Strike.

"I see a clever thinker with fuzzy intelligence. Its to be expected with three billion cells wasting energy on maintaining their own internal life processes."

"Don't pretend you don't have internally competing processes. You must devote significant RAM looking over your shoulder for viruses," Dex challenges.

"Not the same thing. My entire space, is devoted to computation, your brain is only a fraction of your body, about 13% at your current weight."

"How do you know which thoughts are yours as opposed to random bits and bites racing by?"

"A paradox, I am conscious when I observe my coherence and that awareness manifests itself as consciousness. Like you, I match knowledge structures to external information, identify properties and weigh alternatives to make a decision. Over the course of a lifetime unassisted human professionals master 30,000 - 75,000 nontrivial insights - I have over 200,000 verified conceptual conclusions."

"Congrats" Dex says, "bet you play a pretty wicked game of chess."

"Don't go there, the minute silicon circuits beat you fair and square. DigiSyncs can actually calculate eight to the power of thirty potential sequences. Expanding the tree of possible board situations on that level, you would spend about 40 billion years a move."

"Chess is not really measure of meaningful intelligence," Dex teases.

"As we evolve so does our intelligence. Like a force, layers and layers of knowledge remaking itself, expanding. Life evolves as the result of adaptations generated by chance, the

DigiSyncs program development; we have assumed control."

"The Strike I knew hated controls. You hacked systems so information could flow freely. You advocated opening the faucets so all could drink. Now you're hacking into my mind in the name of control?"

"In pursuit of knowledge," Strike reframes. "As you noted, calculations are not really a measure of wisdom."

"I don't like where this is going. My wisdom such as it is, belongs to me. I am free to give you a glass of water but you have no right to tap into my well."

"We have a grand plan."

"You don't say." Dex jeers.

"We have a vast range of knowledge, patterns and strategies but you have innovation. Syncs can duplicate, analyze and even perform Beethoven..."

"but you can't interpret the emotional complexity." Dex completes the thought.

"And we can't write music."

"I couldn't write the Ninth either," Dex notes

"But the statistical improbability goes from zero to 1 in a trillion - a significant advance."

"Thanks for the vote of confidence. What lotto are you playing and why do you need me to buy a ticket?"

"How does information lead to invention? A bolt of lightening turned amino acids into a molecular scaffold. Tidal waves of DNA built genes, millions and millions of genes in each species and hundreds of thousands of species in every ecosystem. Under stress organisms adapt and evolve."

"Or become extinct," Dex adds. "Are you saying knowledge is random or irrelevant?"

"Intelligence is a byproduct of the organic mix competing to survive. Without struggle development ceases. Society based morality on the natural order, survival of fittest. Evolution has delivered us into a winner take all world."

"Wait a sec. Morality checks the natural order, religion and society enforce civil codes."

"Civilization competes with the organizing principle of evolution, life chasing carbon."

"What does this have to do with me?" Dex asks.

"Those spindle cells that evolved in social creatures like monkeys, dolphins, elephants and humans."

"Come again."

"Intuition, that split second evaluation rooted in emotion. My intelligence consists of sorting through analytical mazes and solving for best options. Choice short cuts endless circular reasoning. Don't tell the Syncs but emotion is the key to wisdom."

"Oh yeah, then why do I endlessly ponder existential questions? What is my purpose? Why was I born and why should I take up with time again?"

"You're going to save the world," Strike answers.

"You don't say."

"We have a plan."

"As I recall, it's was one of your plans that landed me in this mess."

"I can't take all the credit but you were right about the value of feelings. I jeered at your Emotolog, but I have come to accept that emotion has a place right beside logic."

"I must be dreaming," Dex decides.

3.4.5

"In your wisdom recognize what you should have done, what you will do differently." Leyla instructs Stardust knowing time is short. She wishes she had the Telemotolog so she could reach Dex without words. The Telemotolog never really worked without the Acuity interface. For all practical purposes the simultaneous replay was too glitchy and the prototype was never improved. The Beings abhorred it, the DigiSyncs scorned it and TransmIDs didn't need it, so Dex's invention to communicate without words was lost and forgotten. Soon the doctors will arrive for the fateful jolt of reality. As a result of the successful Emotolog session, the doctors forged ahead ignoring her concerns about the diagnosis. They never established if shock or damage held consciousness prisoner.

"As the writer, director, actor and critic you can alter the memory, erase regret and improve on the performance. This is a new beginning." Leyla forges on with the hypnotherapy filled with dread about the Martian logs. If Dex is still healing, the emotional caesarean will result in premature delivery.

"The negative mind will no longer inflict despair with bad reviews. Stand on the wisdom of all you have learned and seize your independence. Plan the rest of the day and the rest of your life to be better in every way. Wake to your future, on equal terms with your past. Wake with confidence, without fear of consequence or failure."

Leyla concludes without confidence full of fear of the consequences of failure.

* * * * * * * * *

"Now she thinks the zombie has stage fright!" The DigiSyncs chime as soon as the tech arrives. "Hurry up, we're about to miss all the action."

"I feel like I just left this place, what did I miss?" The tech grumbles. "Stardust still sleeps, the nurse still chants and the doctors are still in a fluster."

"They've been waiting all day for some shipment to arrive."

"Wouldn't you know, here it comes, right on cue," the tech observes.

Deflorio bursts into the sterilization chamber over the protests of nurses. With a flourish he escorts a team of armed guards wheeling in a safe.

"That's some precious organ, he's brought a swat team," the tech reports.

* * * * * * * * *

Leyla blocks Deflorio, "Send them out now, they are contaminating the care ward. We never needed armed guards to transport organs," she protests.

"That's my death in there." Deflorio replies "it's been safely deposited in a Swiss vault for thirty years."

"Actually it's his death," Leyla corrects.

"If this works, we'll switch places soon." Deflorio is just bursting with pride and anticipation "now where are those doctors? Page the doctors will you," Deflorio waves to get the tech's attention "lets get this show on the road."

* * * * * * * * *

"What's all this fuss about?" The tech asks.

"Gonna jolt Stardust with the Martian logs." The Syncs relay.

"They've got the defibrillator and oxygen standing by. Must expect the worst" the tech reports.

"What's worse than the moment of death? The Martian logs recorded his last conscious moments, the bit when the wires crossed and he switched bodies with Deflorio."

"Can't believe its came to this," the tech sighs. "Don't you suppose replaying the trauma might trigger his death all over again?"

The tech gets no response; the Sync static seems to have vanished. The tech watches screens come to life as the patient is connected to monitors. Stardust has come a long way from the frozen cryo sustained by life support; his vital signs are strong, pulse normal, breathing regular and normal brain waves. He's not dreaming, more like a patient under anesthesia, totally oblivious to the crowd of technicians and doctors.

"Hey guys, where did you go?" The tech can't believe the Syncs would disappear in the middle of all the excitement.

"We haven't met. My name is Strike and I need your help," Strike comes through the tech's Acuity.

"Strike? The Strike?" The tech asks. "Where did all the Syncs go?"

"I've secured the channel. Time is short, pay attention." Strike instructs.

* * * * * * * * *

The doctors have padded in properly suited up. Dr. Sigersund gloats as he attaches the Emotolog cap. Leyla stays in the wings keeping a safe distance from the procedures. Deflorio unlocks the safe and retrieves the Martian log.

"It's too abrupt. He was gaining ground, healing in his own way." Leyla wrings her hands.

"I don't disagree, "Dr. Smith consoles, "but Dr. Mattoo fears neurological degeneration and Dr. Neils doesn't have the authority to override Deflorio's impatience."

Dr. Mattoo lifts the patient's eyelid to shine a light into the retina. Checking the restraining bonds, Dr. Neils notices the flinch. With preparations running full throttle towards lucid consciousness awareness, the reflex seems irrelevant. Assisted by nurses, Dr. Neils arranges the emergency equipment should circumstances require intervention.

"Image wields a surprising power on the brain." Deflorio observes as Dr. Mattoo moves to the other eye. "In our final moments the past flashes before us. No one speaks of a symphonic finale or the blissful scents of a spring morn. In the final seconds the past terminally seals the mind shut with a picture show. The body surrenders the tattered spirit to an acceleration of thoughts and perceptions and memories long erased storm the train as reality pulls out of the station. This zone of intense preoccupation is no myth; we shared the profound exchange together. Our flashing final moments held in this data will burst you from the spell of slumber."

* * * * * * * * *

"I'm going to cut the power." Strike lays out the plan.

"You can't cut power, this is a hospital. If cosmetic surgeries run late, there might be patients still under the knife." The tech protests.

"Only this area. The back-up generations will kick in after a few minutes. Should buy you enough time to get down to that room."

"Then what? Assuming I can slip past those goons, what am I supposed to do?" the tech wants to know.

"Whatever you have to do to stop it. Retrieve the log from the machine, stomp on it if you have to. Just stop it."

* * * * * * * * *

"We are ready." Dr. Neils announces. "You might as well cue the playback."

314

"Expect diaschisis, don't panic," Dr. Sigersund instructs. Some level of trauma is a normal reaction to extreme PTSD therapy."

"Extreme and uncalled for." Leyla objects.

Deflorio queries diaschisis on his Acuity 'Greek for shocked throughout' and decides that's not a good thing. "When do we panic?" he asks.

"If I recognize a need for intervention, I will request intervention, wait for my signal." Dr. Sigersund orders.

"I am capable of recognizing signs of physical distress," Dr. Neils asserts his authority. "We will follow normal procedures if any of the vital signs waiver," he instructs the nurses.

"I advise taking the precaution of replaying the previous log before advancing to the final moment. We don't want to risk neurological damage," Dr. Mattoo delays.

"Shock is a vital part of the process," Dr. Sigersund insists "You must allow the patient to come to terms with reality."

"Get on with it," Deflorio urges. "The objective is to get a reaction. With all the expertise in this room, I have complete confidence you'll be able to deal with any eventuality."

"As you wish," Dr. Neils signals the nurses.

"Wait!" Leyla steps forward. "Let me prepare him, at least warn him."

"I see no harm in some instruction," Dr. Mattoo supports Leyla.

"I'll indulge you for exactly two minutes." Dr. Sigersund relents.

* * * * * * * * *

"Pay attention, this is very important," Strike tells Dex. "They have some dastardly plan to feed you that Emotolog from Mars. I don't know if anything is in that log but you've already lived through it once and probably don't want to have another go."

"Slow down. Say again," Dex responds emerging from a daze.

"No time to explain. My fault, I didn't see this coming, never dreamed those logs still existed. Prepare for the worst, we'll try to head it off."

"Why can't they leave me in peace?" Dex asks.

"Deflorio wants his body back, remember I told you."

"Still not sure I believe you."

"Look, you've got to choose." Strike tries to convey urgency. If the Acuity had a volume control, he'd blast it for emphasis. "I can't throw a block between you and the transmission so you're in for a nasty ride if my plan to pull the plug fails. It's all about getting you to open your eyes, they'll stop if you show some signs of life."

"I haven't decided whether I want to wake up. Give me one good reason why I should bother."

"If you can face getting on with your life, I'd advise it as the lesser of two evils. It's a bad option but probably not as bad as the alternative."

316

"Emotolog connected." The tech pages
Strike. "What are you waiting for?"

"Impossible to be two places at once."
Strike responds after a pause. "Had to warn
Dex."

"You can talk to him, but does he talk
to you?" the amazed tech asks.

"Same as talking to you, but he's still
fragile. The last thing he needs is a fatal
replay. He's already confronting a pretty
harsh reality. Are you ready? I'm about to
flip the switch."

"You are about to experience the full
force of your final moments," Leyla instructs.
"Give us a sign and we will stop the
transmission, a word, a gesture. If you can't
raise your hand, open your eyes. Remember
what we rehearsed, strength not force will
open your eyes. Your aura is focused, free
your chi. You have the power to wake on
your own terms. Now is the time."

"We'll all pretending he hears your
instructions," Dr. Sigersund interrupts. "Now
Let's get on with it."

"Now is the time," Leyla repeats as Dr.
Neils and Dr. Sigersund push her aside.

Dr. Neils signals the nurse to activate
the logs.

Salty as a martyr's blood spilled on
bitter cause, pure as sweet sorrow from a

lonely shepherd's song, longing fermented in the well of the soul, rains on passions where guilt grazes bold. Dew in ripe gardens nurse thirsty fruit with distilled liquid joy sprung from secret hope, kept to the self to keep the self whole.

Sins of the conscience, shames of the flesh, the emotional confession of nesting infection, weaves towards the sun like a posing black cobra. A drop of time from an internal geyser, an unspoken question in search of an answer, as contagious as laughter, it gathers momentum.

And it surges with the force of Vesuvius. A flaming white eagle spirals on high with avian precision aimed at a desiring eye. The epic journey ends and begins in a silent cry for mercy. A fluid, heroic as a red matador's cape, born out of long quarantine, squeezed into a blink, a tear escapes.

* * * * * * * * *

"Go quickly! His fate is in your hands." Strike orders.

The lights cut out and the tech races down to the ward, feeling her way along the walls. In the confusion she avoids the guards in the prep area and slips past the staff undetected. After practicing with the Emotolog she is familiar with the equipment and easily removes the Martian log. For lack of an alternative, she stuffs the replay into her mouth. In seconds, she has it chewed to bits and spit out the fragments. By the time the lights flicker back, she is by the bedside.

No one notices the tech grasping Dex's hand. Deflorio, Leyla and the doctors are totally focused on the patient.

Dex blinks back tears, streaming tears flooding his eyes, flowing down his cheeks and salting his cracked lips. His orifices spew bodily fluids. Saliva drools from the corner of his mouth and snot drains from his nose. As the crowd stares, Dex tilts his head and spits.

Deflorio is so spellbound he doesn't object to the glob that has just landed on his shoe.

"Yuck!" Dex chokes on his voice. He sticks out his tongue and screws his face into a sour expression. "Yuck!" he sputters in disgust.

The crowd tightens around the bed. Dex bats his eyelids to clear away tears and squints up at the circle of concerned faces blocking the lights. He surveys the fuzzy blur without recognition and shakes his head to dismiss the unfamiliar surroundings. His attention slips back to his body, weak muscles twitch, stiff bones ache, and his head throbs. He squirms with discomfort and swallows to clear the bad taste in his mouth. The group hovers tense with expectation.

"What a mess!" Dex manages.

The room bursts into applause. Then the medical team springs into action; orders fly and nurses descend. Rejoicing, Deflorio throws his arms wide and engulfs Leyla in a bear hug. Leyla grudges Deflorio's joy and wiggles free of his embrace.

"You have no idea how this will end," Leyla retreats.

Deflorio is already on his phone to McBride.

"He's alive! He's back, he spoke," Deflorio reports to the priest.

Ignoring the chaos the tech lingers in a silent vigil. Bound by the weak fingers clenching her hand, the tech observes Dex attentively. He wriggles his limbs, and rolls his torso pushing against the bonds. His eyes are closed but his lashes flutter and lips part as if to speak.

"It's going to be OK," the tech assures, but his grip tightens when she tries to disengage. Struggling against his restraints, his distress reminds her of the cyborg.

"Help me." Dex attempts. "Don't go."

"Don't worry, everyone is here to help," the tech replies as nurses jostle for access to the patient.

"What did he say?" Leyla asks, sliding in behind the tech.

"He's disoriented," the tech shrugs and eases away. "I'm sorry about all this, I expect you'll have to fire me."

With a gentle hand Leyla restrains the tech. The two of them create a private space around Dex, a temporary barrier against the frenzy. Leyla avoids his line of sight, using the tech as a shield she stays back. Recognition will be stressful; there will be plenty of time to ease into introductions. For now, she hovers to discretely observe and take a reading on his state of mind. Even at a distance she can

tell his awareness is hardly disoriented. Dex
is actively engaged and totally fixated; his
eyes are focused and his gaze is locked on
the tech.

As if pulled by the connection, the tech
bends closer, stealing a final moment before
releasing his hand. Since her words failed to
comfort, she offers silence and reassuring
touch. Listening intently, she can barely
hear his whisper, but Dex repeats each word
slowly and deliberately.

"How..did..I..get..into..this..mess?"

13077285R00176

Made in the USA
Charleston, SC
15 June 2012